SOMEONE TO REMEMBER

ALSO BY MARY BALOGH

The Westcott Series

SOMEONE TO LOVE
SOMEONE TO HOLD
SOMEONE TO WED
SOMEONE TO CARE
SOMEONE TO TRUST
SOMEONE TO HONOR

The Survivors' Club Series

THE PROPOSAL
THE ARRANGEMENT
THE ESCAPE
ONLY ENCHANTING
ONLY A PROMISE
ONLY A KISS
ONLY BELOVED

The Horsemen Trilogy

INDISCREET
UNFORGIVEN
IRRESISTIBLE

The Huxtable Series

FIRST COMES MARRIAGE
THEN COMES SEDUCTION
AT LAST COMES LOVE
SEDUCING AN ANGEL
A SECRET AFFAIR

Classics

THE IDEAL WIFE
THE SECRET PEARL
A PRECIOUS JEWEL
A CHRISTMAS PROMISE
DARK ANGEL/
LORD CAREW'S BRIDE
A MATTER OF CLASS
THE TEMPORARY WIFE/
A PROMISE OF SPRING
THE FAMOUS HEROINE/
THE PLUMED BONNET

The Simply Series

SIMPLY UNFORGETTABLE
SIMPLY LOVE
SIMPLY MAGIC
SIMPLY PERFECT

The Bedwyn Saga

SLIGHTLY MARRIED
SLIGHTLY WICKED
SLIGHTLY SCANDALOUS
SLIGHTLY TEMPTED
SLIGHTLY SINFUL
SLIGHTLY DANGEROUS

The Bedwyn Prequels

ONE NIGHT FOR LOVE
A SUMMER TO REMEMBER

The Mistress Trilogy

MORE THAN A MISTRESS
NO MAN'S MISTRESS
THE SECRET MISTRESS

The Web Series

THE GILDED WEB
WEB OF LOVE
THE DEVIL'S WEB

A CHRISTMAS BRIDE/
CHRISTMAS BEAU
A COUNTERFEIT BETROTHAL/
THE NOTORIOUS RAKE
UNDER THE MISTLETOE
BEYOND THE SUNRISE
LONGING
HEARTLESS
SILENT MELODY

Someone to Remember

A Westcott Story

MARY BALOGH

BERKLEY
New York

BERKLEY
An imprint of Penguin Random House LLC
penguinrandomhouse.com

Copyright © 2019 by Mary Balogh
Excerpt from *Someone to Love* copyright © 2016 by Mary Balogh
Excerpt from *Someone to Hold* copyright © 2017 by Mary Balogh
Excerpt from *Someone to Wed* copyright © 2017 by Mary Balogh
Excerpt from *Someone to Care* copyright © 2018 by Mary Balogh
Excerpt from *Someone to Trust* copyright © 2018 by Mary Balogh
Excerpt from *Someone to Honor* copyright © 2019 by Mary Balogh

Library of Congress Cataloging-in-Publication Data

Names: Balogh, Mary, author.
Title: Someone to remember : a Westcott story / Mary Balogh.
Description: First edition. | New York : Berkley, 2019. | Series: The Westcott series |
Identifiers: LCCN 2019027613 (print) | LCCN 2019027614 (ebook) |
ISBN 9780593099728 (hardcover) | ISBN 9780593099032 (ebook)
Subjects: GSAFD: Love stories. | Regency fiction.
Classification: LCC PR6052.A465 S665 2019 (print) |
LCC PR6052.A465 (ebook) | DDC 823/.914--dc23
LC record available at https://lccn.loc.gov/2019027613
LC ebook record available at https://lccn.loc.gov/2019027614

First Edition: November 2019

Printed in the United States of America
1   3   5   7   9   10   8   6   4   2

Jacket art: photograph of woman by Richard Jenkins; image of building
by Robert Wyatt / Alamy Stock Photo; image of garden by Jianghaistudio/Shutterstock
Jacket design by Katie Anderson
Book design by Kristin del Rosario

Dear Reader,

Welcome to the Regency world of the Westcott family.

Whether this story is your first venture into the series or you are an old friend who has read all or some of the six books that preceded it, I am delighted you have decided to read this novella. It was not part of the original plan for the series, but it caught my imagination anyway and insisted upon being written! I am thoroughly enjoying bringing this whole family to life by telling the love story of one of its members in each book.

The Westcott series was born in my mind with the idea of a crisis situation. What if the head of a family—an earl, no less—had entered into a bigamous marriage when he was a young man, tempted to it because he was in dire financial straits and needed a wealthy wife? What if he justified it, in his own mind, anyway, by the fact that the wife he had married secretly a few years before was dying of consumption?

Would anyone know? There was a daughter from that first marriage, but she was still an infant at the time. He decided that if she was put into an orphanage, no one would ever know who she was.

What if he got away with the bigamy until after his own death more than twenty years later, when his widowed countess sent her lawyer to find and pay off the orphan—presumably a love child from an illicit affair—she secretly knew her husband had been supporting?

What if the countess's son, the new earl, lost his title and fortune after the shocking discovery was made that he was illegitimate?

His sisters would also lose their titles and social status.

The larger family, thrown into turmoil, would somehow have to learn to cope with a new reality. A cousin who had never expected or wanted to inherit the title would find it foisted upon him anyway.

And there would be the added complication of the only legitimate daughter of the late earl discovering who she was at the same time as the family discovered it.

Would the family open—or close—its ranks to her? Would she want to be a part of it?

Someone to Love, *the first book of the Westcott series, deals with just such a catastrophe. Specifically it is the love story of Anna Snow, in reality Lady Anastasia Westcott, the firstborn child of the earl, and Avery Archer, Duke of Netherby, guardian of Harry Westcott, the newly dispossessed young Earl of Riverdale. What would happen if that newly titled orphan fell in love with the man honor bound to protect the dispossessed heir? What if he fell in love with her?*

My plan for the series was to write eight books—for Anna; for Harry and his sisters, Camille and Abigail, and their mother, Viola, the bigamously married Countess of Riverdale; for Alexander, the new Earl of Riverdale, and his sister, Elizabeth; and for Jessica Archer, cousin and best friend of Abigail. Most of them are young people. The eldest is Viola, who is forty-two when her story is being told in Someone to Care.

Someone to Remember, *this additional and originally unplanned-for novella, is different from the others in that its heroine, Lady Matilda Westcott, is in her mid-fifties, considerably older than any other heroine I have ever created. But her story was begging to be told, and I know there are readers who want romances about older heroes and heroines. I have to admit, I absolutely adored writing this story. I do hope you will enjoy it too.*

This story is special to me because of how it called to my imagination. It all started with Matilda, the spinster daughter of a former Earl of Riverdale, who appears in each of the Westcott novels. She is the one who remained single to devote herself to her mother's care, while her younger brother and two sisters married. In all the previous books, she came alive on the page as an overly fussy character, constantly irritating the dowager countess by wrapping shawls about her shoulders and otherwise protecting her from drafts and other hostile elements. She presses smelling salts upon her at the slightest hint of an upset. Uninvited and often unwanted, she always seems to be the one who heads family committees to deal with the crises that arise from time to time within the family. While she and her sisters are planning a grand society wedding for Anna and Avery in Someone to Love, for example, Avery whisks Anna off to a small, obscure church one afternoon and marries her privately. At that point, early in the series, Matilda certainly did not seem like a potential heroine.

That began to change, however, in Someone to Trust, book 5, Elizabeth's story. The change became irrevocable in Someone to Honor, book 6, Abigail's story. What happened was that Matilda started to become a real person to me, and suddenly she was precious.

She was far more than just an aging spinster daughter or sister or aunt to the other characters. She was more than just a fussy woman whose world revolved around her mother and the wider Westcott family. She was a person.

I started to see that she genuinely loved her family and wanted the very best for them all. She was a romantic at heart, as shown in her reactions when some of the family members chose mates the rest of the family found less than ideal. She was happy for Elizabeth and spoke out in her defense when Elizabeth made the shocking announcement that she was going to marry a man nine years her junior. She was happy for Abigail after Abigail married a man who had begun life as the illegitimate son of a village washerwoman.

By this time in the series, I realized I felt very tenderly toward Matilda and wanted her to have her own chance for romance and happiness. I also wanted to know her fully (this, by the way, is how all my main characters begin and grow—through the stories I write for them). What was the story behind her spinsterhood and her fussiness? Had she always been the same? Wasn't she ever interested in marrying? What was her truth? Since she had no reality beyond my imagination, only I could answer those questions—by writing her story.

I had decided after finishing Someone to Honor at the end of last summer that I would do something I had not done before, since I started writing in the 1980s, and take off the whole winter before starting on Jessica's story in the spring. However, I had organized a four-day writing retreat with a group of writer friends in November. I love those retreats, both for the concentrated writing time and for the camaraderie, and hated not to go. But if I did go, I couldn't spend the days twiddling my thumbs while all about me friends were happily tapping away on their keyboards. But what was I to write?

The question soon found an answer, of course. I would write a novella—a long story, a short novel—for Matilda. I thought at first it would be published just as an e-book. I jumped in with enthusiasm and had produced a third of the story by the end of the retreat. It all came together with relative ease despite the looming Christmas season. The hero had already obligingly identified himself in Someone to Honor. It was simply a matter, then, of bringing these two lonely souls together in a warm, romantic love story. Perhaps the imminence of Christmas actually helped me, even though it is not set at Christmastime.

As soon as I finished, I sent the story off to Claire Zion, my editor. After reading the finished novella, Claire liked it so much that she felt it had to be brought out for all the Westcott fans, and not just the e-book readers. Hence, you now hold in your hand the print edition (or maybe you're reading the e-book edition, which we also did).

As I'm sure you have noticed, this book is less expensive than my full-length novels. That's only because it's shorter, not because it's any less important to me than the novels. Matilda is a full member of my beloved *family now! I have grown very fond of her and am glad as many readers as possible can find her story, regardless of their preferred reading format.*

We have also included in this volume excerpts from all six of the Westcott novels already published. If by chance Matilda's story is the first of the series you have read, perhaps the excerpts will entice you to enrich your acquaintance with the family by reading the full stories of six of its members. The hope is that these excerpts will help you pick the next one to read.

If you have already read them, perhaps the excerpts will remind you of each separate story and send you back to reread them in their entirety. I asked on my Facebook page recently how many people are rereaders and was surprised that the overwhelming majority of those who answered are. So am I. There is something very comforting about meeting old friends again within the pages of a loved book. It's a bit like coming home.

But whether you are an old or new fan of the Westcott family, I offer you the below to help you navigate the series:

Someone to Love, book 1, *involves the discovery soon after the death of the Earl of Riverdale, head of the Westcott family, that his marriage of more than twenty years was bigamous and that the son and two daughters of that marriage are therefore illegitimate. The secret, legitimate daughter of his first marriage, who grew up in an orphanage, unaware of her true identity, now inherits everything except the title itself and the entailed properties. That child, Anna Snow, now grown to adulthood, is the heroine of this book, which shows her as she copes with the staggering new realities of her life, not the least of which is the unexpected courtship of the very aristocratic Duke of Netherby, whose stepmother was a Westcott by birth.*

Someone to Hold, book 2, *is the story of Camille, one of the dispossessed daughters of the late earl. As well as losing her title and social status, Camille lost her aristocratic fiancé, who broke off their engagement as a result of the news. The proud, straitlaced, somewhat humorless Camille* has to piece her life together somehow and takes the totally unexpected step of applying for the teaching job at the orphanage in Bath recently vacated by Anna, the half sister she at first deeply resents. There Camille meets Joel Cunningham, Anna's close friend and former suitor.

Someone to Wed, *book 3*, is the story of Alexander Westcott, suddenly and unwillingly the Earl of Riverdale after his second cousin Harry loses the title upon the discovery of his illegitimacy. Along with the title, Alexander has inherited the entailed mansion and estate that go with it, both of them neglected and shabby and in need of a huge influx of money—which he does not have. Resentfully but dutifully, Alexander turns his mind toward the search for a wealthy wife. At the same time, Wren Heyward, a reclusive neighbor who always wears a veil because of a disfiguring birthmark on one side of her face, decides to use the vast fortune she has recently inherited from an uncle to buy herself a husband and some sense of belonging.

Someone to Care, *book 4*, is the story of Viola, the forty-two-year-old former Countess of Riverdale, who reacted to the knowledge that her marriage had been bigamous and her children illegitimate first by running away to live with her brother and then by living quietly in the country with her younger daughter. She has suppressed her anger and her suffering for a few years. But her control finally snaps for no apparent reason at the christening of her grandchild in Bath, and she leaves alone to return home. On the way there, she encounters a man who once, years ago, tried to coax her into an illicit affair. She refused then, but now when he suggests that she run away with him for a brief romantic fling with no strings attached, she asks herself, why not? She does it—she runs off with Marcel Lamarr. As it turns out, however, there are many strings attached to that impulsive decision—for both Viola and Marcel. For each of them has a family that cares.

Someone to Trust, *book 5, is the story of Elizabeth, Lady Overfield, the new earl, Alexander's, widowed sister, who left her abusive husband a year before his death. Now she has decided that she wants to marry again, but not for love this time. She wants a marriage of mutual respect and quiet contentment. However, at a Christmas family gathering in the country, she spends time with Colin, Lord Hodges, whose sister is married to her brother. There is an unexpected chemistry between them, but any thought of romance is out of the question, for Colin is nine years younger than Elizabeth and he too is in search of a bride among the young debutantes of the coming Season. I loved the challenge of dealing with the older woman / younger man dilemma. I also loved creating Colin's mother, the super-narcissistic villain, who first appeared in* Someone to Wed.

Someone to Honor *(make that* Honour *if you have the British edition!) is the story of Abigail, who is still grappling with the way her life completely changed after it was discovered that she was illegitimate. She still does not know quite who she is or what she wants out of life. Then she meets Lieutenant Colonel Gil Bennington, a friend and colleague of her brother's. Gil is a military officer and seems to be a gentleman, but in reality he is the illegitimate son of a village washerwoman and grew up as a gutter rat, to use his own words. He has acquired some wealth and a home in the country, but he is desperate to recover his young daughter from her maternal grandparents, who took her away when his wife died while he was away fighting in the Battle of Waterloo. His lawyer warns him that his best chance of winning the upcoming lawsuit is to marry again so he has a mother, as well as himself, to offer his child.*

I *do hope you enjoy the new story,* Someone to Remember. *I hope you will agree with me that Matilda is a precious person and deserving of her own happily-ever-after even though it has come late in life. And I hope you will agree that Charles is perfect for her and appreciates her as fully as she* deserves. And expect to meet them again in future books—as well as Charles's children, including his first son, Gil Bennington, and, of course, Matilda's family, the Westcotts.

Please look for the next book in the series, book 7, Lady Jessica Archer's story, next year.

All the best to all of you,
Mary Balogh

SOMEONE TO REMEMBER

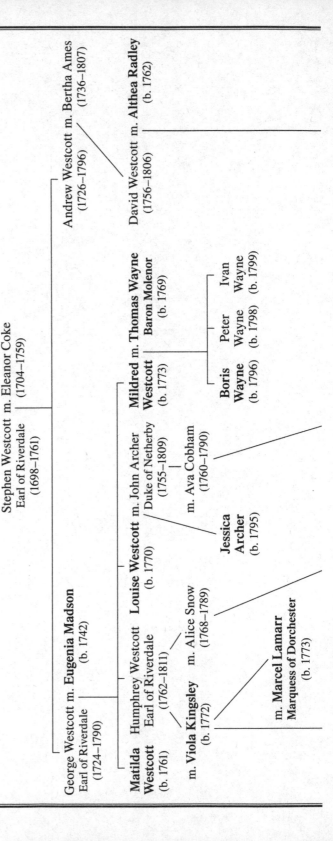

The Westcott Family

(Characters from the family tree who appear in *Someone to Remember* are shown in bold print.)

Stephen Westcott m. Eleanor Coke
Earl of Riverdale (1704–1759)
(1698–1761)

Andrew Westcott m. Bertha Ames
(1726–1796) (1736–1807)

David Westcott m. Althea Radley
(1756–1806) (b. 1762)

George Westcott m. **Eugenia Madson**
Earl of Riverdale (b. 1742)
(1724–1790)

Matilda Westcott (b. 1761)

Humphrey Westcott
Earl of Riverdale
(1762–1811)

m. Alice Snow
(1768–1789)

m. **Viola Kingsley** (b. 1772)

m. **Marcel Lamarr Marquess of Dorchester** (b. 1773)

Louise Westcott m. John Archer
(b. 1770) Duke of Netherby
(1755–1809)

m. Ava Cobham
(1760–1790)

Jessica Archer (b. 1795)

Mildred Westcott m. Thomas Wayne
(b. 1773) Baron Molenor
(b. 1769)

Boris Wayne (b. 1796)

Peter Wayne (b. 1798)

Ivan Wayne (b. 1799)

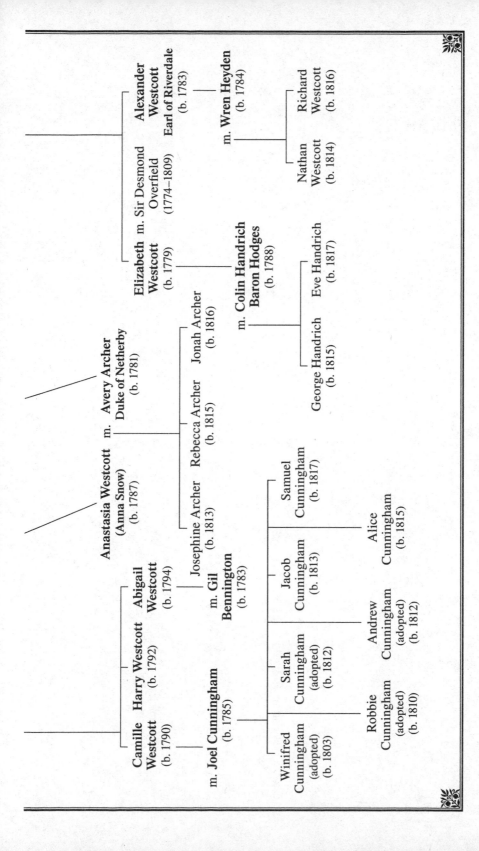

One

Lady Matilda Westcott's day had just taken a turn for the worse. She had not thought it possible, but she had been wrong.

She was sitting behind the tea tray in the drawing room, pouring for her mother and their visitors, whose unexpected arrival had cheered her at first. Alexander, Earl of Riverdale and head of the Westcott family, and Wren, his wife, were always welcome. They were an amiable, attractive young couple, and Matilda was extremely fond of them. Their conversation had followed predictable lines for several minutes—inquiries after the health of Matilda and her mother, and news of their young children and those of Elizabeth, Alexander's sister, and Colin, Lord Hodges, her husband, with all of whom they had enjoyed a picnic in Richmond Park the day before. But now they had changed the subject.

"Wren and I have decided that we really ought to invite Viscount Dirkson to dine with us," Alexander said.

"*Ought?*" Matilda's mother, the Dowager Countess of Riverdale, asked sharply. Matilda meanwhile had gone still, the teapot poised over the third cup.

"As a sort of thank-you, Cousin Eugenia," Wren explained. "Not that any of us need to *thank* him, exactly. Gil is his son, after all. But Viscount Dirkson has had no dealings with Gil all his life and might easily have ignored that custody hearing a couple of weeks ago. His absence might have made no difference in the judge's decision, of course. On the other hand, perhaps it *did* make a difference. And we want him to know that we appreciate what he did. For Abigail's sake. And for Gil's and Katy's sakes. We have invited him for tomorrow, and he has accepted."

"But we would like it to be a *family* dinner," Alexander said. "Not all the Westcotts are in town, of course, but we hope those who are will join us." He smiled his very charming smile, first at Matilda's mother and then at Matilda herself.

Matilda scarcely noticed as she proceeded to pour the third cup of tea with a hand she held steady.

She was invited too.

She should have been delighted. While the last earl, Humphrey, her brother, was alive, the Westcotts had not been nearly as close a family as they were now. He had had little use for any of them, even his wife and son and daughters. And he had done terrible things during his life, the very worst of which was to marry twice. That was not a crime in itself, but in his case it was. His first, secret marriage, to Alice Snow, had produced one equally secret daughter, Anna. His second marriage, to Viola, his countess for twenty-three years, had produced three children—Camille, Harry, and Abigail. The criminal aspect of the second marriage was that it had overlapped with the first by a month or two before Alice died of consumption. As a result Viola and her offspring had ended up dispossessed while

Anna, who had grown up in an orphanage, not knowing even who she was, had inherited a vast fortune, and the whole family had been thrown into turmoil, for the bigamous nature of Humphrey's second marriage had been unearthed only after his death.

May he not *rest in peace,* Matilda was often very tempted to think, even to say aloud. A very unsisterly sentiment, no doubt, not to mention unladylike. She often gave in to the temptation to think it nevertheless—as she did now.

She *should* have been delighted by the invitation, as Alexander was a far different sort of earl than Humphrey had been and had worked hard to draw the family together. However, the dinner was in honor of someone outside the family. Viscount Dirkson. *Charles.* A man Matilda would be very happy never to set eyes upon again for at least the rest of her life.

It had all started when Abigail Westcott, Humphrey's youngest daughter, had arrived unexpectedly in London a few weeks ago with an equally unexpected husband, whom she had married the day before. Lieutenant Colonel Gil Bennington had seemed a perfectly respectable young gentleman—he was a military friend of Harry, Abigail's brother. However, he had proceeded to reveal to Abigail's family that in reality he grew up as a gutter rat—his words—with his unmarried mother, who had scraped together a living as a village washerwoman. The family had been duly shocked. It really, truly *was* shocking, after all. Matilda had liked the young man anyway. He was tall and dark and handsome even if his face *was* marred by the scar of an old battle wound and even if he did tend to look upon the world with a dour expression. She had thought the sudden marriage wondrously romantic. She had fallen into shock only when Lieutenant Colonel Bennington had admitted, when pressed, that his father, with whom he had had no dealings all his life, was Viscount Dirkson.

He had been Charles Sawyer when Matilda had had an acquaintance with him ages ago, aeons ago. A lifetime. The title had come later, upon the death of his father.

But she had had a dealing with him since Gil's revelation—a secret, horribly scandalous dealing that would shock her family to the roots if they knew about it. The memory of it could still turn her cold enough to faint quite away—if she were the vaporish sort, which she was not. Well, it was not a secret from all of them. Young Bertrand Lamarr knew. He was Abigail's stepbrother, not a Westcott by birth but accepted by all of them as an honorary family member.

What had happened was that she, a single lady, had called upon Viscount Dirkson, a widowed gentleman, at his London home, with only young Bertrand as a companion to lend a semblance of respectability to what was in reality quite beyond the pale of it. She had screwed her courage to the sticking point, to quote someone in a Shakespeare play—Lady Macbeth?—though it might not be a strictly accurate quotation. Anyway, she had gone to persuade Charles to do something at last for his natural son, who was about to appear before a judge to plead for the return of his young daughter, who had been taken to the home of her maternal grandparents while Gil was away fighting at the Battle of Waterloo, and was never returned. It was the first time in thirty-six years she had come face-to-face with Charles or exchanged a word with him. After she had said her piece she had left with Bertrand, and she had comforted herself—*tried to*, at least—with the thought that *that* was the end of it. Finished. The end.

Now Alexander and Wren had invited him to a family dinner. And she was a member of the family.

Charles Sawyer also happened to be the only man Matilda had

ever loved. All of thirty-six years ago. More than half a biblical lifetime ago. She was fifty-six now.

All the cups had been filled, Matilda saw, and must be distributed before the tea in them turned cold. Her mother was talking.

"Viscount Dirkson is to be rewarded, then, for fathering a son out of wedlock and doing nothing for him in the more than thirty years since, until he spoke up on his son's behalf before a judge a few weeks ago?" she asked as Matilda set a cup of tea on the table beside her and made sure it was close enough for her to reach but not so close as to be knocked over by a careless elbow.

Wren came to take Alexander's and her cups from the tray and smiled her thanks to Matilda. "He did purchase his son's first commission some years ago, if you will recall, Cousin Eugenia," she said.

The dowager made a sound of derision and batted away her daughter's hand when Matilda tried to rearrange her shawl, which had slipped off one shoulder. "Don't fuss, Matilda."

"And that son is now married to Abigail and is therefore a member of our family," Alexander added, taking his cup and saucer from Wren's hand. "But even aside from purchasing the commission, what Dirkson did a couple of weeks ago was significant. Without his recommendation at the court hearing, Gil might very well not have regained custody of his daughter, and both he and Abigail would have been distraught. Dirkson would surely have attended the hearing for his own sake, of course, since Gil *is* his son. However, Wren and I feel an obligation to thank him on behalf of Abigail's family. Do say you will come too."

"It is nothing short of a miracle that Viscount Dirkson even found out about the custody hearing," Wren said.

But it had not happened by a miracle, Matilda thought as she picked up her own cup and sipped her tea. There was nothing miraculous about her.

"You are very quiet this afternoon, Matilda," Alexander said, smiling kindly at her. "What do *you* think? Will you come to our dinner? Will you persuade Cousin Eugenia to come too?"

Her opinion was rarely solicited. She was merely an appendage of her mother as she fussed over her, making sure she did not sit in a draft or overexert herself or get overexcited, though her mother resented her every attention. Sometimes, especially lately, Matilda wondered whether her mother needed her at all—or even loved her. It was a thought that depressed her horribly, for if the love and care she gave her mother were pointless, then what had been the purpose of her life? And why was she already thinking of it in the past tense?

"I think it is an admirable idea," she said. "You are a worthy Earl of Riverdale, Alexander. You take your responsibility as head of the family seriously. Inviting Viscount Dirkson to dine with as many of the family as are in London is a good way of showing him that we appreciate his speaking up for Gil. It will show him that we consider Gil one of us, that we value his happiness and Abigail's. And Katy's."

Katy was Gil's daughter—and Charles's granddaughter. That realization stabbed a little painfully at Matilda's heart every time her mind touched upon it. He had other grandchildren. Both of his daughters were married and both were mothers. His son, the youngest of his offspring, was as yet unwed. His wife of twenty years or so had died five years ago.

Alexander looked pleased at her praise. "You will come, then," he said. "Thank you."

Yes, she would go, though the very thought made her feel bilious. He was still so very handsome. Charles, that was. Whereas she . . . well, she was an aging spinster, perhaps even an *aged* one, and . . . Well.

"And will you invite Viscount Dirkson's family too?" her mother was asking. "His son and his daughters?"

"It is hardly likely they know of Gil's existence," Alexander said, frowning. "I doubt he would want them to know."

"Perhaps," Wren said, "we ought to inform Viscount Dirkson that he is welcome to bring his children if he wishes, Alexander. Let the decision be his."

"I will do that, my love," he said, nodding to Matilda, who was offering to pour him a second cup of tea. "Yes, thank you. You *will* come, Cousin Eugenia?"

"I will," she said. "Dirkson ran wild with Humphrey as a young man, you know, though he did not have the title in those days. His reputation became increasingly unsavory as time went on. He was not welcomed by the highest sticklers and perhaps still is not."

"I think we will not hold the past against him," Alexander said, a twinkle in his eye. "If he had not fathered an illegitimate child when he must have been a very young man, we would not even be planning this dinner, would we?"

"And Abigail would not have found the love of her life," Matilda said.

"Oh, I think you are right about that, Cousin Matilda," Wren said, beaming warmly at her. "I believe she and Gil are perfect for each other and perfect parents for Katy. No, no more tea for me, thank you. We must be on our way soon. We have taken enough of your time."

"But we have not told you our own very happy news," the dowager said.

"Oh," Wren said. "We must certainly hear that."

And Matilda was instantly reminded of why she had been feeling severely out of sorts even before Alexander and Wren arrived with their invitation.

"Edith is coming to live with us," her mother announced.

"Your sister, Cousin Eugenia, do you mean?" Alexander asked.

"Edith Monteith, yes," the dowager said. "I have been trying to persuade her to come ever since Douglas died a couple of years ago. She has neither chick nor child to keep her living in that drafty heap of a mansion all the way up as near to the Scottish border as makes no difference. It will be far better for her to come to me. She was always my favorite sister even though she is almost ten years younger than I."

"And she is coming to live permanently with you?" Wren asked. "That does indeed sound like good news." But she looked with a concerned frown at Matilda.

Her mother must have seen the look. "It is going to be wonderful for Matilda too," she said. "She will not be tied to the apron strings of an old woman any longer. She will have someone closer to her own age for companionship. Adelaide Boniface will be coming with Edith. She is a distant cousin of Douglas and quite indigent, poor thing. She has been Edith's companion for years."

Aunt Edith had suffered from low spirits since as far back as Matilda could remember, and Adelaide Boniface made good and certain they remained low. If the sun was shining, it was surely the harbinger of clouds and rain to come. If there was half a cake left on the plate for tea, then the fact that half of it was gone was cause for lamentation, for there would be none tomorrow. And she spoke habitually in a nasal whine while the offending nose was constantly being dabbed at and pushed from side to side with a balled-up handkerchief, the whole operation followed each time by a dry sniff. Matilda found the prospect of having her constant companionship, not to mention Aunt Edith's, quite intolerable. She really did not know how she was going to endure such an invasion of her home and her very life.

"I am very happy for you both, then," Alexander said, setting aside his cup and getting to his feet. "Are they coming soon?"

"After we go home to the country at the end of the Season," the dowager told him. "We are certainly happy about it, are we not, Matilda?"

"It will be something new to look forward to," Matilda said, smiling determinedly as Wren hugged her and Alexander kissed her cheek and bent over her mother's chair after assuring her that she did not need to get to her feet.

"We will see you both tomorrow evening, then," he said.

Oh, Matilda thought after they had left, how was she going to *bear* it all? Coming face-to-face with Charles again tomorrow and spending a whole evening in his company. Going back to the country in one month's time to a home that would be home no longer. Could life possibly get any bleaker?

But how could spending an evening in Charles's company possibly matter after thirty-six years? One could not nurse a broken heart and blighted hopes that long. Or, if one did, one was a pathetic creature indeed.

Oh, but she had loved him . . .

All silliness.

"HE IS THIRTY-FOUR YEARS OLD," CHARLES SAWYER, VISCOUNT Dirkson, was telling Adrian, at twenty-two the youngest of his offspring. "It happened long before I married your mother. Before I even knew her, in fact."

"Who was she?" Adrian asked after a pause, a frown creasing his brow, one hand clasping a leather-bound book he had taken at random from one of the bookshelves upon which he leaned. "Or perhaps I ought to have asked, Who *is* she?"

"Was," Charles said. "She died many years ago. She was the daughter of a prosperous blacksmith. I met her while staying with a friend at a house nearby. It was a brief liaison, but it had consequences."

"So all the time you were married to Mother," Adrian said, "you were seeing that woman and *him*. Your other family."

"Nothing like that," Charles assured him. "She would have nothing to do with me when she understood that I would not marry her even though her family had turned her out without a penny. She refused all support for herself and the child. She raised him on the money she made from taking in other people's washing until he went off with a recruiting sergeant at the age of fourteen to join the army. After she died I purchased a commission for him. But he stopped me and cut all ties with me later, after I had purchased a promotion for him. His mother raised a proud son."

"But he managed to rise to the rank of lieutenant colonel after you gave him a leg up into the officer ranks," Adrian said, opening the book briefly before snapping it shut without even looking at it. "And now he has married into the Westcott family. Bertrand Lamarr, that friend of mine from Oxford who came to call a few weeks ago, has a connection to them too. His father married one of them a few years ago. And the lady who came here with him was a Westcott. You took her to look at the garden while he and I were becoming reacquainted. Was it through her that you discovered your . . . *son* had married a Westcott and was in a court battle to regain custody of his daughter? Your *granddaughter*?" He laughed rather shakily and set the book flat on the shelf rather than slotting it into its appointed place.

"Yes," Charles said. "I went to the hearing and said a few words to the judge. Riverdale, head of the Westcott family, seems to believe that what I said made a difference and helped . . . Gil to win his case."

"Gil," his son said softly.

"Gilbert," Charles said. "She named him. His mother."

He had pondered telling his son after a second note had come from Riverdale following the initial invitation. Viscount Dirkson was quite welcome to bring his children and their spouses to the dinner too if he wished, the note had said. Charles most certainly did not wish any such thing. He did not even want to attend himself. Perish the thought. He could not see why the Westcott family felt somehow indebted to him. Gil was *his son*, after all. Katy, as Adrian had just pointed out, was *his* granddaughter. He had not attended that custody hearing for the sake of the Westcotts. He had done it for his son, whom he had never seen before that day but whom he had loved for thirty-four years. Yes. True.

Ah, but he had done it also at least partly for one of the Westcotts, had he not?

For Matilda?

He had rarely been more surprised—no, *shocked*—than he had been a few weeks ago when his butler had come to his dressing room to inform him that Lady Matilda Westcott was downstairs in the visitors' parlor with young Lamarr, Viscount Watley, who claimed to be a university friend of his lordship's son.

Matilda. Here in his own house. Wanting to speak with him. After . . . how long? Thirty years? Thirty-five? It must be the latter or even a bit longer. Gil was thirty-four, and all the drama with

Matilda had been over before he was conceived. In fact there had been a connection. Charles would almost certainly not have engaged in that ill-considered affair with Gil's mother if he had not been raw with pain over Matilda's rejection when she had adamantly refused to stand up to her parents' disapproval of his suit. Within months or even weeks he had gone dashing into the arms of the first pretty woman to take his eye and respond to his flirtations. And he had taken none of the usual precautions when he lay with her. She had taken none either. Perhaps she had not even known such a thing was possible. Or perhaps she really believed he had promised to marry her, though he knew beyond all doubt that he had not.

He had got over Matilda years and years ago, though when they were both in London he had spotted her occasionally, growing ever older and more staid, wasting herself upon a mother who had denied her daughter's happiness and now did not seem to appreciate that daughter's attentions. He had felt irritated every time he set eyes upon Matilda Westcott—the only feeling he had had left for her.

Until, that was, he had stepped a few weeks ago into the visitors' parlor here in his own home and she had called him by his given name instead of his title, a woman of fifty-six who was a stranger and yet was not. He had found himself then remembering the pretty, vital, warmhearted young woman she had once been and had felt an irritation far more intense than usual—for her and perhaps for time itself for robbing her of youth and beauty. And maybe for himself for remembering not just facts but feelings too, most notably the depths of his youthful passion for her and the contrasting pain of his despair at losing her, not because she did not love him but because her parents did not think him worthy of her. And anger. That she had turned him out and there had been no way of getting her to see reason. And present anger that she had come to his home like this without a by-your-leave and with only young Lamarr's connection to Adrian as an excuse.

He had been angry that he could still remember those feelings. For it had all been a lifetime ago. And why should he remember? He had known scores of women both before and after her and even after his marriage.

Why should it annoy him that Matilda had grown old? No, not old. That was both inaccurate and unkind. Besides, she was almost the exact same age as he. She had grown middle-aged—to the shady side of middle age, to be more precise. She had never married. Why not, for God's sake? Had no one measured up to the expectations of dear Mama and Papa? Yet their two younger daughters had married well. Had Matilda been too valuable to them, then, as the family drudge? Had it pleased them to sap all the life and youth and passion out of her until she became as she was now?

But why should it annoy him, what had happened to Lady Matilda Westcott? A bruised heart did not remain bruised for very long. He had soon learned that. He had forgotten her before that summer was even over. Gil's mother had had successors. His reputation as a rake had been well earned.

"So," Adrian said, "is he going to be in your life now? As a semi-respectable member of the Westcott family? Is that what this dinner is all about?"

"The dinner," Charles explained, "is Riverdale's way of thanking me for appearing at the custody hearing and perhaps having some small part in enabling my . . . son to get his daughter back from her grandparents. He does not need to thank me. None of them do. I do not really want to go to the dinner, but it would seem the civil thing to do."

"And you want me to go with you," Adrian said.

Charles shrugged, picked up the quill pen from the desk before him to trim the nib, changed his mind, and set it back down. "I thought I ought to tell you at last," he said, "before word somehow leaks out, as it well might, and you learn the truth from someone else. The existence of my natural son makes no difference to my feelings for you and your sisters."

"I have a half brother twelve years my senior," Adrian said, as though he were only now understanding what Charles had told him several minutes ago. "Does he look like me?"

"No," Charles said.

"No." Adrian laughed. "How could he? I look like Mama. Does he look like you?"

"Yes," Charles said. "But he has a facial scar." With one finger he traced a line across one cheek and down over his chin.

"The crusading hero," Adrian said. "I suppose it makes him irresistible to women. And he is tall and dark like you, is he? I suppose you are going to grow close to him now."

"I very much doubt it," Charles said. "He does not have a high opinion of me, and I cannot blame him."

"Do you have a high opinion of him?" his son asked.

Charles hesitated. "Yes," he said. He pushed his chair with the backs of his knees and got to his feet. "You may come to the dinner with me if you wish, Adrian. I will be pleased if you do. I will understand if you do not."

"Do you intend to tell my sisters?" Adrian asked.

Neither of them was in London at present. Barbara, the elder of the two, was in the country with her husband and children to celebrate the fortieth wedding anniversary of her parents-in-law. Jane had discovered herself to be with child just before the start of the

Season and had remained in the country until she recovered from the bilious phase that had plagued her also with her first child.

"I do," Charles said. "In person when the opportunity arises." And for the same reason that had persuaded him to tell Adrian. The truth was bound to come out now that Gil had surfaced in his life, even though his son planned to live year-round in Gloucestershire. It was better that the news come from their father.

Adrian nodded and pushed away from the bookshelves. "I'll come," he said. "Bertrand will be there, you said?"

"Lamarr?" Charles said. "Viscount Watley? Very probably, since his father is married to the former Countess of Riverdale."

"Then I'll come," Adrian said again. "Just as long as your other son will not be there too."

"No," Charles said. "He has already taken his wife and daughter home to Gloucestershire."

"At your expense?" Adrian asked.

"No," Charles told him. "He is apparently independently wealthy. So is his wife."

"I have to go out," his son said abruptly, making his way toward the door. "I was supposed to be somewhere half an hour ago."

"Adrian." His son stopped, his hand on the doorknob, and looked back at him. "I adored you from the moment I first saw you all swaddled up in your mother's arms, your cheeks red and fat. I have not changed my affections since."

His son nodded again and was gone.

He was not good with words of affection, Charles thought. He had not been a good husband. They had not married for love, he and his wife, and they had lived very separate lives. They had always been polite to each other, but there had been no real warmth or affection between them.

It had been otherwise with his children. He had always loved them totally and unconditionally, and still did. He had spent time with them when they were young. He had taught them to ride and had taken Barbara hunting with him on several occasions. He had taken Jane and Adrian fishing. He had taken them all swimming and tree climbing—the latter when his wife was well out of sight. He had read to them before they could do it for themselves. Perhaps, he thought now, he had lavished upon his legitimate children all the time and affection Gil's mother had refused to allow him to lavish upon his firstborn.

He picked up the quill pen again, though he did not resume his seat, and turned it in his hand, brushing the feather across his palm.

He loved his firstborn son with a dull ache of longing. But he wished all this had not happened to churn up pointless emotions— Gil's sudden appearance in London with a wife, terrified that he might lose his daughter forever if the judge ruled against him; Charles seeing his son for the first time across that small courtroom where the hearing had been held, the Westcott family in their rows of chairs between them; the stiff, awkward breakfast meeting the following morning at Gil's hotel, arranged by Gil's wife; the almost certain knowledge that they would never see each other again.

Matilda.

He wished he did not feel angry with her, irritated with her for aging and making him want to lash out at someone or something for a reason he could not even fathom.

Passion was for young men. He resented the strong emotions that had been coming at him from all directions during the past few weeks. His life, at least for the previous ten years or so, had been on the placid side as he surrendered to middle age, prepared to enjoy his grandchildren, and rejoiced in how well his children were settling into meaningful lives. His relative contentment with life had included happiness for his firstborn, who had survived the unimaginable brutality of the Napoleonic wars.

He did not want strong emotions to erupt now at his age.

He did not want to have to look again into the wounded eyes of his younger son, who had just discovered the existence of an older half brother. He did not want to have to tell Barbara and Jane, and that was an understatement.

He did not want to go to this infernal dinner at Riverdale's house on South Audley Street. He did not want to have to talk about Gil with the Westcotts. He did not want to spend an evening in company with Matilda.

Especially that. In fact, without that, the dinner would be merely an inconvenience.

He had loved her . . .

But it was all foolishness.

Two

Eighteen members of the Westcott family—though not all of them actually bore the name, or, in some cases, even the blood—were assembled in the drawing room at the house on South Audley Street where Alexander, Earl of Riverdale, had his town residence. They ranged downward in age from the dowager countess, who was in her middle seventies, to Boris Wayne, twenty-one years old, eldest son of Matilda's sister Mildred, newly down from Oxford and eager to cut a figure as a dashing young man about town, much to his mother's frequent consternation.

There were plenty of persons, in other words, among whom to hide. But they nevertheless seemed thin cover to Matilda as Alexander's butler announced Viscount Dirkson and Mr. Adrian Sawyer, his son, whom she had met very briefly a few weeks ago when she made her call upon his father. She took up her accustomed position behind her mother's chair and busied herself with her usual tasks, checking to see that her mother was comfortable and in no danger of a draft from the opened door even though it was not the time of year when one was likely to take a chill from such exposure. She attempted to be invisible, to blend into the scenery.

Charles stepped into the room ahead of his son. He was a remarkably distinguished-looking man and was drawing all eyes his way. Well, of course he was. He was the newcomer, the guest of honor. He had just walked in among a crowd of people who all claimed some sort of kinship with one another. Nevertheless, he looked perfectly at ease as he smiled and bowed to Wren and shook Alexander by the hand. His hair was still thick and predominantly dark, though it was nicely silvered at the temples. Although he was not slim in the way a young man is slim, he had an excellent figure, the extra weight well distributed about his person. His evening clothes were expertly tailored.

All told, he was an extremely attractive man and Matilda dearly wished she had thought of some excuse not to come, though *what* excuse she did not know. She had always been notoriously healthy. She had never, all her life, laid claim to the vapors or heart palpitations or any of the other ailments many women trotted out anytime they wished to avoid an activity they considered tedious.

She *wished* her mind was not so full of buzzing bees.

She turned her attention toward Mr. Adrian Sawyer, several inches shorter than his father and fuller faced, fair-haired rather than dark—a pleasant-looking young man. He too was smiling as he bowed to Wren and said something that caused her to twinkle back at him. What reason had his father given him for their attendance at this family dinner? Had he told him the truth? Bertrand was making his way toward his former university friend, and the two shook hands warmly before Bertrand bore him off to introduce him to Estelle, his twin sister, and to an openly eager Boris.

Seeing Alexander begin to lead Charles about the room to make sure he knew everyone—though he surely did—Matilda stepped farther behind the chair and bent over the back of it to adjust her mother's shawl.

"Don't fuss, Matilda," her mother said just as the two men arrived before her chair.

"The Dowager Countess of Riverdale," Alexander said, "and Lady Matilda Westcott."

"I have an acquaintance with Viscount Dirkson," Matilda's mother said, her voice regal and a bit chilly, "though it has been a while since we last spoke. I did see you in the judge's chambers a couple of weeks ago but you did not remain after the proceedings were over. You used to be a friend of my son's."

"I did indeed, ma'am," he said, bowing to her. "The late Riverdale and I were acquaintances for a number of years. I also know Lady Matilda. How do you do, ma'am?"

He was looking very directly at her over her mother's head, and Matilda felt as flustered as a girl at her first *ton* party, her heart pounding hard enough in her bosom to rob her of breath, her brain spinning and fluttering with a thousand bees' wings so that no sensible answer presented itself immediately to her tongue and lips. No one was looking at her, she told herself. Not with any particular attention, anyway. And why should they? She was just Matilda. And why be so flustered? She had actually called upon him and stepped into his garden with him and spoken with him there less than a month ago. But that was half the trouble. What must he have thought of her bold presumption?

"I am well, I thank you," her mother said in just the words Matilda ought to have uttered in the brief moment of hesitation that had followed his question.

His eyes remained on hers a moment longer before he looked

down to acknowledge her mother's reply, and then he stepped away with Alexander to shake someone else by the hand.

Matilda leaned over the back of the chair again to adjust her mother's shawl, remembered that she had just been told not to fuss, and straightened. She, who never wept, even when there was good cause, wanted to weep now when there was none.

"It is easy to see where Gil got his height and his looks, is it not, Matilda?" her former sister-in-law, Viola, said, moving up to her side. "He and Abby and Katy arrived safely home in Gloucestershire. I had a letter today. Abby loves the house and the village and the countryside. I have rarely if ever had such an exuberant letter from her. I do believe she is going to be happy."

"I *know* she will be," Matilda said, patting Viola's arm. "She already is. They both are. He has a way of looking at her and she at him, and they have the child. And their cottage in the country with a garden full of roses."

"Now if I can just see Harry happily settled I will consider myself the most blessed of mothers," Viola said.

Her son, Harry, had very briefly been the Earl of Riverdale following his father's death—before it had been revealed that his birth was illegitimate.

"He will have his own happily-ever-after, never fear," Matilda assured her.

"You cannot be certain that anyone will be happy, Matilda," her mother said. "What do you know of marital bliss, never having been married yourself?"

Matilda did not wince, not outwardly at least.

"But Matilda knows a great deal about *love*, Mother," Viola protested, linking her arm through her erstwhile sister-in-law's. "I will take her word about Abby and Gil's future because I want to agree with her and actually do. And I agree about Harry."

Charles was bending his head to listen to the conversation of the small group to which he had been led. He was smiling, his eyes crinkling attractively at the corners.

He had fathered Gil very soon after she sent him away, even though he had sworn undying love and fidelity when he went. And for years afterward he had had what Matilda believed to be a well-deserved reputation as a rake and a gamester and a man who lived hard and behaved recklessly. He had perhaps mellowed with age. She could not know for sure. But surely her father had been right to refuse his consent to their marrying and her parents had been right to insist that she put an end to her acquaintance with him. *Acquaintance!* Ah, it had felt like far more than that. But surely she would have been miserable had she married him.

Wouldn't she?

Love would not have been enough.

Would it?

But they were pointless questions to ask herself. She could not know the answers. There was no going back to do things differently. There was no knowing how happy or unhappy their marriage would have been. There had been no marriage.

Dinner was being announced and Matilda entered the dining room with her mother. Fortunately she was able to sit halfway along the table, some distance from Charles, who was seated beside Wren at the foot. Unfortunately, perhaps, she had not thought to go to the other side of the table so that she would be on the same side as he and therefore unable to see him every time she looked up from her plate and turned her head that way. But it did not matter anyway.

He was never looking back at her when she did inadvertently glance at him. He was always politely focusing his attention upon Wren to his left or Louise, Dowager Duchess of Netherby, Matilda's middle sister, to his right. Conversation was lively along both lengths of the table.

Matilda discovered without surprise that she had little appetite. She also felt like bawling for no good reason whatsoever—again. She sincerely hoped she was not about to develop into a watering pot at her advanced age.

IT WAS A SOMEWHAT MORE PLEASANT EVENING THAN CHARLES had anticipated. For one thing Adrian was taken almost immediately under the wing of young Bertrand Lamarr, who introduced him to Lady Estelle, his twin sister; to Boris Wayne, Lord Molenor's son; and to Lady Jessica Archer, half sister of the Duke of Netherby, who was married to a Westcott. And since Adrian was a young man of generally even temper and easy manners, he appeared to be right at home with all of them and actually enjoying himself.

The dinner was excellent, the conversation pleasant. He had agreeable table companions. Only at the end of the meal was the subject of Gil raised when Riverdale got to his feet, a glass of wine in his hand.

"We Westcotts are always ready for an excuse to gather together," he said when everyone had fallen silent and turned his way. "We are happy this evening to have Viscount Dirkson and Mr. Sawyer with us too. Perhaps none of us needed to be present in the judge's chambers for the custody hearing a couple of weeks ago. Perhaps young Katy would have been released into Gil and Abigail's care even if we had all stayed away. But I am glad we went. Even if our presence did not weigh with the judge, at least we demonstrated to the newly married couple that we care, that we consider them family, that we will concern ourselves with their well-being and stand with them whenever it is threatened for any reason. It is what we Westcotts do for our own. It is what no doubt you do for your own, Viscount Dirkson. We are happy that your son came with you this evening. Shall we drink a toast to family—to all branches of it no matter how slight the connection?"

They drank, even Adrian, who looked steadily at his father as he did so.

The ladies withdrew to the drawing room after the toast, leaving the men to their port and their male conversation. In the drawing room later, the Marchioness of Dorchester, Gil's mother-in-law, came to sit beside Charles. She spoke of the difficulties her daughter had faced after the discovery that her father had married her mother bigamously. She spoke too of her conviction that her daughter's marriage to Gil would be a happy one for both of them.

"Ma'am," Charles said, "you do not have to convince me, if that is indeed what you are attempting to do. I agree with you." They smiled at each other, two parents linked by the marriage of their offspring.

He conversed with other members of the family too, even the Dowager Countess of Riverdale after she had beckoned to him, almost like a queen summoning her subject. He was not fond of that particular lady, though he had had no dealings whatsoever with her for many years and it would be foolish to hold a grudge for what she had done more than half a lifetime ago. But even this evening she had annoyed him. He had seen her as soon as he walked into the drawing room earlier, perhaps because Matilda had been standing behind her chair beside the fireplace, and Matilda was the Westcott he had least wanted to encounter this evening. But as he had approached with Riverdale to pay his respects, she had bent over the back of the chair to adjust her mother's shawl about her shoulders. The old lady had batted away her hands and admonished her not to fuss, a thinly disguised impatience in her voice, though she must have been aware that she might be overheard.

Or perhaps she had not been aware. Perhaps she was so accustomed to treating Matilda that way that it did not strike her as inappropriate behavior before a stranger. But then she had compounded her disregard for her daughter. Charles had acknowledged the older lady and turned his attention to Matilda and asked her how she did. But it was the mother who answered, leaving her daughter with nothing to say and perhaps feeling foolish. He had felt irritation with both of them, with the dowager for behaving as though her daughter did not even exist and could not possibly be the object of his inquiry, and with Matilda for meekly accepting it.

Was this the life for which she had renounced him all those years ago? But why should he care? It was all ancient history. Good God, he had had a full life since then. Matilda was living the life she had chosen, as the spinster daughter who had remained at home, the prop and stay of her parent in old age.

But who would care for Matilda in *her* old age?

He would have rather enjoyed the evening if she had not been there. But every moment he was aware of her and hated the fact. He had been aware during dinner and had deliberately avoided looking her way and perhaps meeting her glance. He had relaxed briefly while the men were alone together after dinner. But then he had been aware of her again in the drawing room.

He had no real idea *why*. He had been involved in a brief, passionate romance with her when they were both very young, had been rejected by her father when he had asked to pay his addresses to her, had been rejected by *her* afterward to the extent that she had told him firmly to go away and refused ever to speak to him or so much as look his way ever again. And that had been the end of that. It had been surely the sort of disappointment that most men, and probably many women too, suffered during their volatile youth. He had not pined with unrequited love for long. Maybe a few days. Perhaps a few weeks. No longer than that. He had promptly got on with his life.

And it had happened all of thirty-six years ago, for the love of God. Why was it, then, that he was so aware of her now and so irritated by her—and for her? Society was full of aging, fussy spinsters who were used by their relatives and lacked the spirit to fight back. But none of the others irritated him or aroused ire in him on their behalf.

She was standing over at one end of the room, talking with a couple of the other ladies. After they had moved away she remained there, straightening a pile of sheet music on top of the pianoforte. Then she looked across the room toward her mother. Perhaps, Charles thought, this needed to be settled—whatever *this* was. He strode toward the pianoforte before she could hurry away to see if her mother's shawl needed straightening again.

"How *do* you do, Matilda?" he asked, emphasizing the one word. She had not been given the chance to answer the question earlier.

"Oh." She looked into his eyes and kept her gaze there. "My mother thought you were addressing her."

"Even though I was looking at you?" he said. "Does she imagine you are invisible?"

She drew breath and closed her mouth. Then she drew breath again when it must have become obvious to her that he was waiting for her answer. "I do not suppose so. I do not know what you expect me to say."

"I expect you to tell me how you are," he said. "It would be the courteous thing to do, to answer a question politely asked, would it not?"

She tipped her head slightly to one side, and he was instantly assailed by memory. It had been a characteristic gesture of hers when she was twenty, and apparently it still was.

"I am well," she said. "Thank you."

"Why did you not say so when I asked earlier?" And why was he pressing the point? He had no idea except that he was still feeling the irritation she seemed to arouse in him.

"My mother answered," she said.

"To inform me that *she* was well," he said. "Does she always answer questions that are addressed directly to you?" He frowned at her.

"It would perhaps have embarrassed her if she had realized it was me you were asking," she said. "Charles, what is this about?"

It was a good question. He did not have an answer. She looked her age, he thought. But she was not actually a faded creature, as one might expect her to be under the circumstances. She was tall, still as straight backed as she had been as a young woman, her posture elegant, even proud. She was no longer slender. But she was well proportioned and elegantly dressed. Her face was virtually unlined, her hair still not noticeably graying. She was what might be called a handsome woman. She had been pretty as a girl, with a spark of animation to make her beautiful in his eyes. She might have married any of a dozen eligible men during that first Season of hers. She had not married him. She had not married anyone else either. Or during all the Seasons after that.

"Are you happy?" he asked her, his tone sounding abrupt even to his own ears.

She frowned but said nothing.

"I expected every time I opened the morning papers for a year or more afterward," he said without stopping to explain what he meant by *afterward*, "to see a notice of your betrothal to someone rich and eligible and respectable. It never happened, even after I stopped specifically looking. Are you happy?"

"I scarcely know what to say," she told him. "I make myself useful. My mother needs me, and it is a comfort to my sisters to know that she has constant companionship."

He gazed steadily at her. He had his back to everyone else in the room. But he did not suppose his conversation with her was being particularly remarked upon. Why should it be? He had conversed with most of the rest of the family by this stage of the evening. Why not with Lady Matilda Westcott too? No one in this room with the exception of her mother would remember their brief, intense courtship. And even if anyone did, it was a long time ago.

What would life have been like if they had married? It was impossible to know. So much would have been different. Everything would have been. Gil would not exist. Neither would Adrian nor Barbara nor Jane. Nor any of his grandchildren. But perhaps other children and grandchildren who had never been born would have had existence in their stead.

"Do you live to serve, then?" he asked her.

"There are worse ways to spend one's life," she told him.

"Are there?" It was not really a question he expected her to answer. "Why did you not marry?"

She recoiled slightly before recovering and looking beyond him to smile briefly at someone he could not see. "Perhaps," she said, "no one asked."

"That is nonsense," he said. "And untrue. *I* asked."

Her eyes focused fully upon him again. "Perhaps there was no one I wished to marry," she said.

"Not even me?"

He watched her draw a slow breath. "Your son—Gil—was born a mere year or so later," she said. "Whether I wished to marry you is not the point. The point is that I was wise not to do so."

That was inarguable. He had been known as wild even before he met her. But it had been the wildness of a very young man testing his wings and sowing a few wild oats, if that was not a hopeless mingling of metaphors. His real notoriety as an unsavory character and a rake came afterward. Would it have happened if he had married Matilda? He could not know the answer. He had not married her.

"It was wise, then," he said, "not to marry anyone else either?"

"Perhaps," she said.

"But perhaps not? Do you regret remaining unmarried?" He could not seem to leave the matter alone.

"Regrets are pointless," she said.

"Yes." She did regret it, then?

"The tea tray has been brought in," she said, looking beyond him again, "and Wren is pouring. I must go and add the correct amount of milk and sugar to my mother's cup and take it to her. She likes her tea just so."

And no one else was capable of doing it quite right? No one else knew the exact number of grains of sugar or drops of milk? He did not ask aloud. He stood aside and let her pass. As she did so he got a whiff of her perfume, so subtle that it could not be detected unless one was close to her. He was rocked by the memory of that same perfume and a shared kiss behind a potted aspidistra on the balcony outside a ballroom where they had danced a minuet together. A brief, passionate kiss. Lady Matilda Westcott had always—*almost always*—been carefully chaperoned by her mother.

Why would he remember that kiss when he had surely forgotten hundreds of others and the women with whom he had shared them? She had pressed her lips to his and brought her bosom against his chest, her spine arching inward beneath his hands. And he had smelled her perfume and been lost in sensual bliss—and an intense sexual desire that had never been fully satisfied.

Why was he remembering? Just because of that whiff of perfume?

Three

Matilda took her mother a cup of tea, made just the way she liked it, as well as a piece of cake, and stayed close even though there was no need to. Both her sister Louise and cousin Althea, Alexander's mother, were seated close to her and engaging her in conversation. The younger women were agreeing that this evening's gathering had been a good idea of Alexander's and that it was encouraging that Viscount Dirkson had come and had even brought Mr. Sawyer, his son, with him.

"Well, I do *not* like it," Matilda's mother said. "All I can say is that I hope it is not a case of like father, like son. Viscount Dirkson was a crony of Humphrey's, which is *not* a great recommendation even though Humphrey was my son."

"Mama, do not upset yourself." But when Matilda would have handed her mother the smelling salts she always kept in her reticule, her hand was pushed aside.

Mr. Adrian Sawyer spoke up at that exact moment. He was addressing his father, but loudly enough to draw everyone's attention.

"Bertrand is getting up a party to go out to Kew Gardens to-morrow, Papa," he said. "He wants me to go with them. Will you mind terribly if I do not after all accompany you to Tattersalls, as I promised I would? May we make it next week instead?"

"And who is to be of this party, pray, Bertrand?" Louise asked, raising her voice.

"Well, my sister and Adrian for sure, Aunt," Bertrand replied. "And Boris."

"And me," added Jessica—Lady Jessica Archer, Louise's daughter. "I may go, may I not, Mama, instead of going visiting with you?"

"And my particular friend, Charlotte Rigg, to make numbers even," Estelle, Bertrand's twin sister, said. "I am sure her mama will let her come. I believe she has designs upon Bertrand." She laughed as he grimaced. "Her mama, that is, not Charlotte herself."

"Oh bother," Louise said. "That will mean I ought to accompany the party in order to reassure Mrs. Rigg that it is properly chaperoned. There are some ladies I particularly wished to call upon tomorrow."

"Oh, Mama," Jessica protested, "we will all be cousins and siblings. There will be absolutely no need of a chaperon. Besides, I am twenty-three years old."

"A veritable fossil," Avery, Duke of Netherby, said on a sigh, looking with lazy eyes at his half sister through his jeweled quizzing glass.

"But Miss Rigg is neither anyone's sister nor anyone's cousin," Louise pointed out. "Nor is she twenty-three. I doubt she is even nineteen. And her mother will not be able to accompany her. I heard just this afternoon that she has taken to her bed with a nasty chill."

"Well, bother," Jessica said.

"I daresay I could accompany the young people," Charles said, causing all eyes to turn his way—including Matilda's, though she had been trying to ignore him, having been considerably discomposed by that strange conversation of theirs. Heavens, did he seriously believe the Westcott family, not to mention Mrs. Rigg, would consider him a suitable chaperon for a group of six that included three young ladies, none of whom was related to him? But he was not finished.

"Provided there is a lady who is prepared to come as cochaperon, of course," he said.

"But if I go, as it seems I must," Louise said, "you may save yourself the trouble, Lord Dirkson. I—"

"I suppose I could—" Viola began at the same time.

Charles cut them both off.

"Perhaps Lady Matilda Westcott?" he suggested, turning his eyes fully upon her. "If the dowager countess can spare her for a few hours, that is."

What? *What?*

"Me?" Matilda said foolishly, spreading a hand over her bosom while she felt all eyes turn her way. Though she was really aware only of his eyes and of the disturbing feeling that she might well swoon. Yet she gave no thought to the smelling salts in her reticule.

"Oh yes, do come, Aunt Matilda," Jessica cried, turning eagerly toward her. "It is really rather dreary to be on an outing with one's own mama as chaperon." She laughed and looked fondly at Louise. "No offense intended, Mama. I am sure you felt exactly the same way when you were my age."

"Oh yes, please do come, Aunt," added Bertrand, who had informed her a few weeks ago that she was a great gun after she had ridden in his sporting curricle all the way to Charles's house without clinging or squawking in alarm. It had actually been one of the most exhilarating experiences of her life. She only wished he could have sprung the horses. "You can keep a strict chaperonly eye upon Estelle." He grinned at his twin.

"*Chaperonly?*" His father, the Marquess of Dorchester, raised his eyebrows.

"Will you please come, Aunt Matilda?" Boris asked. "I have a hankering to see the pagoda at Kew. I have never been there."

"May I add my pleas, ma'am?" Mr. Sawyer added, smiling sweetly at Matilda. "And you will be comfortable with Papa, will you not, since you know him?"

It seemed to Matilda that the room grew suddenly silent and that all eyes turned accusingly upon her. Perhaps she was imagining it. But her cheeks felt as though they had caught fire.

"It is a very slight acquaintance," she hastened to explain. "I met your father, Mr. Sawyer, when my brother was still alive and I had just made my debut into society." She wondered if he would remember her calling his father Charles rather than Lord Dirkson when she had appeared at his house with Bertrand a few weeks ago. And heavens, she willed him not to mention that visit. Her mother and the rest of the family would be scandalized at the very least. "We danced together at a few balls that Season. It was many years ago, as you may imagine. I would be delighted to play chaperon for Jessica and Estelle and Miss Rigg tomorrow if I may be spared. It is ages since I was last at Kew. Mama?"

"Of course you can be spared, Matilda," her sister Mildred said. "I will spend the afternoon with Mama."

"I do not need anyone to cosset me," their mother protested.

"I will spend the afternoon with you anyway," Mildred said. "You may cosset me if you prefer. At least I will be able to relax, knowing for once where Boris is. He will be under the eagle eye of my sister."

"Mama," Boris protested, clearly mortified.

"Then it is settled," Bertrand said, rubbing his hands together. "We merely have to make arrangements for Charlotte Rigg to come with us."

"Oh, there will be no problem over that," Estelle assured him. "Not when her mother is too sick to take her anywhere herself and Aunt Matilda will be accompanying the party. There is no one more respectable."

"Thank you, Estelle," Matilda said. "You make me sound very staid and very dull."

"You are not dull at all," that young lady cried, startling her by rushing at her and catching her up in a hug. "Or staid."

"What I want to know about," Boris said, "is your flighty youth, Aunt Matilda, when you were in town with Uncle Humphrey and made your come-out and knew Lord Dirkson. Was everything very different back then?"

"Oh yes, indeed," Matilda said, slightly dizzy over the fact that everyone's attention was upon her. "We lived in caves, you know, and wore animal skins."

"And hunted down our food with stone mallets," Charles added to the great delight of the young people.

Matilda, catching his eye and noting the twinkle there—oh she *recognized* that twinkle—felt suddenly giddy with joy.

Joy?

When had she last felt joyful? When she had also felt youthful? A long, long time ago. Back when they lived in caves and rubbed sticks together to make fire. Even before the time of bows and arrows.

"And did you waltz at those balls, Aunt Matilda?" Boris asked.

Alas, no. The waltz had not been invented until long after she was young.

"We stamped about barefoot to the beating of drums," Charles answered for her, actually grinning for a moment.

Matilda laughed aloud and then felt horribly self-conscious. For though the young people and most of the adults were laughing too, Charles's eyes were fixed upon her, and suddenly he was not laughing at all. His eyes had even stopped twinkling.

Ah, but she wished, wished, *wished* the waltz had become popular thirty years or so before it had. It was surely the most romantic dance ever. She wished there was the memory of waltzing with him, even if only once.

"IT WAS DECENT OF YOU TO OFFER TO ACCOMPANY OUR PARTY," Adrian said the following morning as he rode his horse alongside his father's through the streets of London.

"I shall enjoy seeing Kew on my own account," Charles said. "I just hope you will not feel constrained by my presence."

"Not at all." Adrian grinned. "If I wish to become amorous, I am sure I will discover some bushes behind which to slink while you are looking the other way."

"You fancy one of the ladies, then, do you?" Charles asked.

"Lady Jessica Archer has a court of admirers large enough to fill our drawing room," Adrian told him. "I would be totally lost in the crowd. And I do not *fancy* Lady Estelle Lamarr, though she is exceedingly pretty and I like her. I do not believe I have met Miss Rigg, though I may recognize her when I see her. I have no intention of fixing my interest for many years yet."

The group was to gather at Archer House on Hanover Square, home of the Duke of Netherby, Lady Jessica's half brother. They were to take one carriage, provided by young Bertrand Lamarr's father. The ladies would ride in that. The men would accompany it on horseback. And they had perfect weather for the excursion. After a few cloudy, blustery days, the sun was shining and the wind had died down at last. It was going to be a warm day, though probably not oppressively hot.

Why the devil *had* he made the offer to accompany the young people? Obviously he could not be the sole chaperon of a group of unmarried young ladies. Yet without them there would have been no need of chaperonage at all. He could fulfill his role only if there were an older lady with him, yet he had no wife. Had he imagined the shocked silence with which his offer had been received? He knew why he had made it, of course, for he had already had a lady chaperon in mind.

Strangely, he had not really thought of the implications of his suggestion until later. It had been such a spur-of-the-moment thing. It had hardly occurred to him that he was dooming them both to spending the day in company together. He had thought only that *Matilda* was free to go with the young people, that she would probably be well accepted by them all since she was the mother of none of them. He had thought that she would probably enjoy a day out with young people, free of her own mother. He had thought that she would enjoy a day at Kew. She had enjoyed it thirty-six years ago. And yes, Adrian, there were bushes there behind which a couple could slink for a quick kiss.

He had wanted her to be *visible*. They were a decent lot, the Westcotts, but they had one collective shortcoming that had irritated him all evening. None of them saw Matilda. Oh, they did not ignore her. She was a part of their family and was included in all their activities and conversations. But none of them *saw* her. None of them, with the exception of her mother, had seen her, lovely and graceful, eyes bright, cheeks flushed with animation, dancing a min-uet. None of them *knew* her. A presumptuous thought, no doubt, when he had had no dealings with her for well over thirty years and had known her even all that time ago for only a few brief months.

But she was a *person*, by God, even if she was past the age of fifty. Even if she was a spinster. She deserved *a life*.

But now he was stuck with being in company with her all day. It was not a happy thought, though he had found himself dressing with greater than usual care this morning—to his great annoyance when he had realized it.

"I think I want to meet him," Adrian said abruptly.

Charles turned his head to look at his son.

"Lieutenant Colonel Bennington," Adrian explained. *"Gil."*

"He lives in Gloucestershire," Charles told him. "I doubt he will want to meet you, Adrian. He has no desire to see me ever again."

"A man can travel," Adrian said. "A man can knock on a door. It can remain closed to him, of course, but he can do those things."

Charles frowned. "And will you?" he asked as they turned their horses into Hanover Square.

His son shrugged. "Maybe," he said. "Maybe not."

There was no further chance to consider what Adrian had just said. Dorchester's traveling carriage as well as a cluster of horses was drawn up outside Netherby's house. A chattering group of young people was gathered on the steps and out on the pavement while the young Duchess of Netherby and the dowager duchess, Lady Jessica's mother, looked on from the top step, presumably preparing to wave them on their way. Lady Matilda Westcott was standing by the open door of the carriage.

He had once told her, Charles remembered suddenly, that pale blue was her color, that she should wear it as often as possible.

Where the devil had that memory come from? She was wearing it now. It might have been thought to be too youthful a color for a woman of her age, but the dress and the spencer she wore over it were smart and elegant, neither youthful nor dowdy. She wore a small-brimmed navy blue bonnet, neat, with no added frills or flowers or feathers. She had spotted him and inclined her head, rather prim mouthed. He wondered if she regretted agreeing to his suggestion. But she had done it without hesitation. And then she had made that light, humorous answer about living in caves and wearing animal skins to the question one of the young people had asked about life when they were young. And then, when he had added his own silliness, she had laughed aloud with what had sounded like genuine glee.

And, ah . . .

She had been Matilda in that moment, as she had once been. As though all the years between had fallen away.

"Mr. Sawyer," Lady Estelle Lamarr cried gaily, addressing Adrian as they rode closer. "There you are. You are almost late. And you see? We have added two more members to the party. Mr. Ambrose Keithley and Dorothea, his sister, have agreed to join us." Miss Rigg and the Keithleys were identified and made their bow and curtsies.

"How do you do, Lord Dirkson?" Bertrand Lamarr called, grinning up at Charles. "Both Mrs. Rigg and Lady Keithley accepted you without question as a chaperon for their daughters."

"I believe, Bertrand," the dowager duchess said, "it was the fact that Matilda was to go along with the group that persuaded both of them. Good morning, Lord Dirkson, Mr. Sawyer."

Charles touched his hat to the ladies and smiled at Matilda. Her lips grew even primmer. Even her kid gloves, he noticed, were pale blue. Had she dressed with as much care as he had this morning? Had she remembered what he had told her about the color? Or had she discovered for herself over the years that it suited her?

"If the horses are not to stage a rebellion at being kept waiting so long," she said, *not* specifically addressing Charles, "we should perhaps think of being on our way."

"Oh yes, indeed," Lady Estelle cried. "You will sit on the seat facing the horses, Aunt Matilda. We are all agreed upon that. The rest of us drew spills, and Jessica won the seat next to you, the lucky thing. Charlotte, Dorothea, and I will squeeze onto the other seat, our backs to the horses."

"How fortunate the gentlemen are," Miss Keithley said, "being able to ride the whole way in the fresh air. We ought to have drawn also for the middle seat. Now we will have to squabble over it."

"Not in my hearing," Matilda said. "You may occupy it on the way there, Miss Keithley, and Estelle on the way back."

"Bravo, Aunt Matilda," young Boris Wayne said. "You keep them in line."

Miss Keithley laughed and climbed into the carriage. The other three young ladies lost no time in following her, all talking and laughing at once.

"Matilda," Charles heard the dowager duchess say to her sister, "I hope you know what you have taken on. I doubt they will stop giggling all the rest of the day."

"I expect to survive the ordeal, Louise. I was once young myself," Matilda replied before looking, obviously startled, at Charles, who had dismounted in order to hand her into the carriage. "Thank you, Lord Dirkson."

She rested her hand lightly upon his outstretched one and he closed his fingers about it. It was a slim, long-fingered hand and warm through her glove. And then she was inside the carriage and turning to sit beside Lady Jessica, and the coachman was putting up the steps and closing the door before climbing to the perch and gathering the ribbons in his hands.

Charles mounted his horse again, and the whole cavalcade set off on its merry way to Kew. Adrian was already laughing with the other young men, perfectly at his ease.

Now *this*, Charles thought, was a new experience. The rake turned chaperon.

BERTRAND HAD THOUGHT OVERNIGHT OF A FRIEND OF HIS WHO would be sure to want to join them. Perhaps more significant, Matilda had understood from the studied carelessness with which he had made the explanation, the friend had a sister who was very pretty and vivacious and had danced a set with Bertrand at her come-out ball a month or so ago in addition to several since then. So the carriage was more crowded than originally planned, and three of the young ladies were forced to sit squashed together on the seat opposite the one she shared with Jessica. Their spirits did not seem to be in any way dampened by discomfort, however.

It was a merry group indeed. Matilda had half forgotten how the very young behaved when they far outnumbered any older persons. She might have tried impressing a more sober decorum upon them and thus securing some peace for herself, but why should she? She was actually pleased to discover that her presence seemed not to have any inhibiting effect upon the spirits of her charges.

"Mama was not at all inclined to permit me to come," Miss

Keithley said when the carriage was nicely under way, "even though Ambrose was to come too. I almost *died*. But then she was told that *you* were to chaperon us, Lady Matilda."

"Oh dear," Matilda said, twinkling back at the girl. "Does that mean I have a reputation as something of a dragon?"

It was a quite unwitty remark, but it nevertheless set off a renewed gust of giggles from all four of her fellow travelers.

"Not at all," Miss Keithley assured her. "Mama said you were *eminently respectable*—her exact words."

"Ah, a dragon, then," Matilda said. "I shall try not to breathe fire over any of you, however. Provided, that is, you all display your most sedate conduct from this moment on."

For some reason that suggestion called for another burst of merry laughter, and Matilda felt happy for no reason she could explain. She had not felt at all happy all through a night of disturbed sleep. She had never been a chaperon. More to the point, she had never been a chaperon *with Charles Sawyer*. Whatever had possessed him to offer her name when Viola had been about to suggest going with the young people and Louise had been about to make a martyr of herself by agreeing to go herself? Mama had not been at all pleased. She had told Matilda on the way home last night that she ought to have put that man in his place with a very firm refusal. Since he was going too on this ramshackle excursion to Kew, who was going to chaperon Matilda?

Mama, Matilda had protested. *I am fifty-six years old.*

And Viscount Dirkson is a rake, her mother had retorted.

Was a rake, Matilda had said. *His own son is to be of the party, Mama.*

She had lain awake wondering why he had suggested her name and why she had agreed with such alacrity and what she would do if any of the young people misbehaved. Surely that would not happen, though. They were all properly brought up young persons. And she had wondered what she and Charles would talk about if they happened to be paired together, as was surely very likely since the young people would want to be with one another. She had wondered if he would offer his arm and if she would take it. The very thought had interfered with her breathing and she had wondered if she could develop a head cold or smallpox or something similarly dire overnight so that she could send her excuses and beg Viola to go in her stead. But there was her notoriously healthy constitution. No one would believe her.

But now she felt happy and carefree, almost as though she were one of these youngsters herself. Almost as though she had suddenly shed thirty-six years and might start giggling too at any moment. Goodness, they would all look at her as if she had sprouted another head.

"One thought bothered me last evening," she said. "The excursion was planned to include six young persons. But it was going to be impossible, I thought, for the six to be sorted out in such a way that *two* were not going to be paired with either a sibling or a cousin. What a dreadful waste of an outing and lovely weather *that* would have been."

Again the delighted, trilling laughter.

"But now that the number has increased to eight," Matilda continued, "you may each walk with a gentleman who is not related to you in any way at all."

The laughter this time was mingled with a few blushes.

"And that includes you, Lady Matilda," Miss Rigg said. "For there are ten of us in all, are there not?"

"Well, goodness me, yes, you are quite right," Matilda said, hoping she was not about to become one of the blushers. "Now let me see. I need to avoid Boris Wayne, as he is my nephew, and Bertrand Lamarr, since he is my former sister-in-law's stepson. Does that make him in any way my relative? Hmm. Maybe not, but he does call me Aunt Matilda. He is very handsome, is he not?"

"He is," Miss Keithley said with a scarcely disguised sigh.

"Bertrand and I both consider you our aunt," Estelle told Matilda. "And do not tell him he is handsome or his head will swell."

"But you will be paired with Lord Dirkson, Lady Matilda," Miss Rigg told her in all seriousness, as though there were any alternative.

"I suppose you are right," Matilda said, "since he is the only one close to me in age. Well, he is rather handsome too, is he not?"

"I think Mr. Sawyer is nice looking," Estelle said. "He has kind eyes and a sweet smile."

"Was Viscount Dirkson really a friend of Uncle Humphrey's?" Jessica asked. "And did you really meet him all those years ago, Aunt Matilda, and dance with him at balls? I think he must have been very handsome as a young man. He must have looked a bit like Gil but without the scar. Did you fancy him?"

"*Fancy?*" Matilda said, raising her eyebrows. "Is that the sort of language your mama encourages you to use, Jessica?"

But Jessica only laughed with glee, as did the other three. "Were you in love with him?"

"Oh, head over ears," Matilda told her. "So was every other girl on the market that year, and probably a few who were not. But there were many other very gorgeous young men to ogle too. I am convinced men were more handsome in those days."

"Oh, Aunt Matilda," Jessica said, still laughing, "is that the sort of language Grandmama encouraged you to use? *Ogle?*"

"Touché," Matilda said, and patted her niece on the knee.

The attention of the young ladies turned beyond the windows at that point. They would have claimed to be admiring the scenery, no doubt, if asked, while what they were really admiring was the gentlemen, who often rode within sight of the windows. They did it deliberately, Matilda believed, in order to see and be seen. Oh, she had forgotten so much about the mating rituals of the very young. But how easily the memory of it all came back—the preening and flirting, the fan waving and pretended indifference, even disdain.

Men always showed to advantage on horseback, provided they had reasonably trim figures and good posture and well-muscled thighs and rode as though they and the horse were a single entity.

All of which *Charles* had and did. The thought was in Matilda's mind before she could guard against it. He was fifty-six years old, for heaven's sake. But he was still gorgeously handsome and attractive. Though probably only in her eyes. She doubted any of her companions were sparing him a glance when there were Bertrand and Boris to gaze at, and Mr. Sawyer and Mr. Keithley.

She wondered if he had noticed she was wearing pale blue. She *hoped* not, or, if he had noticed, for after all he had eyes, she hoped he did not remember once telling her that she should always, always wear blue of the palest shade because it accomplished the seemingly impossible and made her even prettier and more desirable than she already was. He had actually used those words—*more desirable*. She had been shocked and thrilled to the core. But how foolish to think that he might remember. So many years had passed. She had not chosen her outfit deliberately for that reason. She had tried three different dresses first—the dark green, the tan, and the dark blue—before she had instructed her maid to pull this one from the back of her wardrobe. She had worn it only once before even though she had possessed it for two years. She had concluded after that one occasion that it was too youthful. But today she had tried it on and had felt immediately happy in it. She might be going as a chaperon, but she was not *ancient*. Not quite, anyway. And she wanted to look her best.

She had deliberately not asked herself why.

It felt very strange not to be with her mother. Not to be watching her every moment to make sure she was comfortable and warm and not in need of a shawl or a fan or a cup of tea. Not to be a shadow whom no one really saw except her mother, who was more often than not irritated with her for constantly fussing. Why did she do it, then? Because she needed to be needed by someone? It felt wonderful to be free of all that. The whole of today—well, the rest of the morning and the afternoon anyway—stretched ahead of her with nothing further to do except watch eight young people who really would not need any watching at all and enjoy the beauties of Kew Gardens, which she had not seen for ages. And on a perfect day, with scarcely a cloud in the sky or a breath of wind.

A whole afternoon to spend in Charles's company. And she was not going to feel self-conscious about it or fearful that he would find her dull, though he surely would. For *he* had asked *her*. She had not even thought of volunteering her services. She was going to enjoy herself, though she was feeling somewhat apprehensive about the end of the journey and the pairing up that would happen as soon as the men had dismounted and the ladies had stepped down from the carriage. She was perhaps the only one who knew exactly with whom she would be paired.

She was going to enjoy herself anyway. And if he thought he was going to throw her onto the defensive as he had done last evening, then he was going to have a rude awakening. She did not owe Charles Sawyer an explanation for *anything* she had done with her life. If anyone owed an explanation, it was he. Though that was not quite right. She, after all, was the one who had broken off both their romance and their acquaintance—because she would not have been able to carry on with the latter without the former. She had dismissed him and thus set him free to do and to be whatever he wished. He had done just that. But she would not even *think* of the past for the rest of today.

"This is going to be *such* fun," Miss Keithley said. "It is the first time I have been out without Mama since we came to London."

"But if you think your mama is a strict chaperon," Matilda said, "wait until you discover what I am. Dragons may appear mild in contrast. You may well beg your mother to accompany you everywhere you go for the rest of the Season."

A renewed burst of happy giggles greeted her dire warning and she smiled.

And then stopped smiling.

They had arrived.

Four

Bertrand Lamarr and Boris Wayne wanted to go straight to the Chinese pagoda and climb to the top.

"Two hundred and fifty-three stairs," Boris said, "winding around the center."

"And spectacular views from each story," Bertrand added.

"Are there really golden dragons on the roofs?" Miss Rigg asked. But she wanted to go first to the orangery because it had been recommended by a cousin.

"But it is said to be too dark inside for the fruit to flourish," Miss Keithley told her.

"I want to see some of the temples," her brother said. "We missed them when we came last year because everyone else wanted to see the pagoda."

Lady Estelle Lamarr wanted to see Kew Palace, and Lady Jessica Archer would prefer the Queen's Cottage.

"All the royals used to have picnics in the gardens there when they were children," she said. "Queen Charlotte used to arrange them."

"It is such a beautiful day," Adrian said, "and the gardens are so well laid out and so full of varied trees and plants and green expanses of grass that I would be content just to stroll about without any particular destination, seeing what is to be seen as we come to it."

Everyone had expressed a preference almost before Charles had handed Matilda down from the carriage and turned it over with all the horses to the care of the grooms and the coachman.

"I daresay we can spend at least a couple of hours here," he said, "before feeling the need to seek out a late luncheon or early tea, whichever seems appropriate when the time comes. There will be a chance to see everything and even just to relax and look about us and enjoy the sunshine. Lady Matilda, you are the only one who has not voiced an opinion. With what shall we start?"

"Me?" she said, spreading a hand over her bosom. Charles guessed that her preferences were not often consulted. "Well, I do not mind."

"The pagoda, Aunt Matilda," Boris said, grinning at her.

"The Queen's Cottage."

"The temples."

"The orangery."

"Kew Palace."

They all clamored to be heard, and there was much laughter interspersed with the raised voices. Ambrose Keithley was elbowing Bertrand Lamarr in the ribs for some unknown reason and was being elbowed back. Miss Keithley had raised her parasol and set it spinning behind her head. Adrian was pretending the poke of it had caught him in the eye as he clapped both hands over it. Matilda held up a staying hand, and miraculously order was restored.

"You all have a great deal of pent-up energy," she said. "It needs to be used. Two hundred and fifty-three stairs, did you say, Boris? Perfect. We will begin with the pagoda. Besides, I want to see those dragons even if they *are* only gilded wood and not solid gold."

"But you have to climb to the top, Aunt Matilda," her nephew said, waggling his eyebrows at her.

"Was there any question of my *not* doing so?" she asked. "*Of course* I will be climbing to the top. Let us go. I did not agree to chaperon you all just in order to stand here procrastinating for the rest of the day."

And they all paired up and moved off along a wide grassy avenue in the direction of the pagoda, which was clearly visible from most parts of the park. Charles offered Matilda his arm. She looked smart and prim, her manner brisk. Yet there was about her a suggestion of exuberance that one did not see when she was playing the part of aging spinster daughter tending her mother's needs. He had been a bit afraid that the journey here in a carriage filled with flighty, giggling young ladies would sap her of all energy and patience. The opposite seemed to have happened.

She looked at his arm before slipping her hand through it, then glanced up at him. "I have not climbed to the top of the pagoda since—" She closed her eyes briefly before turning her head away. She did not complete the sentence.

Since they had done it together when they were twenty?

"Neither have I," he said.

He had been to Kew a number of times since then, of course. He had even been close to the pagoda. He had been urged a few times to climb it but had always declined. He had never really asked himself why. Was it fanciful to imagine now that it was because he had once climbed it with Lady Matilda Westcott?

"It was a day much like today," he said.

"Yes," she said softly. And then, a little more firmly, "Was it? I cannot remember."

They walked behind the young people, who were, as she had observed, full of high spirits. They were in pairs, but they were chattering as a group.

"*Have* you forgotten, Matilda?" he asked.

"Yes," she said.

"We were in a group like this," he said. "I believe there were six of us, not counting the parents of one of the young ladies—I cannot recall who. But they were not *your* parents. They were a little more indulgent. Your brother was one of our number."

"I have forgotten," she said.

"Whoever those parents were," he said, "they did not climb higher than the second story. They remained there while the rest of us wound our way to the top. The others did not remain there long. They went clattering back down the stairs almost immediately, leaving the two of us to enjoy the view."

"I will take your word for it," she said. "I have no interest in the distant past. I am here now. It is a beautiful day, and I want to enjoy everything as it is."

"Very well," he said, briefly covering her hand on his arm.

He had kissed her, surrounded by carved wood and vast sky and green expanses below. It had not been their first kiss, but it was the first one that could be prolonged. He had told her, his mouth against hers, that he loved her. And she had told him after he had kissed her that she loved him.

They were words he had not spoken to any other woman. He had grown up fast after Matilda and had abandoned such immature, sentimental drivel.

Her mouth now, he saw when he glanced at her face, was set in a prim line.

"We will enjoy everything as it is now, then," he said. "Were you driven to near insanity on the journey here?"

He was startled by her sudden smile and the twinkle in her eye as she looked back at him.

"Not at all," she said. "What a delight young people are, Charles."

"Giggling?" he said. "And chattering?"

"Well," she said, "I giggled and chattered right along with them." She looked self-conscious suddenly and turned her head away, hiding her face behind the brim of her bonnet. "Why not? It seemed the best form of self-defense."

Matilda! Ah, Matilda. What had her parents done to her? Or was that unfair? If Barbara or Jane had wanted to marry a young man as wild as he had been at the age of twenty, would he have given his consent? He knew he would not. But would he also have forbidden them all future contact with that young man? Would they have obeyed him without question if he had?

Ought he to have waited? If he had given up his wild ways and approached her the following year, would he have been able to persuade her to change her mind? And her father his? And her mother hers?

"*Why* did you not marry, Matilda?" he asked.

Her head turned sharply back toward him. "I never *wanted* to," she said.

"You wanted to marry me," he reminded her.

"I was young," she said. "And foolish."

Even now, ridiculously, it stung.

"You never loved anyone else?" he asked her.

"No." She frowned.

"Was it that you never wanted to marry?" he asked her. "Or was it that you never found a man to love?"

"Enough," she said. "Please, Charles, enough."

And he was a bit horrified to see that her eyes were rather bright, but not from the sunshine or the pleasure of the outing.

"I beg your pardon," he said. "Forgive me."

"And why should you care?" she asked him. "You fathered a *son* very soon after. And there were other women. Many of them. One could not help hearing about them. And you married a few years later and had children and grandchildren, all the while acquiring an ever worsening reputation as a rake among other things. Much you loved *me*, Charles. I will be forever thankful that my mother and father talked sense into me. My life as it has been is *far* better than it would have been if I had married you."

Every word felt like a blow. And every word was true. Except four of them, spoken with biting sarcasm—*much you loved me*. Literally they were true, but she had not meant them literally.

He *had* loved her, but he had proved it in the worst possible way, by going completely to pieces after she would have nothing more to do with him. He could not even blame immaturity. His unsavory reputation had been well deserved for years and years.

"I am sorry," he said. "I am so sorry."

"We have arrived at the pagoda," she said, and she smiled brightly at the young people, who had stopped walking and stood in a group to admire it from the outside.

"There are ten stories," Miss Keithley said. "I counted them."

"Impressive, Dorothea," her brother said. "You can count that high."

"I am not sure I will be able to step out onto any of those balconies," Miss Rigg said, "if that is what they are called. Not on the higher stories anyway. They must be terrifying."

Each story had a balcony outside it and a protruding roof above. But it was not necessary to step outside to appreciate the views. There were tall, round-topped windows all about each story.

"Take my arm," Boris said to her. "I promise not to let you fall."

"That is kind of you," she said. "But will we be able to climb the stairs two abreast?"

They all stepped inside to find out, exuberant and chattering. They had not yet worked off much of their overabundance of energy, it seemed.

"I love the dragons," Matilda said, looking up at the series of roofs. "They *look* as if they are made of gold."

"Do you really want to go to the top?" Charles asked. "You are under no obligation."

"Oh, but I am," she said. "I was challenged by my nephew and accepted."

"Is he in the habit of issuing challenges to you and grinning and waggling his eyebrows at you?" he asked.

"Oh good heavens, no," she said. "He has always treated me with the utmost respect as his mother's elder—*considerably* elder—sister. I believe he is enjoying teasing me."

"And you are enjoying being teased," he said.

"Yes." She sighed. "Sometimes it is a little lonely being a staid maiden aunt." But she colored rosily as she said it and looked as though she would dearly like to recall the words. No one really liked to admit to loneliness. And perhaps no woman liked to admit to being a maiden aunt, as though those two words described everything there was to know about her.

"You are not my aunt, fortunately," he said. "You are Matilda."

"Oh." She looked at him a little uncertainly, her head tipped slightly to one side.

"Shall we go after the young people," he asked, "and make sure none of them try hanging from the balcony rails by their fingertips? I would hate to fail during my first stint as a chaperon."

"Oh goodness me, yes," she said. "What a horrid thought. And it is just the sort of thing young men do to impress young ladies. Not hanging *from* the balcony rails, perhaps, but certainly *over* them. The mere thought of it gives me heart palpitations."

They huffed and puffed their way up the stairs, winding about the interior middle of the pagoda, stopping only once, briefly, at the fifth level to look out through the windows while they caught their breath. Loud exclamations of wonder as well as the habitual laughter came from the floors above.

"Oh," Matilda said, "I had forgotten how much higher a tall building seems from the inside than it looks from the outside. And we are only halfway up."

"Are you sure you do not want to claim that you won half a challenge?" he asked her, almost hoping she would say yes. Sometimes one forgot that being fifty-six years old was a little different from being twenty.

For answer she turned and continued the climb. Coming up behind her, Charles admired beneath the pale blue of her dress the sway of her hips, still shapely though no longer youthful. And he admired the fact that she kept her spine straight and climbed steadily upward without slowing. By the time they came out on top, the young people were moving about the full circle of the room, looking out and exclaiming at the height and pointing out to one another all the landmarks they could see both within Kew Gardens and beyond.

"It is a bit like being up in a hot air balloon," Adrian said, "except that there is more than empty air beneath our feet."

"You have been up in a balloon?" Lady Estelle asked him.

"Yes," he told her. "Last year. It was exhilarating and frankly terrifying. But I lived to tell the tale."

"If I did not know differently," Lady Jessica said, "I would swear this pagoda is swaying. Would someone please assure me that it is not?"

"I think it is," Bertrand said, staggering and then grinning at her. "You had better hang on to me, Jessica, and stop me from falling."

She tutted and slapped his arm.

And everyone was ready to go down and set out on another adventure.

"AFTER COMING ALL THIS WAY UP," CHARLES SAID, "I INTEND TO stay awhile and admire the view at my leisure. My leisure is going to last at least ten minutes."

"It takes that long to recover your breath?" Mr. Sawyer asked, grinning rather cheekily.

"And that too," his father admitted.

"But you do not all have to wait for us at the foot of the pagoda," Matilda said. "We can do our duty quite adequately from up here. It makes a splendid watchtower. I daresay there is not a square inch of the Gardens that will be invisible to us."

Mr. Keithley groaned aloud and clutched his chest.

There were lots of trees, of course, and a person could not see into them or under them from up here. But young people must be allowed some time alone together. And what could they get up to in ten minutes? Though of course it would take about that long again to get down from here, and then one would no longer be able to see to all corners of Kew, let alone into all the crannies. But—

"I trust you all to behave yourselves as young ladies and gentlemen ought," she added in her severe Aunt Matilda voice. Not that she had ever been a severe aunt. She had never interfered with her brother and sisters or her in-laws concerning the ways they chose to deal with their children.

"That was very sly of you, Aunt Matilda," Boris told her. "Now you have forced us to be good."

"Not that we would ever dream of *not* being good," Dorothea Keithley said as she followed Mr. Sawyer down the winding staircase. "Don't look at me that way, Ambrose."

"Do you have eyes in the back of your head?" her brother protested, offering his hand to Jessica to help her onto the top stair.

Soon they were all gone, clattering downward noisily and cheerfully.

"We will all gather outside the orangery in half an hour's time," Charles called down after them.

And Matilda was aware of the sound of wind all about the outside of the pagoda, and of nothing else. She stepped up to one window and gazed down upon trees and lawns and the red-bricked front of Kew Palace. She moved to the next window and saw temple follies among the trees and land stretching to infinity beyond the Gardens. She moved again and simply gazed. She was aware of the warmth of Charles's right arm along her left, though they were not touching. She could smell his cologne.

"Oh, there they are," she said, pointing downward. "They have stayed all together."

"I can spot no budding romance between any of them," he said, "with the possible exception of Bertrand Lamarr and Miss Keithley. They are merely enjoying one another's company."

"Yes," she said.

"In a similar situation we were only too eager to snatch time for ourselves," he said. "And we were fortunate enough to have a pair of chaperons who were happy to remain well below the top story of the pagoda."

He had kissed her here, maybe on this very spot. He had told her he loved her and she had not for a moment doubted the truth of his words. She had told him she loved him and had meant the words with all the passion of her young heart. But not a month later she had sent him away, told him she would not speak with him or even see him again. She had told him when pressed, when it had seemed the only way to convince him, that she did not love him, that she never really had.

"*Did* you mean it?" he asked now, and she knew he had turned his face toward hers, was no longer looking at the view but at her. "I have often wondered."

"Did I mean what?" she asked, but she knew what he meant. It was as though he had read her thoughts.

"That you loved me," he said.

She frowned and watched a horse and cart inching along a ribbon of roadway on the distant landscape.

"I do not remember," she said. "Are you talking about the time we were here together all those years ago? How am I to recall what I said or what I meant?"

"You told me you loved me," he said, "after I had said I loved you. And then, not long after, you turned me away. But the cruelest cut of all came with the words you spoke as you did it. You did not love me, you said, and never had. But you did love me when we were here. You did mean it, did you not?"

From beneath contracted eyebrows she returned his gaze. Why was the answer important to him? "You have lived a lifetime of memory-bringing events since then," she said. "You fathered Gil. You married Lady Dirkson and had children and then grandchildren. You lived through years filled with . . . with riotous living. Why try to remember now what happened or did not happen here years and years ago when we were young and foolish and could not possibly have known our own minds? Why bother to remember? We have scarcely seen each other since. We have spoken only a few times, all of them very recently. What is the point of all this, Charles? If we ever had a . . . a chance, it is long gone. Those things happened to other people in another lifetime. We are not the same people now. Not even close."

"*Were* we foolish?" he asked her. He had turned to look downward again. Matilda could see the young people, still in a group together, making their way along a grassy avenue toward one of the domed temples. "But yes, of course I was. I was young and in love and then hurt as only the young can be. I was blinded by hurt. Instead of waiting for a year and then trying during the next Season to get you to change your mind and to get your father to see that I had changed, I immediately leaped into wild pleasure seeking in an attempt to forget you and soothe my bruised sense of self. I never did try to win you back. Yes, I was foolish. Were you?"

"Foolish?" she said. "No. I had always been obedient to my parents. I had always believed they knew what was best for me and loved me. I believed them when they told me you were no suitable husband for me, that your wild debaucheries would bring me nothing but misery."

"Debaucheries?" He turned to look at her again. "At *that* stage of my life? Hardly. So you were *wise* to break off with me? To tell me you did not love me?"

"Yes," she said.

He was looking steadily at her, and almost inevitably she had to turn her own head and look back.

"Tell me," he said, "that that at least was not true. And please do not tell me you do not remember."

"Why should I remember?" she asked. "It was a lifetime ago. Oh, Charles, *of course* I loved you. We were young as these young people are young now." She gestured with one hand toward the window, though she did not look out. "You were handsome and you were paying court to me. You danced with me and talked endlessly with me and smiled and laughed for me alone, it seemed. Of course I loved you. It would have been strange if I had not."

"But you stopped?"

"Of course I stopped," she said, remembering her broken heart, her shattered dreams, her conviction that she would surely not be able to live on. "Did you imagine that I have been nursing a tendre for you all these years? Do you see me as a poor, frustrated spinster, sighing herself to sleep each night with memories of the one man with whom she shared a romance when she was no more than a girl? That is both absurd and insulting."

"Did I say I imagined any such thing?" he asked. "I am sorry. I have upset you."

"I am not upset," she said, swiping at her cheeks with the heels of both gloved hands and feeling the humiliating wetness of tears there—she, who never wept.

"Let us not talk or even think about all the years between," he said. "I loved you when we were last here together, Matilda, and you loved me. It is a bitter memory because of all that came so soon after. But there is a very definite sweetness about it too. We were a young couple in love. I have never been in love since."

"What nonsense," she said.

"Perhaps," he said. "But true nevertheless. I do not believe you have either, have you?"

"Me?" she said. "Of course I have—No, I have not. Is there anything shameful about that? I had chances. But I would not marry without love. I was a stubborn young woman."

"Yes," he said. "I know."

"Well," she said, "it *is* a sweet memory, Charles. It was also something that happened to two people who no longer exist."

"But we do," he said. "We are those very same two people thirty-six years later. There are gray hairs—more for me than for you—and lines carving themselves on our faces and somewhat thickening figures. But you still look very good. Perhaps I can say so because I look at you through fifty-six-year-old eyes. To me you look good, though I would like to see your mouth primmed less often and smiling instead—as it has smiled today whenever we are in company with the young people. I would like to kiss that mouth again."

She stared at him as though she were welded to the floor. She was too shocked to smack his face. At the same time she felt a renewed rush of awareness—of their aloneness up here, of the last kiss they had shared here, of *him*, of his solid presence, of his continued good looks, of his maleness. Of his *mouth*. But she was middle-aged. On the far side of middle age, in fact. Kissing was for the young. She no longer knew how to do it. The last time she had been kissed was . . . thirty-six years ago. It would be embarrassing. It would be bizarre. It would be . . .

She licked her lips, and his eyes dipped to follow the gesture. Her nipples were tingling. There was an ache between her thighs. She had not experienced such things for many years. She was past the age . . . But even before then she had suppressed the nagging needs that brought her nothing but empty frustration and misery. She could not now . . .

She took a step closer to him, and when *he* stepped closer to *her*, she ignored the instinct to jump back in fright and she let herself rest against him instead, closing her eyes as she did so. Even through his coat and waistcoat and shirt she could feel that he was warm and firm muscled and male. She felt enclosed by the smell of him, his cologne, the starch that must have been used on his cravat and neck-cloth, the essence that was Charles himself. It was ridiculous, perhaps, to feel that it was all somehow familiar, but it was nevertheless. With her thighs she could feel the powerful muscles of his own. With her lower legs she could feel the supple leather of his Hessian boots. It was all surely sufficient to make her swoon—if she knew how to do it.

She would remember this, she thought, just as she had always remembered the last time. She would remember for the rest of her life. With her dying breath she would remember that she loved him, that she had always loved him even if there had been days, weeks, even perhaps months through her life when she had not thought of him a single time. Oh no, never months. Or even weeks. Love never quite goes away. It was always there, dormant, waiting to be revived. Broken hearts were always aching to be mended.

His arms had come down along hers and he found her hands with his and twined his fingers with hers as their arms rested against their sides. He lowered his head and tipped it slightly to one side.

She felt his breath against one cheek and opened her eyes. His own searched hers from a mere few inches away and somehow she did not feel like an embarrassed and dried-up old spinster for whom such things were merely a present embarrassment and a dream of what might have been a long time ago and could never be again. He did not look like an aging man who surely should be past such things.

"Allow me?" he murmured, his lips almost against hers.

For answer, she shut her eyes again and closed the distance. And—

Oh my.

Oh my.

Oh . . . *my goodness me.*

Her thoughts were no more coherent than that for however long the kiss lasted. It was probably a few seconds. No, surely longer than that. Minutes? Hours?

Had it been like this all those years ago? All the physical sensations? All the emotional yearnings? All the inability to *think*? But if it had been, how could she possibly have let him go?

Ah, how could she have let him go?

Charles.

"Charles?"

He had moved his mouth away from hers and was gazing at her with eyes that were impossible to read. They were still touching along their full length. Their fingers were still entwined at their sides. It had been really, she thought, by any objective standard, a rather chaste kiss. It had also been nothing short of earth-shattering. No, that was far too mild a term. It had been *universe*-shattering.

For her anyway.

He, of course, must have participated in a thousand such kisses with as many women.

Don't exaggerate, Matilda.

Was it an exaggeration?

"We are neglecting our duty," she said.

A wave of something so fleeting that it was impossible to name passed across his face. Amusement, perhaps? Regret? Longing? None of those? All of them?

"You are the one who told the young people you trusted them," he said. "I would have remained right behind them, treading upon the heels of the last in line."

"Oh, you would not," she said. "You were the one who told them you needed ten minutes up here before following them."

"Because I am an old man and needed to catch my breath and give my arthritic knees a rest," he said.

"Nonsense." She was very aware that they were still touching each other, front to front, and their fingers were still tangled up together.

He released her and took a step back. There was definite laughter in his eyes now. "I am sorry for discomposing you, Matilda," he said.

"You have done no such thing," she assured him.

"There is another reason why you are cross, then?" he asked.

"I am not cross," she protested, running a hand over the front of her dress and making sure her bonnet was still straight. "But we came as chaperons and . . ."

"And ended up needing some of our own," he said. "Come. We will go down. I will go first so that you do not have to peer into the abyss with every step."

Oh. *Oh.* He had surely said exactly the same thing the last time. But how ridiculous to believe that she could remember such a trivial act of gallantry thirty-six years later.

"Thank you," she said, and wanted to weep.

Yet again.

Five

During the week following the excursion to Kew Gardens, Charles concentrated upon getting his life back to normal. The only trouble was that he was not sure it was going to be possible—not, at least, if *normal* meant the way it had been until a month or so ago.

For one thing, he had let go the mistress he had employed since not long after his wife's death. He had paid her off abruptly the very evening after Matilda had made her unexpected call at his house, though at the time he had not believed there was any connection between the two events. He had assumed that he would replace his mistress soon. But he had not done so in the ensuing weeks, though he was not at all sure celibacy suited him. Neither was he sure it did not. Actually, it was sex for sex's sake that no longer satisfied him, but he did not know what *would* satisfy him instead. Or if he did, he was not willing to give it serious thought.

For another thing, there was Gil. His son had been in his life for thirty-four years, in a purely peripheral way, but that had changed with all the business over the custody battle and then the breakfast to which his son's wife had invited him and his first-ever face-to-face meeting with his son. To say that meeting was uncomfortable would be to severely understate the case, but it had been difficult afterward to accept the possibility that he would never see Gil or hear from him again.

But hear from him he had a couple of days after Kew—or at least *about* him from Abigail, Gil's wife. She had written a letter filled with cheerful details about the Gloucestershire village in which they lived and their house and garden, which was dominated by both the sight and smell of roses. Interspersed with those details were seemingly random anecdotes about Katy, his granddaughter. And there had been one mention of Gil, who was being transformed from soldier to farmer, complete with muddy boots, for which Abigail had scolded him when he stepped inside the house with them one day without cleaning them off adequately on the boot scraper outside the door. Charles found reading the letter painful more than pleasurable, yet he read it at least a dozen times in the course of the rest of the day.

Then there was Adrian, who had renewed the friendship he had enjoyed with Bertrand Lamarr at university. He had also become friendly with Lamarr's sister and with Boris Wayne. The four of them had apparently called upon the Dowager Countess of Riverdale the day after Kew in order to thank Lady Matilda Westcott for accompanying them and making the day such fun for them—Adrian's word. She had apparently tried to persuade her mother to put her feet up on a stool while they were there, but the dowager had declared she was quite capable of keeping her feet on the floor and became quite cross with her daughter for fussing.

"And *I* ended up feeling quite cross too," Adrian reported. "There were none of the smiles and twinkly eyes from Lady Matilda that we saw yesterday, or the mock severe admonitions. I think the dowager countess stifles her, Papa. It is a shame, and it is not right. It is not easy to be a woman, is it? Especially a spinster. I wonder why she never married."

"Perhaps she chose not to," Charles suggested.

"But the *alternative* . . ." his son protested.

Charles ended up feeling irritated himself—but as much with Matilda as with her mother. Why did she behave like that? Why had she allowed herself to become the stereotypical fussy spinster daughter of an autocratic mother? He did not want to think about Matilda. He wished he could erase the memory of the day at Kew, especially of that half hour or so at the top of the pagoda. He did not know what to make of what had happened there. She had aroused in him memories that had been so deeply buried that he would have thought them completely obliterated if her reappearance in his life had not brought them flooding back. Not just memories of facts, however, but memories also of feelings and passions that should be laughable now but were not.

Matilda! There was no way on earth he wanted to become involved with her again. It would be ridiculous. And his guess was that she would agree with him.

Then there were his daughters. Barbara and her family returned from her in-laws' anniversary celebrations on the same day as Jane arrived in town with her family after recovering from her bouts of nausea. They came together the following day to call upon Charles, bringing their children with them. He talked and played with all three of his grandchildren and admired various toys and treasures they had brought with them for his approval—including the proud treasure of a bruise the size of a bird's egg acquired from slipping off the back of a pony that had become suddenly frisky. The children were then taken up to the nursery by Barbara's nurse, and Charles was left alone with his daughters. Barbara had an invitation for him. Her birthday was coming up soon.

"I know," Charles said. "I never forget birthdays, do I?"

"I wish every man were like you in that regard, Papa," Jane said, shaking her head, and clucked her tongue. "Wallace, for example." Wallace, Lord Frater, was her husband.

"Instead of having a family dinner at home as usual," Barbara continued, "we are going to have a family celebration at Vauxhall Gardens. Edward has reserved a box and we will feast there and listen to the orchestra and dance and watch the fireworks. It must be three years or more since I was last there."

"We went last year," Jane said. "But I am always happy to have an excuse to go to Vauxhall. It is sheer magic if the weather is good."

"Oh, the weather will be perfect for my birthday," Barbara assured her. "It would not dare be otherwise. Adrian will be coming. He has asked Lady Estelle Lamarr to accompany him. Do you know her, Papa? She is making her debut this year, though she is well past the usual age. I have seen her once or twice. She is a beauty—very dark coloring."

"I have an acquaintance with her," Charles said. "Her twin brother was at Oxford with Adrian."

"It would be lovely, in order to keep numbers even," Barbara said, "if you would invite someone too, Papa."

"Mrs. Summoner, perhaps?" Jane suggested.

Mrs. Summoner, who had been widowed about the same time as Charles had, had signaled on several occasions that she would not mind indulging in a discreet affair with him. She must be all of twenty years his junior. He held up a staying hand.

"If I must bring someone," he said, "I will choose for myself. I shall ask Lady Matilda Westcott."

He did not quite know what made him say it—and he certainly did not know if she would accept—except that he had been trying to pluck up the courage to talk to his daughters about something they needed to know, and this would make it somewhat imperative that he say it now.

"Lady Matilda Westcott?" Jane frowned. "Do you mean *Abigail* Westcott, Papa? But she is no longer *Lady* Abigail, is she? She lost the title several years ago. Besides, she is too young for you."

"And she has recently married, I have heard," Barbara added.

"I said Lady *Matilda* Westcott," Charles told them. "She is Abigail Westcott's aunt—Abigail Bennington now. She recently married Lieutenant Colonel Gil Bennington. My son."

They stared at him blankly.

"Did you say '*my son*'?" Jane asked, and laughed.

"I did," he said. "Gil Bennington is my natural son. He was born thirty-four years ago, before I even met your mother. His mother was the daughter of a village blacksmith. She raised him without my assistance, though assistance was offered. The only help I ever gave him came after her passing, when I purchased a commission for him in the foot regiment in which he was a sergeant. He refused any further help not long after that. I saw him for the first time a few weeks ago after he arrived in London with his new wife. They came to appear before a judge who was to decide who would have custody of his daughter. She was living with her maternal grandparents at the time. Now she is with Gil and his wife. I was at the hearing. I spoke up in Gil's defense. He has since taken his family to their home in Gloucestershire."

It all came out in a rush.

Jane's smile had disappeared. Both daughters were staring blankly at him.

"You have a *son*?" Jane asked. "Apart from Adrian?"

"Does Adrian *know*?" Barbara asked. "Dear God, it will kill him."

"He knows," Charles said. "He came with me last week to a dinner given by the Earl of Riverdale and his wife. A number of the other members of the Westcott family were there too. It occurred to me when I was invited that the truth was almost bound to leak out at last and that it would be better that you all hear it from me than from *ton* gossip."

His daughters were looking identically stunned, rather as Adrian had looked when Charles told him.

"And you are going to invite Abigail Bennington's *aunt*, one of the Westcotts, to Barbara's birthday party?" Jane said.

"Unless Barbara objects," Charles told her. "Obviously I have not asked her yet. She may say no even if I do."

"Lady Estelle Lamarr has some connection with the Westcott family too, does she not?" Barbara said, frowning in thought. "Her father married the former Countess of Riverdale a few years ago? Abigail Westcott's mother?"

"Yes," he said.

"And Adrian is bringing her to Vauxhall," Barbara said. "Yet he *knows*."

"Yes," Charles said again.

"Oh goodness." Barbara sat back in her chair and placed her palms against her cheeks. "I feel as though I were in the middle of some bizarre dream. We have a *half* brother, Jane."

"If you happen to have a feather about your person," Jane said, "someone could easily knock me over with it. How is it possible we never knew of this? And how *could* you, Papa? Oh, of all the dreadful things. Whatever will Wallace say when I tell him? What is he like, Papa? Though I am not at all sure I want to know."

They were none too happy, Charles realized. It was unsurprising. He was not himself. He had kept the secret for so long that it felt disconcerting to have the truth out in the open to upset his children. His wife had never known.

"I believe he is a good man," he said.

He proceeded to tell them some facts about his son. And he wondered as he did so whether he ought to ask Matilda to go to Vauxhall with him and thus keep alive the connection between her family and his. Perhaps his children would resent it. Though Adrian did not seem to do so. Quite the contrary, in fact.

How would she answer if he did ask her? Would she accept? And what would it mean if she did? It was to be an intimate event *with his family.* Would anyone get the idea that he was *courting* her? And would he be?

WHEN MATILDA RECEIVED A WRITTEN INVITATION TO JOIN MRS. Barbara Dewhurst and her family for an evening at Vauxhall Gardens in celebration of her birthday, she thought at first that the lady must have mistaken her for someone else. But only for a second.

"You look as if someone had just died, Matilda," her mother said from across the breakfast table. "Whatever has happened?"

Matilda looked up blankly. She would have loved to take the card upstairs to digest its contents in the privacy of her room, but it was too late for that. Apparently her face had betrayed her.

"Who is Mrs. Dewhurst?" her mother asked after Matilda had read the invitation aloud.

Matilda knew. She had known when Charles married and whom he married and where. She had known when each of his children were born—and married. She knew when his wife had died. For someone who had obliterated him entirely from her mind and memory over thirty years ago, she knew a lot about him. And she had suffered a great deal over each milestone in his life while denying every pang.

"She is Viscount Dirkson's elder daughter," she explained.

"But why would she be inviting you to join a family party?" her mother asked. But she did not wait for an answer. She set down her half-eaten slice of toast, dabbed at her mouth with her linen napkin, and sat back in her chair, regarding her daughter the whole while. "Do you have the viscount himself to thank for this?"

"I do not know any more than you do, Mama," Matilda said. Except that he had kissed her, and she had had a hard time both eating and sleeping in the week since, poor pathetic creature that she was.

"You fancied yourself in love with him once," her mother said.

"Oh goodness." Matilda laughed and stirred her coffee, even though the cup was already half-empty. "That was a long age ago, Mama." She looked up as she set the spoon in the saucer. "But I did not *fancy* myself in love with him. I loved him with my whole heart and soul."

Her mother continued to regard her steadily, and Matilda waited for the tirade of anger and ridicule that was bound to be coming. Instead her mother set down her napkin beside her plate and sighed.

"I know," she said.

Matilda lifted her cup, changed her mind, and set it back down on the saucer. She raised her eyes.

"I am not sure I knew about the 'heart and soul' part at the time," her mother said. "Though I understood it later, when you would have nothing to do with any of the many perfectly eligible gentlemen who would have courted you in the years after. I told myself it was infatuation. I told myself you were merely *in* love, something girls fall in and out of a dozen times before they settle into a sensible marriage."

"I fell only once," Matilda said. Oh goodness, she and Mama never talked like this.

"Yes, I know," her mother said again. "He ran wild with Humphrey, Matilda. Humphrey was my own son, but I was never blind to his many faults. Viscount Dirkson, or Charles Sawyer as he still was in those days, was a year older. I blamed him for leading Humphrey astray, or deluded myself into blaming him. My heart broke at the prospect of you marrying him and having to endure a wretched marriage for the rest of your life. I was not wrong about him. He grew worse than just wild as the years went on."

"I know, Mama," Matilda said.

"But," her mother said, "I have always lived with the guilt of denying you that misery—or that happiness. For it is impossible to know if his life would have proceeded differently if you had married him. Did he love you heart and soul too?"

"I believed so," Matilda said. "Indeed, I knew so."

"Being a parent is a hard job," her mother told her. "One so very much wants one's children to be happy. One wants to do all in one's power to prevent their being miserable. But where does wise guidance end and blind interference begin?"

Matilda frowned across the table at her mother. "You and Papa did the right thing," she said.

"Did we?" Her mother lifted her napkin again and proceeded to fold it neatly. "You were my firstborn, Matilda. I hesitate to say you were my favorite, for you were *all* my favorites at different times and in different circumstances. But you were special. You were my . . . my *firstborn.*"

Matilda found herself blinking back tears. Her mother *never* talked this way. And she had never been a demonstrative parent. She had never before said that she loved her eldest daughter, let alone that she had been the favorite.

"I must go and send an answer to Mrs. Dewhurst," Matilda said, getting to her feet. "I will decline, of course."

"Why?" her mother asked.

"I do not belong with that family," Matilda said. "I would feel embarrassed and awkwardly out of place."

"Why?" her mother asked again. "It is obvious that it was Mrs. Dewhurst's father who suggested your name. Why else would she have thought to ask you? I daresay she does not even know you."

Matilda could think of no answer. *Why* had he suggested her? He had said nothing during or after the journey home from Kew about seeing her again. There had been nothing from him since. She had assumed he was bitterly regretting some of the things he had said. Not to mention that kiss.

"Did you enjoy the day at Kew?" her mother asked.

"Yes, of course I did," Matilda said. "The young people were delightful. I was touched when Mr. Sawyer came the following day with Boris and Bertrand and Estelle to thank me. It was thoughtful of them."

"And was Viscount Dirkson delightful?" her mother asked.

Matilda sat back down. "He was pleasant company, Mama," she said. "I believe all the young people liked him."

"But did you, Matilda?" her mother asked.

"Yes, of course," she said. *He kissed me. Me, a fifty-six-year-old spinster.*

"Then you must go to Vauxhall with him and his family," her mother told her.

"Mama," Matilda began, but her mother held up a hand.

"Matilda," she said, "you have driven me to the brink of insanity several times in the years since your papa died."

"I know," Matilda said. "I want to care for you, Mama, but I know you resent my every move."

"You drive me insane with *guilt*," her mother said. "Believe me when I tell you I did not understand just how much you loved him, Matilda. Perhaps the advice your father and I gave you was sound. It seemed so at the time. But I have looked upon you in all the years since as a millstone of regret and guilt about my neck. We ought to have advised you and then trusted you to make your own decision. We ought at least to have put a time limit on our refusal. We could have insisted that your young man wait a year before applying to your father again for permission to address you."

"Mama!" Matilda cried, hearing only that she had been a millstone about her mother's neck.

"Matilda," her mother said, getting to her feet while her daughter shot to hers in order to rush to her assistance—an impulse she reined in before she had taken more than two steps. "Matilda, *I love you.* When I snap at you, it is because my heart hurts for you and I know I am to blame for everything you have become. Now, I am going to my sitting room to read the morning papers. I can get up the stairs with the assistance of the banister rail and my own feet. You are to go to the morning room to write to Mrs. Dewhurst. You are to thank her for the kind invitation and inform her that you will be delighted to make one of the party. Or you may write to refuse. The choice is yours."

Matilda, dumbfounded, watched her mother leave the room. For the first time in what must be years she did not rush after her to offer assistance that was not solicited. It took a great deal of resolution.

She accepted the invitation. Having placed it on the silver tray in the hall and drawn the attention of the butler to it, she went up to her room and lay down on her bed, something she never did in the daytime, and stared up at the canopy.

I love you.

Not in the voice of a man from years and years ago, but in her mother's voice. For perhaps the first time ever. If her mother had said it before, Matilda had no memory of it. She had always chosen to believe it must be true anyway, though she had doubted of late. But oh, the craving to hear those words from one's own mother. And now they had been spoken.

I love you.

Matilda rolled over onto her side, hid her face against the pillow, and wept.

I love you.

Why did he want her to go to Vauxhall with his family?

Did he regret that kiss at the top of the pagoda in Kew Gardens?

I love you.

He too had spoken those words to her once upon a time long, long ago.

Life, her dreary, endless life, had suddenly become too full of emotion to be borne. She was not accustomed to strong emotion. She did not know what to do with it.

Except weep.

Something she never did.

She wept.

AS SOON AS HE HAD HEARD FROM BARBARA THAT MATILDA HAD accepted the invitation to Vauxhall, Charles wrote to inform her that he would bring his carriage to her mother's house and escort her there himself. He did not look forward to calling at the house, but it was the correct thing to do, and he was not really afraid of the dragon. Was he? But when he arrived on the appointed evening and was conducted to the drawing room, it was to find that the dowager countess was alone there.

His heart sank even as he girded his loins for battle.

"Ma'am," he said, making her a bow.

She looked him up and down from her chair beside the fireplace, her expression stern, even hostile.

"Lord Dirkson," she said. "Your daughter has a lovely evening for her party."

"She is fortunate," he said, "considering the fact that we have had nothing but drizzle and blustery winds for the last several days."

"Tell me," she said. "Did I make a mistake all those years ago?"

Her words took him completely by surprise. He did not know for a moment how to answer. "I understood," he said, "that the Earl of Riverdale, your husband, rejected my suit because my wild ways made me an ineligible suitor for his daughter. I was twenty years old. I behaved as a large number of young men behave at that age. Wildly, that is. I was prepared to reform my ways after I had made the acquaintance of Lady Matilda. Whether I would have done so or not cannot be known for sure. I daresay you believed at the time that you were acting in the best interests of your daughter. Subsequent events would seem to have justified you in that opinion."

"You loved her?" she asked.

"I did, ma'am," he said. "Very dearly. I do not expect you to believe me."

"Age does not necessarily strengthen a person or insulate her from pain," she said. "My daughter is as fragile now as she was then, Viscount Dirkson, even though she may appear to be set in her ways and incapable of deep feeling."

Matilda did not appear that way to him in either regard.

"Are you asking me my intentions, ma'am?" he asked.

She did not reply for a moment as she looked steadily at him. "I am," she said then.

He felt like a young man again, being hauled up before suspicious parents as he pursued their daughters. It was a little bizarre. But one thing was clear. The old dragon cared after all. He did not like her, but she cared. At least he assumed she did. Perhaps she was only anxious at the possible loss of her longtime slave.

"They are honorable, ma'am," he assured her. "I have no wish to hurt Lady Matilda. I will do all in my power not to do so. I never did hurt her, if you will remember. I am not the one who ended our connection."

What the devil was he saying? Was he committing himself to something? Events of the past couple of weeks or so had left him with the uneasy feeling that he was being drawn into some sort of trap. But . . . a trap of whose making? Not Matilda's, certainly. Not her mother's either, or any of her family's. Of his own, then? He was the one, after all, who had suggested first himself and then Matilda as chaperons for that youthful excursion to Kew. He was the one who had suggested her name to Barbara.

"Do you still love her?" the dowager asked him.

He raised his eyebrows. "I *care* for her, ma'am," he said.

She narrowed her eyes and then nodded curtly. "Matilda is an adult," she said. "She has been an adult for many years. It is time I learned not to interfere in her life. I am sure you would agree with that, Lord Dirkson."

"I am sure, ma'am," he said, "that your concern for her arises from love."

He was sure of no such thing. But before she could reply, the door behind him opened and he turned in some relief to watch Matilda hurry into the room, her evening gown an icy, shimmery silver gray, a blue cashmere shawl over one arm, her hair styled with simple elegance, her posture more erect even than usual, her cheeks slightly flushed, her lips in a prim line.

And dash it all. He fell in love. Again.

Six

They crossed the river by boat instead of by the bridge, a convenience Matilda had always considered unromantic ever since it opened a few years previous. Charles took her shawl from over her arm just when she was starting to feel a bit chilly and wrapped it around her shoulders. For a moment he kept his arm about her, holding the shawl in place, but he soon removed it and sat more decorously beside her, making light conversation. It must be twenty-five or, more likely, thirty years since she had been anywhere escorted by a gentleman alone. She had been relieved that her mother had not suggested her maid accompany her. How humiliating it would have been if that had happened in his hearing.

He had arrived a bit early. She had not been quite ready. But she had hurried, alarmed that he was going to have to face her mother alone in the drawing room. And sure enough, Mama had been looking severe when she arrived there, and he had been looking stern. He had not told her—and she had not asked—what had transpired between them. Merely a stilted, banal conversation about the weather, she hoped.

"Oh," she said now. "Just look." They were foolish words, since they were facing the opposite bank of the Thames and he would have to be blind not to see the dozens of colored lanterns strung through the branches of the trees of Vauxhall Gardens, swaying in the breeze, their reflections shivering across the flowing water. "Is it not sheer magic, Charles?"

"It is indeed," he agreed, but when she turned her head to look at him it was to find that *he* was looking at *her*, his eyes shadowed by the near darkness and the brim of his tall hat.

She smiled and turned her face away. He had used to do that all the time. She had questioned him about it once. *Why are you always looking at me?* she had asked. He had had a ready answer. *Because there is nothing and no one in this world I would rather look at.* Foolish, flattering words that had warmed her to her toes. She did not ask the same question now. Who knew how he would answer?

"It was very kind of your daughter to invite me to join her birthday celebrations," she said. "Her card mentioned the fact that it is to be a *family* party."

"Immediate family, yes," he told her. "Barbara and Jane will be there with their husbands. Adrian has invited Lady Estelle Lamarr. And I have invited you. Social events are always better when there is an even number of men and women."

"Will Estelle indeed be here too?" she asked, pleased. "I had not heard. I like your son, Charles. He is a very pleasant young man."

"He likes you too," he told her. "He says you have a permanent twinkle in your eyes."

"Oh," she said, "I do not."

"No, I know," he said. "But you ought to, Matilda. You were

born to arouse happiness in those around you. You used to do it. When I won your affections—for a short while at least—it was against brisk competition."

"That is so untrue," she protested.

"You were unaware of your own charms," he told her. "It was one of the endearing things about you. You were much admired, Matilda, largely because of the sparkle of happiness you exuded."

He must be wrong. Oh, surely he must. She had had other suitors, of course, a tedious number of them after she had sent him away. But she was Lady Matilda Westcott, eldest daughter of the Earl of Riverdale. She came with a large dowry. She was extremely eligible. The attention she received had not been at all surprising. There had been nothing personal about it. He was quite wrong about that.

"This is a silly conversation," she said.

He laughed—and her insides turned over. "Then it is a good thing it is at an end for a while," he said as the boat drew in to the bank and all the magic and pleasures of Vauxhall awaited them, as well as the nervousness of meeting his daughters and their husbands as a member of their family party just as though . . . Well, just as though Charles were *courting* her.

She was *so* unaccustomed to being out alone, Matilda thought. For a moment she longed for the prop of her mother to fuss over. Then she set her hand in Charles's, got carefully to her feet against the sway of the boat, and stepped out onto the jetty. She rearranged her shawl about her shoulders as an excuse to release her hand from his, straightened her spine, and nodded briskly to indicate that she was ready to proceed. Colored lanterns swayed above their heads. The distant sound of music enticed them to come closer.

"Matilda." He offered his arm. "I chose you as my companion

for this evening because I wanted you here. Everyone will be prepared to like you. You need not look as though you were about to march into battle."

"Do your daughters *know?*" she asked as she took his arm. "About Gil, I mean?"

"Yes," he said.

"And they know he is married to my niece?" she asked.

"Yes," he said. "And to Lady Estelle Lamarr's stepsister. They know. They are dealing with the knowledge."

As was she, Matilda thought. She was still dealing with it, with the knowledge that Charles must have fathered Gil a mere few months after declaring his undying love for and fidelity to her.

They strolled along a wide avenue in the direction of the rotunda, surrounded by other people, their senses assailed by the sounds of music and voices and by the sight of colored lamplight. She was here with a companion who was not her mother. She was here with a man who had deliberately chosen her. She was here with *Charles.* Whoever could have predicted any of this?

"Do you remember," he asked her, his voice low, "the last time we were here together, Matilda?"

How could she possibly *not* remember? The magic, the exhilaration, the pure joy of that evening. The heady feeling of being young and in love. The anticipation of a lifetime of love together. She had never doubted his eligibility, even though she knew he had been embroiled in some pretty wild escapades with Humphrey. He had been heir to a viscount's title, after all. And that evening had been one of the very few times they had been able to snatch more than just a few short moments alone together. They had wandered along one of the narrower, darker paths among the trees until they had stopped and he had kissed her.

"It was a long time ago," she said.

He did not answer. They had reached the rotunda with its tiers of open-fronted boxes arranged in a horseshoe shape about the dance floor. The orchestra was positioned in the center.

"It looks as if we are the last to arrive," he said. "But everyone else was coming via the bridge. My children, it would seem, have no sense of romance."

"And you do?" The words were out of her mouth before she could rein them in.

He turned his head to smile at her. "And I do," he said.

Then they were at the family box and Matilda was being presented to Mr. and Mrs. Dewhurst and Lord and Lady Frater, all of whom smiled amiably at her and shook her hand. Mr. Sawyer shook her warmly by the hand too, and Estelle beamed at her and kissed her cheek.

"It was only half an hour ago that I learned you were coming here too with Viscount Dirkson, Aunt Matilda," she said. "I was so delighted. Is this not the perfect evening for Vauxhall?"

"It is indeed," Matilda agreed. "And may I wish you a happy birthday, Mrs. Dewhurst?"

She was a pretty young lady and favored her mother in looks, as did her brother. Lady Frater more closely resembled her father.

"Thank you, Lady Matilda," Mrs. Dewhurst said. "But will you call me Barbara, please? And I am sure my sister would rather be called Jane than *Lady Frater*."

"I would indeed," that young lady said. "Do come and sit down, Lady Matilda. The food will be arriving shortly. Vauxhall always has the *best* ham. And strawberries."

"Edward will pour you and Papa some champagne," Barbara said as her husband got to his feet.

Oh, this, Matilda thought, gazing about her at Charles's family and beyond the box at the sights and hearing the sounds of Vauxhall, was wonderful. *Wonderful.* She was going to tuck every single detail away in her memory to hoard for the rest of her life.

Her eyes rested briefly upon Charles's face and she smiled.

THE THING WAS, CHARLES THOUGHT, THAT MATILDA LOOKED every bit her age. She had attempted nothing to minimize it. And she behaved with a certain primness. At the same time there was something almost youthful about her—a certain innocence and wonder over her surroundings. There was no bright sparkle in her eyes, very little laughter, not a great deal of conversation, very few outright smiles. But . . . What was it about her? At every moment while they ate supper and listened to the music and watched the dancers and conversed, she looked . . . happy? Was that a strong enough word? She looked as if she really wanted to be here. She appeared fully present. She looked upon his children, his sons-in-law, her stepniece, as though she really liked them and was enjoying being with them. She looked very little at him, but when she did it was with almost a questioning expression, as though she did not quite know why she was here with him, but for this evening anyway was contented that it be so.

He suspected there had been very little joy in Matilda's adult life. And very few outings that did not include her mother or other members of the Westcott family.

He sensed that his daughters liked her, even knowing of her connection to Gil. He knew that Adrian did.

"I want to dance," Barbara announced after the remains of their supper had been cleared away. "And the next one is to be a waltz. Come, Edward."

"I believe almost every dance at Vauxhall is a waltz, Barbara," Wallace said. "Jane?" He held out a hand for his wife's.

"Have you been approved yet to dance the waltz, Lady Estelle?" Adrian asked. "I know this is your first Season."

"I have," she told him.

"I am not sure the rules apply so strictly here at Vauxhall anyway," Charles said as Lady Estelle got to her feet and set her hand in Adrian's. He turned his head. "Matilda?"

"Oh," she said, "I have never waltzed. The dance was not even performed in England until a few years ago." There was a certain wistfulness in her voice.

"But you know the steps?" he asked her.

"Yes, of course," she said. "I always think it must be the most romantic dance ever invented. Young people now are very fortunate."

"I do not believe," he said, "there is any prohibition upon the not-so-young waltzing too." He stood and extended a hand for hers.

"I would make a cake of myself," she protested. "And humiliate you."

"Matilda." He leaned a little toward her. "Do you not trust me to hold you and lead you and prevent you from tripping over your own or anyone else's feet? And do you not trust yourself to perform the steps you have seen and yearned to dance?"

"I have not yearned—"

"Liar," he said softly, smiling at her. "Your eyes give you away."

"Oh, they do not," she protested.

"Waltz with me," he said.

She raised her hand and placed it in his. She primmed her lips and squared her shoulders and he almost laughed. But it was not the moment for laughter. Only for tenderness. He knew that the bright, youthful star that had been the young Matilda was still locked within her, long repressed. All the warmth and vitality and love he remembered were still there too. He was not imagining it. It was not wishful thinking on his part. His Matilda still existed, but she had grown older, as he had, and he was not sorry for it. He was no longer interested in youthful beauty and allure. A fifty-six-year-old Matilda suited him perfectly. But the *real* Matilda, not the one shaped by her sense of duty to her mother and the perceptions of her family, who saw her merely as a spinster sister or aunt.

"You will be sorry," she warned him.

"Only if you are," he said. "I am wagering on my ability to make sure that you are not."

He led her onto the floor with a number of other people, including his son and his daughters, and waited for the music to begin. He looked up, beyond the colored lanterns, and saw the moon, almost but not quite full, and stars against a black sky.

"Look," he said, and she gazed upward with him.

He lowered his eyes to her face and the music began. He placed a hand behind her waist while hers came to rest on his shoulder. He took her other hand in his and held her firmly, close to but not quite touching his chest. And he led her into the steps of the waltz, tentatively at first, avoiding any fancy twirls. She kept her eyes on his, though she was not really seeing him, he knew. She was concentrating upon the steps she had seen performed but had never danced herself. And then she smiled fleetingly and then more brightly, and he knew she was seeing him and beginning to enjoy herself.

He led her into a simple twirl, and she laughed. With pure delight. He smiled back into her eyes. She was warm and vital in his arms, and he was where he wanted to be more than anywhere else on earth—not at Vauxhall specifically but within the loose circle of Matilda's arms. He was where he had surely always yearned to be, long after he had consciously and then unconsciously let go of the memory of her and his passion for her.

"Neither of us is going to be sorry," he murmured beneath the sounds of music and voices and laughter.

"No," she said. And then, with a touching sort of wonder in her voice, "I am *waltzing*, Charles."

He felt a curious tickle in his throat as though—alarming thought—he was about to weep.

"*We* are waltzing," he said.

And Vauxhall wove its magic around them.

ALL ABOUT THEM COUPLES OLD AND YOUNG, PLUMP AND THIN, rich and not so rich, were waltzing. And Matilda waltzed with Charles among them.

She would not feel self-conscious because she was a staid spinster who always sat among the chaperons on the rare occasion when she attended a ball with her mother, or because she was past the age of fifty. She was not past the age of wanting to waltz or to indulge in a little romance. She was not too old to enjoy the feel of a man's hand at the back of her waist, his other hand in hers, the whole of the waltz to be danced face-to-face, almost body to body. She could feel his heat. She could smell his cologne as well as something equally enticing that seemed to be the very scent of him. She was not too old to feel the pull of his physicality. Or to dream.

Or to fall in love.

Though perhaps it was impossible to fall into anything one was already in. To fall in love again, then. Could one fall in love twice, with the same man, when one had not really stopped loving him the first time? Was it possible . . .

"What is amusing you?" he asked, and Matilda shivered at the low intimacy of his voice against her ear. He knew, as many people did not, that in order to make oneself heard amid music and a babble of voices, one needed to pitch one's voice beneath the general hubbub rather than try to shout over it.

"I am merely enjoying the waltz and the myriad sensations of being here at Vauxhall on a lovely evening," she told him.

"No," he said. "There was *amusement* in your face, Matilda. Something tickled you."

"Oh," she said, "I was wondering if it is possible to have the same feelings twice in a lifetime about the same subject, or whether that would mean that really there had been only one feeling spread over a long period of time, even if perhaps it was dormant for a while, and not two separate feelings at all."

And if he could interpret *that* it would be a wonder.

He led her into a series of twirls that had her marveling that this accomplished female dancer, who did not once trip over her own feet or anyone else's for that matter, was *she*. Matilda Westcott. Though she knew it was really the accomplished dancing of Charles that made her look good.

"I can see why you were so amused, then," he said. "Those were enormously amusing wonderings."

His eyes were laughing. Oh, he had used to do that all the time. And Matilda could not stop her own laughter from bubbling out of her. Then his mouth was smiling too and all sorts of lines showed themselves on his face, mostly at the outer corners of his eyes. Wrinkles in the making. Or, rather, laugh lines. Very attractive ones.

And she had never—oh, surely she had never before in her whole life, even when she was in love at the age of twenty—been happier than she was now, at this precise moment. Waltzing at Vauxhall. With Charles. She wanted to pinch herself. No, she did not. If this was a dream, she did not want to wake up. Ever.

But the waltz came to an end. Life always forged onward whether one wished it to do so or not. Matilda returned on Charles's arm to the box, only to have her hand solicited for another waltz by his son.

Oh my. She was about to refuse. No one ever danced with Matilda. She never expected it. But now *two* partners in one evening? She might never recover from the vanity of it all. Charles, she could see, was extending a hand for his elder daughter's and leading her out into the dancing area.

"Well, thank you," she said. "I have just danced my first waltz, you know. I hope I do not make a cake of myself and a spectacle of you during the second."

He laughed as they took their place on the dance floor. "I am my father's son in some ways," he said. "I will see to it that you come to no harm, Lady Matilda."

"Ah," she said, "but can you also see to it that *you* do not?"

He laughed again.

He was as good a dancer as his father, she decided after they had waltzed for a couple of minutes without talking—and without mishap—though he was *not* Charles, of course. He was not quite as tall and he was fairer of coloring and considerably younger. She doubted he had ever given his mother a moment's anxiety over wild oats he was sowing. Though he had been a mere boy, of course, when his mother died.

His eyes were upon hers. "You know my half brother, Lady

Matilda," he said. "When you came to our house that day with Bertrand Lamarr, it was to tell my father about the custody hearing, was it not?"

"Yes," she said. "I thought he might be able to help. It was very much in the balance, you see, whether the judge would order that the little girl remain with her grandparents or be restored to her father."

"The little girl," he said. "My niece. My half niece."

"Katy, yes," she said.

She guessed that he was still grappling with the knowledge that there was another member of his father's family he and his sisters had known nothing of until very recently. Just as they, the Westcotts, had had to deal with the appearance of Anna, Humphrey's only legitimate daughter, in their midst six years ago. It had not been easy. It had been harder for some of them than for others.

"Lady Matilda," he said, "tell me about your niece."

She thought for a moment that he was moving on to another subject. "Estelle?" she said. "She is not really my—Oh, you are asking about Abigail, are you?"

"About Mrs. Bennington, yes," he said.

"She is the youngest of my brother's children," she told him. "She was always sweet and quiet, but a happy girl, I thought. She was on the brink of making her come-out into society when her father died and the discovery was made that he had never been legally married to her mother. She seemed to be the one who took the blow the best. She remained quiet and sweet. But her happiness was gone. And actually she became quieter than she had been— withdrawn and insistent upon being left to live her life her own way. We were all worried. My heart ached for her with that helpless feeling one gets when one wants desperately to help while knowing that all one's efforts to do so are not wanted and are therefore useless."

The story of her life.

"Ah, but she would have known herself loved," he said. "That is invaluable in itself, ma'am."

He was a kind young man, she thought. Some young lady was going to be very fortunate when he decided to settle down.

"And then this year she met Gil Bennington," she told him, "and married him without a word to her family—except her brother, who was the sole family member at her wedding. None of us were quite easy in our minds about it, for he is a taciturn, stern, dour man, very military in his bearing. But it became clear to us at the custody hearing and afterward that he loves his daughter to distraction and probably—*very* probably—Abigail too. And she glows with happiness, though she is as quiet and reserved as ever. There is a certain look about two people in love, Mr. Sawyer."

Matilda was surprised to realize that they were still waltzing, surrounded by other couples. She had forgotten her fear of tying her feet in knots.

"She is my half sister–in–law," he said. "If there is such a relationship."

"Your father loves you and your sisters no whit the less for the fact that he also loves his natural son," she told him. "Love is not a finite thing to be equally apportioned among a limited number of people. It is infinite and can be spread to encompass the whole world without losing one iota of its force. And goodness, just listen to me. If you wish for life advice, come to Aunt Matilda. Tell all your friends."

He laughed. "It is a jolt to the system, you know," he said, "to discover at the age of twenty-two that one has a thirty-four-year-old brother. And now I will not rest until I have met him. And Mrs. Bennington. And Katy."

Matilda smiled. How she liked this young man. Under other circumstances he might have been hers. But no. What a stupid, ridiculous thought. He was the son of Charles and his late wife.

"When you and my father knew each other as young people," he said, "were you in love, Lady Matilda? And what an impertinent question that is. Do please ignore it."

She continued to smile at him as Charles and Barbara danced by, laughing over something one of them had said.

"We were both very young," she told him. "Just twenty. Whatever was between us, Mr. Sawyer, was over long before your father met your mother. I saw very little of him during the years of their marriage, and even that little was from afar. We never spoke. There was never anything between us."

"Except when you were very young," he said. "As though young love is foolish and not to be taken at all seriously. I am twenty-two, Lady Matilda. Only two years older than my father was then. I know I am young. I know it will be years before I acquire any serious sort of wisdom. But the feelings of the young ought not to be dismissed or made light of. They are very real. I am sorry that something happened—and I am *not* going to ask you what it was—to separate you and my father. I like you."

Matilda smiled and blinked her eyes rapidly. Was it because of something to do with life after the age of fifty-five that she was becoming a watering pot these days?

"Thank you," she said. "It was not your father's fault, you know. It was mine. But it is also ancient history. *Very* ancient."

They lapsed into a not-uncomfortable silence for what remained of the waltz. How lovely it felt to be *liked*, Matilda thought in some surprise. One tended to imagine sometimes that only being *loved* was of any significance. But there was something enormously touching, something genuine, about being told that one was liked. By a young man who had no reason to feel anything at all for one.

Charles's son.

After the dance was over and while the orchestra took a break they all indulged themselves with the strawberries with clotted cream for which Vauxhall Gardens was famous. And then Jane suggested a walk, something they all agreed they needed after feasting upon such rich foods. Besides, during the darkness of evening there was about Vauxhall a beauty that beckoned one beyond just the area around the boxes.

They all set off together, Mr. Sawyer and Estelle leading the way along the broad, tree-lined avenue, well illumined by the light from the colored lanterns, Charles and Matilda bringing up the rear "like a couple of conscientious chaperons," Charles remarked.

"However," he added a minute or two later, "I believe it is to Barbara that the Marquess of Dorchester entrusted Lady Estelle's care this evening. That leaves us free of all responsibility, Matilda."

For some reason his words left her feeling breathless.

The avenue was crowded with revelers. It was difficult for a group of eight to remain together. But she and Charles did not need to try. Both his daughters were with their husbands. Estelle was under the care of one of them and being escorted by surely a very respectable young man.

How lovely, Matilda thought, to be without responsibility and walking alone with a man in the crowd.

As she had been with the same man in the same venue thirty-six years ago.

Seven

Thirty-six years ago they had walked this avenue with a group of other young people. Oddly—or perhaps not so strangely considering how long ago it had been—Charles could not recall who any of the others had been, though he thought Humphrey had been there. The parents of one of the young ladies had chaperoned them, but they had been a cheerfully careless pair and had enjoyed the pleasures of Vauxhall on their own account without keeping too close an eye upon their charges, a fact that had delighted those charges.

Charles and Matilda had turned off onto a side path, narrower than the main avenue, more thickly enclosed by trees, more sparsely lit by lanterns, and close to being deserted. They had been able to walk side by side, but only because each had an arm wrapped about the other's waist. Her head had come to rest upon his shoulder after a while until, in a small clearing to one side of the path, they had come to a halt and he had kissed her.

He had stopped short of making full love to her, and she had indicated just as he was pulling back that she would not have allowed it anyway. But they had shared a long and passionate embrace before that moment. Afterward, while they were recovering their breath, his forehead against hers, her hands spread over his chest, he had told her again that he loved her, that he wanted to marry her. She had said yes, oh yes, oh yes, she wanted to marry him too. She would love him with all her heart forever and ever.

Soon after, they had returned to the main avenue to rejoin their party and begin living happily ever after. Less than a week later he had called upon her father . . .

"Matilda," he said now as they walked along the main avenue, "how long did it take you to stop loving me?" For she *had* loved him. He had doubted it for a long time, when the pain was raw, but no longer.

"About as long as it took you to stop," she said. "Gil was born the following year."

"I dealt with my unwanted love in a thoroughly unbridled and immature way," he said. "I suppose I remained immature long after the age at which most men settle down. Until ten years or so ago, in fact. I did not love Gil's mother, though I do not want to speak disrespectfully of her. She was not a woman of loose morals. I believe she genuinely thought I loved her and would marry her. She punished me very effectively when she understood that I did not and could not."

"By keeping you away from your son?" she said.

"Yes."

"Are you telling me, then," she asked him, "that all the behavior for which you became notorious was because of me? Did I hurt you so very badly?"

"I was hurt," he admitted. "But my behavior was mine to own. You were not responsible for any of that, Matilda."

"Humphrey always assured me whenever I asked," she said, "that you were not hurt at all, that you had been lying to me when you told me you loved me, that you were incapable of love just as he was. You were a capital fellow in his estimation. He told me to grow up to the real world and not expect love outside the pages of a book."

"And you listened and believed?" he said. *She had asked her brother about him?*

"I did not look for love from any man," she said.

"Because of me?" he asked.

"No, of course—" She stopped. "Yes. Because of you."

He drew a slow breath and let it out on an almost audible sigh.

"Your mother treats you poorly, Matilda," he said. It might seem to be a non sequitur, but it was not. "You gave up love and marriage in order to be treated with impatience and irritability even before strangers? Do you not regret—"

"Regrets are pointless," she said sharply. "My mother is sometimes impatient with me because I *coddle* her. I have fully realized it only lately. I have always been so determined to show my love and devotion, to make my life seem meaningful, that I have treated her, at least in recent years, like an old woman rather than as a person of dignity still able to be in charge of her own life. I have been a severe trial to her—as she has been to me. Don't judge from the outside, Charles. She has her own demons to deal with. She feels guilty for blighting my life. My presence forever at her side and my . . . fussy behavior are a constant reproach to her. I could have behaved differently all those years ago. I could have fought for myself instead of giving in so meekly to my parents' fears and commands. I could have married someone else of whom they *did* approve. Oh, but regrets are pointless, Charles. Must we spoil this most wonderful of wonderful evenings by talking of the past?"

The avenue was crowded. They dodged other revelers and probably annoyed a number of them with their slow pace. The orchestra had resumed its playing, but the music was almost drowned out by the sounds of raised voices and laughter.

Perhaps her mother was not such an ogre, then, Charles thought. Apparently she had a conscience. Perhaps she loved her eldest daughter after all. Probably she did, in fact. And Matilda loved her in return, even though her mother had blighted her life—an interesting choice of words. No, he must not judge. Close human relationships were often a great deal more complex than they seemed to outsiders. His own relationship with his wife, for example, had been far from simple, far from one-faceted. On the whole it had been a decent marriage, even though he had been a wayward husband much of the time and she had told him even before they wed that she had no real interest in men but recognized the necessity of conforming to society's expectations by marrying him. Yet they had produced three children who had grown into affectionate, sensible adults of whom they had both been proud.

"We will not spoil the evening," he said. "It *is* wonderful, is it not?"

He could not be sure in the dim, swaying light of the lanterns, but it looked to him as though her eyes had filled with tears. And how much she had revealed about her feelings!

. . . this most wonderful of wonderful evenings.

Ah, Matilda.

"Come," he said, turning her onto a side path just as he had more than thirty years ago. "Let us seek a little more privacy."

He could not be sure it was the *same* path. But it did not matter. It was narrow as the other one had been, a little too narrow for two people to walk comfortably side by side. He drew his arm away from hers and encircled her waist with it. Far from showing any outrage or resistance, she set her own arm about him and very briefly rested the side of her head against his shoulder.

Just like last time.

"This is better," he said. "The noise seems more muted here."

"Yes," she said. "Charles—"

"Mmm?" He waited for her to continue.

"Surely this is impossible," she said.

"*This?*"

"It surely is," she said. "Impossible. More than three decades have gone by. I am *old*."

"I take exception to that word," he told her. "For if you are old, then I am older. Three months older, I seem to recall. We are not old, and even if we are, we are not *dead*. Only in that circumstance would I be forced to agree with you that this is impossible. Though perhaps I would be unable then either to agree or to disagree. I would be dead. We are *alive*, Matilda."

"But this sort of thing is for young people," she protested.

"Slinking into the trees to set our arms about each other's waist?" he said. "Embracing?"

"Oh, not that," she said hastily. "It would be most unseemly."

And she sounded so like a prim, middle-aged spinster that he smiled into the darkness. He loved her primness. But only because there was also her passion. And passion very definitely lurked within her. It had shown itself briefly during their kiss on top of the pagoda. And in some of her looks and words since—*this most wonderful of wonderful evenings*, for example.

"Most," he agreed.

"You are laughing at me," she said.

"Yes."

She turned her face toward his, though he doubted she could see his laughing eyes. "That is unkind."

"Is it, my love?" he asked her.

"*Charles!*" Her voice seemed half agony, half outrage.

"Do you not want me to call you that?" he asked. "My love?"

"Ch-a-a-arles."

He stopped walking. There was a little open-fronted rain shelter in a small clearing to the right of the path, a bench inside it, a lantern suspended from the branch of a tree before it to illumine the interior. He led her toward it, though he did not sit down with her. He faced her instead and laced his fingers with hers at their sides, as he had done at the pagoda. He could see her face dimly, as she would be able to see his. She was gazing wide-eyed at him.

"That was no answer," he said. "Do you not understand that is what you are to me—my love?"

"Oh," she said, "you cannot possibly love me, Charles."

"I do not see why not," he said. "And apparently it is possible. I have tested the idea and can find no flaw in it. Do you love me, Matilda?"

He watched her lick her lips, lower her gaze, first to his mouth, then to his neckcloth. "Of course I do," she said, sounding almost cross.

"You cannot possibly," he told her, and her eyes shot up to look accusingly into his again.

"I never stopped," she said. "Do you think I did—or could? I followed all the events of your life from afar and lived for the few glimpses I had of you down the years. I bled a little inside every time

I heard something about you that reaffirmed my conviction that I had done the right thing by refusing to have anything more to do with you. The pain dimmed as time passed until there was almost no pain at all. The memories dimmed until they became almost unconscious, lost somewhere in the recesses of my mind. But always, always, I have known that I love you, ridiculous as it seemed to be, ridiculous as it would have seemed to anyone who had ever suspected."

He had turned very still inside. His love for her must have lain dormant in him for more than half his life, but he had given it almost no thought since a year or so after she had rejected him. He had given *her* no thought, or almost none. Yet his love must not have completely died—or why had it been revived so easily now in all its intensity? Why was it that after such a brief time he was surer than he had been of anything else in his life that he loved this woman who was his age and looked it and dressed without glamour or obvious allure? Yet to him she seemed the most beautiful woman on earth. Why was it he had fallen in love only twice in his life, and with the same woman? It shook him to the core that even though she was the one who had rejected him all those years ago, she had remained true to him ever since. For he knew she must have had numerous chances of marriage to other men, at least during the ten years or so after him.

"Matilda." He sighed and drew her to him, one arm about her waist, the other about her shoulders. "You put me to shame with your steadfast fidelity."

"But I am the one who sent you away," she said.

"For reasons that seemed sound to you at the time and possibly were," he said. "How can either of us be sure I would not have turned out just as I did even if we had married? I do not *believe* I would have, but I cannot be certain. Perhaps we needed to wait until we were older. We might have had a very unhappy marriage if we had wed when we were young."

"And we might not have," she said, infinite sadness in her voice.

"You said earlier that regrets are pointless," he said, resting his forehead against hers. "You were right."

"Yes," she agreed.

And he kissed her.

She kissed like someone who had never kissed before, with slightly pursed lips and stiffened limbs—even though they had kissed at Kew. But there he had not had his arms about her. Perhaps she felt more threatened this time. He raised his head.

"Put your arms around me," he said. She had her hands clutched about his upper arms. She tipped her head slightly to one side in a familiar gesture before releasing her hold and sliding one arm beneath his about his waist and wrapping the other about his neck.

"Charles," she said. "I am no good at this. I will only make a cake of myself."

"I do not believe there is a manual," he said. "Or any rules at all, in fact. Just kiss me, my love, and I will kiss you."

"You ought not to call me that," she said.

"My love?" he said. "Why not?"

She pursed her lips, looked as though she was about to say something, and changed her mind. "I keep waiting to wake up," she said at last.

"So do I," he told her. "But while we are both asleep, shall we share the dream?"

She tightened her arms about him. "Very well," she said so primly that he almost laughed.

He smiled instead and kissed her again, drawing her against

him, moving his hand lower down her back to draw her closer yet. He probed the seam of her lips with his tongue, and when they trembled apart he explored the inside of her mouth, stroking and circling her tongue. She moaned low in her throat, and he could feel one of her hands tangling in his hair.

And though she was different from the way she had been at the age of twenty, there was something about her that was unmistakably Matilda, and he knew he had never really stopped loving her. It was why he had never fallen in love with anyone else. For always, somewhere in the recesses of his being, there had been Matilda. And now—yes, it was like a dream—he held her in his arms again.

They were gazing into each other's eyes then in the dim, pink glow of the lantern, her head tipped back.

"I never did ask you to marry me," he said. "Your father said no, and then you sent me away, and the question remained unasked."

"Yes," she said. "I am so sorry, Charles. I know now that you suffered just as I did."

"Can we put the omission right at last?" he asked her. "Will you marry me, Matilda?"

Her eyes widened and she took a step back, dropping her arms to her sides. "Oh," she said. "But it is impossible."

"Why?" he asked.

"There is your family," she said. "And mine. There is . . . our age."

He turned his head to eye the bench inside the wooden shelter and led her to sit there. He took one of her hands in his and held it on his thigh. "Shall we dispense with the last objection first?" he said. "Is there an age limit upon love and marriage? If we wish to spend the rest of our lives together, does it matter whether we are twenty or fifty-six—or eighty?"

"People would laugh," she said.

"Would they?" He stroked his thumb over her palm. "How strange of them. *Which* people, exactly?"

"They would laugh at *me*," she said.

"I cannot think of anyone who might," he said. "But in the unlikely event that someone did, would you care?"

She frowned in thought, her eyes upon his. "I think I might," she said. "If I became the subject of a sneering on-dit with the *ton* I believe I might mind."

And the thing was that such a thing was possible. Lady Matilda Westcott was known to the *ton* as a staid, fussy, aging spinster who hovered constantly over her mother. *Would* she be seen as a figure of fun if she suddenly announced her betrothal and went about looking as she looked now? Like a woman in love? All April and May?

"Then I suppose you will have to decide which course of action you would prefer," he said. "Would you rather keep your familiar image and thus be largely invisible to the *ton*? Or would you prefer to announce your engagement to me and become the sensation of the hour and very much *not* invisible?"

"Oh," she said, still frowning. "Oh dear."

"Thirty-six years ago," he said, "you were given no choice at all. You were told what to do and you did it. You have lived with the consequences ever since. Now, after all these years, you do have a choice. You can continue as you are. Or you can marry me. *You* have the choice, Matilda."

"But it is still impossible," she said. "For we are not the only ones concerned. There is your family. And mine."

"My children like you," he told her. "I know Adrian does. He has told me so. And I sense that Barbara and Jane do too. They do not often like the women I escort. For they always look upon them as potential wives, and they all come up wanting in one way or another."

"Surely I would quite as much as anyone else," she said. "They cannot help but compare other women to their mother. They surely cannot *want* you to marry again."

"I believe you are wrong in that," he said. "Much as I do not deserve such good fortune, I have children who love me and wish to see me happy. They loved their mother, but they accept the fact that she is gone while I am still here. And what of the Westcotts, Matilda? They seem a decent lot on the whole. Why would you expect them to object to your finding happiness at last?"

"Oh," she said, "it is not that they do not wish for my happiness. But to them I am just Matilda. Or Aunt Matilda. I am the sister who stayed home to look after my mother while the other two married. They would all . . ."

"Laugh?" he suggested when she did not immediately complete the thought.

"No." She was frowning again. "Not that. They would not be so unkind. But they would be . . . incredulous."

"And perhaps a little bit happy for you?" he suggested.

"I am not sure," she said. "They certainly might doubt my judgment. When they first learned that you were Gil's father they immediately recalled your unsavory reputation."

"It was a well-deserved notoriety," he said, "and has been hard to shake, even impossible in some circles. I can understand the concern they will feel for you. However, if you decide to marry me, they will learn that I have changed. Perhaps some of them already know it. They all treated me with warm courtesy when I attended Riverdale's dinner."

"But you were not my betrothed then," she said.

"And I am now?" He smiled at her. "Then I will have some work ahead of me. I will have to persuade them that I love you, that you are all the world to me and always will be. And you, if you decide to marry me, will have to show them that you are not *just* sister Matilda or Aunt Matilda but *Matilda* without any qualifiers, a person in your own right, free to make your own choices. A person deserving of happiness. *If,* that is, you love me more than you fear change or the incredulity of your family and society."

"Oh, Charles." She sighed.

He released his hold on her hand, set his arm about her shoulders, and drew her head down onto his shoulder.

"Two simple questions," he said. "First, do you love me?"

"You know I do," she said. "I always have."

"Second," he said, "do you *want* to marry me?"

There was a long silence before she answered. "Yes," she said at last.

"One somewhat more complex question, then," he said. "*Will* you marry me, Matilda?"

"Oh," she said.

He waited.

"Yes," she said then, her voice barely audible. "Oh yes, Charles, I will."

He released the breath he had not realized he was holding. "Then let us rest upon that for tonight," he said. "We love each other. We are to marry and spend the rest of our lives together. Sometimes life really is that simple."

"But—" she began.

He set one finger across her lips. "No buts. Not tonight."

"And tomorrow we awaken from the dream?" she asked against his finger.

"There is a funny thing about tomorrow," he said. "It never comes. Have you noticed? For when the day that ought to be tomorrow arrives, it is actually today. And today we are in love and planning to marry."

She gazed at him and then laughed—with that delightful merry sound that could always make his heart turn over. "How absolutely absurd," she said. "You have set my head in a spin."

He grinned at her and kissed her again before sitting quietly with her, gazing out into the pink-hued darkness and listening to birdsong and the distant sounds of music and voices and laughter.

"We are going to be *married*?" she asked him after a while. *"At last?"*

"At long last," he said softly, his cheek against the top of her head. "And it will be good, Matilda. I promise."

"Yes." She smiled, and in the glow of the lamp he watched one tear trickle down her cheek and disappear beneath her chin.

He did not show that he had noticed. He closed his eyes instead and rested a little longer upon his happiness.

Eight

Charles had been very wrong about tomorrow. It *did* come. It also became today in the process, as Charles had said it would, but it was very different from yesterday's today.

Oh goodness, she was beginning to think like him, in a head-spinning way. Suffice it to say that today—*now*, this morning—was very different from yesterday, last evening. Then she had been caught up in the magic of Vauxhall Gardens and all things had seemed possible. It had been the most wonderful evening of her life. It had culminated in fireworks and in a journey home in a darkened vehicle, their hands clasped upon his thigh. It had ended with a warm kiss as the carriage drew to a halt outside her door. And the unspoken promise of happily-ever-after.

This morning she was Matilda Westcott again, a little pale and droopy eyed because she was not accustomed to late nights or to dancing and kissing handsome gentlemen and agreeing to marry them. She was not used to laughing and even giggling a time or two. Oh dear, had she really behaved in such an unseemly manner, as though she were a *girl*? Whatever must everyone have thought? Today the idea of marrying Charles seemed utterly absurd. He could *not* have been serious, or, if he had been, today he would be feeling a certain horror at what he had said on the impulse of the moment.

This morning she was feeling elderly and frumpish and mortally depressed and irritable and not at all herself. She wanted to be herself again. Instead she felt like weeping.

"Your evening out," her mother said, setting down the letter she had been reading and regarding her daughter across the breakfast table, "must not have been a great success."

"I would have been happier if I had stayed at home," Matilda said. "I worried about you being alone." With a rush of guilt she realized she had spared her mother scarcely a thought all evening. And now she had lied and made herself feel worse.

"I was alone with a houseful of servants and a library full of books," her mother said. "Matilda, I do not *need* you."

Well, there. She had been justly punished for her lie.

"I only love you," her mother added.

Her mother *never* talked like this. Matilda frowned and looked down at her plate. She was rather surprised to see half a slice of toast spread with marmalade there. She could not remember eating the other half, or anything else for that matter.

"It was a pleasant enough evening," she said. "Vauxhall is always worth a visit. Mrs. Dewhurst appeared to enjoy her birthday. Everyone was very amiable and kind."

I waltzed. I laughed. He kissed me—and I kissed him back. I accepted his marriage proposal.

"And Viscount Dirkson?" her mother asked.

"He was amiable and kind too," Matilda said, getting to her feet.

"Mama, let me get you a fresh cup of coffee. That one has grown cold while you have been reading your letter."

"I do not need a fresh cup," her mother said with a flash of her old irritability. "Don't fuss, Matilda. I am sorry if the evening was not everything you hoped it might be. I am . . . sorry."

"I had no expectations," Matilda said. "And it really was very pleasant."

But her mother was on her feet and making her way toward the door. It was time for one of her meetings with the housekeeper to discuss the meals for the coming days and other household matters. She had never allowed Matilda to take over those responsibilities from her. Neither had she ever offered to share them.

Matilda went to the morning room to write letters to her nieces, Camille in Bath and Abigail somewhere in Gloucestershire in her country cottage, which she shared with Gil and Katy. Charles's son and granddaughter. There was no getting away from him, was there?

But did she want to? Had she not accepted a marriage offer from him last evening? Had he not held her hand all the way home in the carriage and kissed her before his coachman opened the door and set down the steps? He had not said anything about seeing her again, though. But surely he meant to. It would be most peculiar if he did not, even if he had changed his mind.

As he surely must.

Oh, he had been wrong about tomorrow. Tomorrow definitely came, and it was not the same as yesterday. But what happened to *today* while one made the contrast between *yesterday* and *tomorrow*? Strange thoughts.

He could not *possibly* love her.

There was no way on earth he could really want to marry her.

Just *look* at her.

* * *

THE FIRST VISITORS ARRIVED EARLY IN THE AFTERNOON. IT WAS not unusual for Matilda's sisters to call, as they were attentive to their mother and knew she enjoyed hearing the latest on-dits that had not yet found their way into the morning papers. It was unusual for them to come together, however, as they did today, and for Louise to bring her daughter, Jessica, and Anna, Duchess of Netherby, her stepdaughter-in-law, with her. And no sooner had the four of them arrived and exchanged greetings and weather reports and seated themselves than Viola, Marchioness of Dorchester, Matilda's former sister-in-law, was ushered into the room too.

"It seems we all had the same idea this afternoon," she said, and kissed cheeks, asked after the dowager's health, and commented upon the fact that it would be a lovely day if the wind were not so cutting. "I knew you at least were here, Louise. Your carriage is outside the door."

"Thomas came home from White's Club this morning," Mildred said, "with word that you were seen at Vauxhall last evening, Matilda, in company with Viscount Dirkson. You were strolling along the main avenue with him, apparently without even your maid for company. I thought whoever told Thomas that must have been mistaken, but when I called upon Louise, she informed me that Jessica danced with young Bertrand Lamarr last evening, and he told her when she asked about Estelle that she had gone with Mr. Sawyer and one of his sisters for a birthday party at Vauxhall Gardens. And Mr. Sawyer told Bertrand while they were waiting for Estelle to finish getting ready that his father had invited *you* to accompany him, Matilda."

"I was charmed, Aunt Matilda," Jessica said.

"Yes, I was there," Matilda said. "It was a pleasant evening."

"Only pleasant?" Viola smiled warmly at her. "Estelle was bubbling over this morning about all her experiences there. And she was very happy that you were there too. She told us about how you appeared very different from how she had always thought of you. About how, both at Kew Gardens last week and at Vauxhall last evening, you were full of sparkle and laughter and *fun*—her words, I do assure you. *Did* you enjoy yourself?"

"Well, I did." Matilda felt horribly uncomfortable. She was not accustomed to being the focus of anyone's attention, even her family's. "It was a birthday party, and they are a close family and were greatly enjoying the occasion and one another's company. How could I not show pleasure too? It would have been uncivil to look bored or even just solemn."

"Aunt Matilda." There was sheer mischief in Anna's smile. "Do you have a *beau*? I do hope so."

"Anna," Louise said reproachfully.

"Oh, do say it is true, Aunt Matilda," Jessica said, a spark of mischief in her eyes. "I thought when we were at Kew that Viscount Dirkson was particular in his attentions toward you."

"And we heard, Matilda," Viola said, "that you *waltzed* last evening. More than once. With Viscount Dirkson more than with anyone else."

"I believe you are in love," Jessica said, laughing and clapping her hands.

"Jessica." Her mother's outraged voice put an instant end to her merriment. "Your aunt Matilda is *not* a figure of fun. She is a lady of mature years and must be treated with the respect that is her due. The very idea of her being in love, as though she were a giddy girl. And with Viscount Dirkson of all people."

"I must agree with Louise," Mildred said. "I cannot stand by and listen to my sister being teased upon such a matter. She is far too mature to be in love or to *have a beau*. And she is far too sensible to lose her head over a man like Viscount Dirkson. He may have reformed his ways in recent years, but he once had a very unsavory reputation indeed and even now ought not to be welcomed into society with wide-open arms. It was probably unwise of Alexander and Wren to invite him to dine with us. Just consider what followed. He had the effrontery to suggest that Matilda share the duties of chaperon with him for the young people's excursion to Kew. And when I heard this morning that he had taken her to his daughter's birthday celebration, I was very angry. You ought not to be subjected to such disrespect, Matilda, and I am sorry it has happened. I shall ask Thomas to have a word with Viscount Dirkson. It would not hurt, Louise and Anna, if you persuaded Avery to do likewise."

Matilda sat quietly in her chair, fighting the urge to jump to her feet to fuss over her mother for some imaginary need.

"Thank you," she said. "Thank you for coming and showing your concern. You speak *of* me as a mature woman, Louise. And you too, Mildred. Yet you speak *to* me as though I were a child, someone lacking in the knowledge and experience needed to command her own life and make her own decisions. You speak of me as though I were someone who needs a *man*, a family member, to protect me from all the wicked harm that awaits me beyond my doors."

"Well, you must admit, Matilda," Louise said, "that your experience of life is severely limited. You have lived all your days with Mama, and Papa while he was alive, sheltered within the safety of home. We *care*. We do not want to see you the subject of gossip."

"We could not bear to see you humiliated," Mildred added. "Or hurt. We love you, Matilda. You are our *sister*."

Matilda drew breath to answer, but her mother spoke first.

"And Matilda is my daughter," she said. "My firstborn. The eldest of you all. Quite old enough to decide for herself what she wants to do with her life, even if it is only to go to Kew Gardens with a party of young people and the father of one of them, a man whose reputation once set him beyond the pale of polite society. Or even if it is to go to Vauxhall under the escort of the same man and in company with his son and daughters and their spouses. She is old enough to decide for herself whether she will sparkle and laugh and have fun, as Estelle put it. Such careless language, Viola! And Matilda is old enough to decide whether she will waltz under the stars. *She is old enough*. Perhaps it is disrespectful, Louise and Mildred, to question the judgment of your elder sister."

There were a few moments of incredulous silence while everyone—Matilda included—gawked at the dowager countess. *Gawked* was the only appropriate word.

"I really meant no offense, Matilda," Louise said at last. "You must know that. I am merely concerned for you. Of course you may . . . But do you have an *attachment* to Viscount Dirkson?"

"Is it true," Jessica asked, "that you were once in love with him, Aunt Matilda?"

"And that you are again?" Anna asked. "But we are embarrassing you. Do forgive us. We really *do* care, you know. If we did not, we would not tease you. We care about your happiness. And about you. Do let us shift the subject a little. Were there fireworks last evening? Were they as amazing as they usually are?"

But before Matilda could answer, the butler appeared in the doorway—no one had heard his discreet knock—and they all turned to hear what he had to say.

"Viscount Dirkson, my lady," he announced, and Charles came striding into the room.

* * *

CHARLES HAD SEEN THE TWO CARRIAGES OUTSIDE THE DOOR. HE had even recognized one of them as belonging to the Duke of Netherby. For a moment he considered driving his curricle right on by and returning later, but there was always a chance that he had already been spotted from the drawing room window. Besides, he had no reason to hide from the Westcott family. Indeed, he had every reason not to.

He was a bit disconcerted a few minutes later, however, when he stepped into the drawing room on the heels of the butler and found the room seemingly full of ladies. All of them were members of the family. Matilda, he was happy to see, was not hovering behind her mother's chair today but was seated very straight backed on the edge of another chair, two spots of color in her cheeks.

"Ma'am." He bowed to the dowager countess and looked around at the others. "Ladies. Matilda." He smiled at her.

She looked back at him with what he could describe only as acute embarrassment as everyone else rushed into greetings, which varied from subdued to effusive. He guessed they had been talking about him before his arrival. He wondered if Matilda had *told* them, as he had told his children—Adrian last night, Barbara and Jane this morning.

"Estelle was bubbling over at breakfast about last night's visit to Vauxhall," the Marchioness of Dorchester said. "What an inspired idea it was, Lord Dirkson, to choose that venue at which to celebrate your daughter's birthday."

"It was entirely her idea, ma'am," he told her. "But it was indeed a lovely evening. Was it not, Matilda?"

"It was," she said, and surely it was not his imagination that all attention was suddenly riveted upon her. Her hands were clasped tightly in her lap. Her lips were in a prim line. "It was lovely."

Ah, she had not told them.

"I came to assure myself that you had taken no chill or other harm," he said.

"It was kind of you," Louise, Dowager Duchess of Netherby, told him, "to invite Matilda."

"Kindness had nothing to do with it, ma'am," he said. "Or if it did, it was on Lady Matilda's part. She was kind enough to accept my daughter's invitation to be one of the party."

"Oh," Lady Molenor, Matilda's youngest sister, said. "The invitation came from your daughter, did it?"

"It did," he said. "At my suggestion."

"Estelle's invitation came from Mrs. Dewhurst too," the marchioness said. "At the suggestion of Mr. Adrian Sawyer, I believe. She had a splendid time."

"Do have a seat, Lord Dirkson," the dowager said, indicating an empty chair.

"I do not intend to stay, ma'am," he said. "I came to pay my respects and to ask Lady Matilda if she will drive with me in my curricle in the park later."

"Oh," the Dowager Duchess of Netherby said, "my sister has never ridden in a curricle. She would be terrified."

"I have, Louise," Matilda said. "I rode up with Bertrand one afternoon several weeks ago, and far from being terrified, I found it to be one of the most exhilarating experiences of my life."

"Matilda?" Lady Molenor said. "Impossible."

"With Bertrand?" the marchioness said. "Well, the rogue. He said nothing to us."

"Bravo, Aunt Matilda." The young Duchess of Netherby laughed. "How splendid of you."

"Indeed," Lady Jessica Archer agreed. "How did he persuade you to do something so daring, Aunt Matilda?"

"Exactly when was this?" the dowager countess asked eagerly.

Matilda was stretching her fingers in her lap and then curling them into her palms again. "Thank you," she said, looking at Charles and ignoring the questions her family had for her. "That would be delightful."

"Matilda—"

"Oh good, Aunt Matilda."

"Are you sure, Matilda—"

She continued to ignore them all. She licked her lips, her eyes still upon Charles, though it was clear she was addressing everyone when she spoke. "Last evening Viscount Dirkson asked me to marry him and I said yes."

Well, that silenced them—for a few moments anyway.

Charles smiled slowly at Matilda, and she frowned back at him.

Part of his attention was caught by the sound of the dowager countess, her mother, drawing breath. He waited for the tirade that was sure to come.

"Well, thank God for that," was what she actually said.

MATILDA THOUGHT HER FINGERNAILS MIGHT WELL BE DRAWING blood from her palms, but she could not seem to relax her hands. She thought her heart might beat a path through her chest cavity and ribs. She held her mouth in a firm line so that she would not . . . what? Laugh? Why would she feel an irresistible urge to laugh when she was so tense that her jaw felt locked in place?

She gazed upon Charles and could hardly believe he was the same man as the one with whom she had danced and laughed last evening. And kissed. The one with whom she had stood beyond the rotunda to watch the fireworks while exclaiming all the while in childish superlatives at the splendor of it all. The one who had stood behind her at last and encircled her waist with his arms so that she could rest the back of her head against his shoulder and not grow dizzy as she gazed upward—despite the fact that they might have been observed by half the *ton*, or even three-quarters.

Today he was an immaculately clad gentleman, handsome, solid of build, somehow remote from her. Except that . . . He had named her alone when he had entered the room and greeted everyone. He had *smiled* at her. He had come to make sure she had taken no harm last evening, though from what she might have taken harm she did not know. He had neatly turned the idea that *he* had been kind to invite *her* to Vauxhall into one in which *she* had been kind to *him* by accepting Barbara's invitation. And he had come—he had said it in front of her mother and sisters and sister-in-law and nieces—to invite her to drive in his curricle with him in Hyde Park. It must be thirty years or more since any gentleman had invited her to do that.

She was fairly bursting with her love for him. All last night's and this morning's anxieties had fallen away. *He had come.* And he had smiled and called her by name. He wanted her to go out with him. He still loved her.

Tomorrow had not come after all. It was still today. Eternally today in which to be with Charles, to enjoy his love, to return it in full measure, to . . .

"*Thank God*, Mama?" Mildred said.

"I thought my punishment was to be eternal," her mother said.

"It is the millstone I have carried about my neck for well nigh forty years. I thought I would carry it to my grave."

"Whatever are you talking about, Mama?" Louise asked. "Are you well? Matilda, is Mama ailing?"

"Stop fussing," their mother said. "Start talking about a wedding instead. It must be a grand one. I will not stand for anything less. Matilda must have her grand wedding at last. And if you have anything to say to the contrary, Lord Dirkson, I would suggest that you keep your tongue between your teeth and allow the women to do what women do best."

He actually grinned as he clasped his hands behind his back. "Plan weddings?" he said.

"Precisely." She nodded briskly.

"Mama—" Matilda began.

"Ma'am." Charles spoke again. "I am quite prepared to allow the world to turn upon its axis as it always has done. However, I feel compelled to speak out on two points before I lose my voice altogether, and I fear that time is imminent. First, Matilda and I did not get as far as discussing our wedding last evening. I have no idea what sort of ceremony she wants or where or when she wants it to happen. She must make that choice—with me. I will not allow her to be bullied into giving in to what her family and mine may think appropriate. And second, when the women sweep in to organize us, as they no doubt will unless Matilda chooses to elope with me, it must be remembered that there are women in both the Westcott and Sawyer families. My daughters, despite my dire warnings this morning, very probably have my wedding half-planned already."

"I am still in shock," Anna said, getting to her feet. "But a very pleasant shock. Aunt Matilda! I cannot tell you how pleased I am for you. And you too, Lord Dirkson. Avery and I slipped off quietly to marry one afternoon, you know, while Grandmama and the aunts and cousins were busy planning a grand wedding for us. I was never happier in my life." She leaned over Matilda's chair and hugged her warmly. "And Abigail married Gil in the village church at home just a few weeks ago with no one present except Harry and the vicar's wife. I believe she will always treasure the memory. Perhaps you—"

"Thank you, Anna," Matilda said. "But I want a *wedding*."

She had not thought of it until now, when she had been almost afraid to believe in the truth of what had happened last evening. But it was true. All her life she had dreamed of a grand wedding, but for most of that time that was all it had been—an ever-fading dream. And, for the last twenty years or so, entirely faded.

"Then a wedding is what you will have, my love," Charles said.

My love? Oh. In front of half her family.

"St. George's it will be, then." Louise clapped her hands as though to draw the attention of thousands. "We must have the banns called next Sunday. It is already rather late in the Season and we do not want to wait until it is over and most of the *ton* has returned to the country. If Matilda is to be married at St. George's, the pews must be full to overflowing. Oh goodness, we must let Wren know and Elizabeth and Althea. They will want to be involved in the planning."

"We must arrange a meeting with Mrs. Dewhurst and Lady Frater," Viola said. "They will have ideas of their own. They already do, according to Viscount Dirkson."

"Alexander will want to host the wedding breakfast," Anna said. "But I know Avery will insist that the ballroom at Archer House has more room."

A *ton* wedding at St. George's on Hanover Square? A wedding breakfast in the ballroom at the town house of the Duke of

Netherby? Matilda started to feel anxious again. Surely, oh surely, she would be the laughingstock. She had not meant anything quite so grand. Just a definite wedding with . . .

"Matilda," Charles said. "My curricle is outside your door. Why wait until later to go for our drive? I have the distinct impression that our presence here is de trop. Will you come now?"

"Yes." She got to her feet. "Oh yes. Thank you."

How many times had she participated in family conferences and family planning committees? She had usually been at the forefront of them all, busy planning how to extricate some family member from disaster or how to help them celebrate an event in their lives. Was she now to be the object of such family activity?

Oh. It did feel good.

"Matilda," Charles said when she joined him downstairs after going to fetch her bonnet and gloves and reticule, "I will not allow you to be bullied, you know. Even by me. Especially by me. You are looking worried, even a little stricken. There is no need. You must tell me as we drive what you want. And you shall have it. You are the bride. You are to make the decisions."

You are the bride.

She felt that growingly familiar urge to weep. She smiled instead as he handed her up to the passenger seat of the curricle and she remembered that heady feeling of being much farther off the ground than she had expected. The feeling of danger and exhilaration. She laughed aloud.

"But everyone would be so disappointed," she said, "if we were to run off with a special license to marry in secret. Besides which, *I* would be disappointed. And they would be upset if they planned and planned and I disapproved of everything. My family would be upset. So would Barbara and Jane. I think a marriage is for two people, Charles. But a wedding is for their families and friends. Shall we just let them plan?"

"It would save us a lot of anguish," he said, grinning at her as he took his place beside her. "When I walked into that room awhile ago and saw you, I feared you had changed your mind. You looked brittle and severe."

"But only because I was convinced *you* must have changed *your* mind," she said.

"Absurd," he told her.

"Absurd," she agreed, and they both laughed as though someone had just made an extremely witty remark.

"Charles," she said, laying a hand on his arm as he leaned down, took the ribbons from his young groom, and gathered them in his hands, "I wish we were in the country. I wish I could ask you to spring the horses."

He turned his head to look into her face, his own still filled with laughter. "*Do* you, my love?" he asked her.

"I know you are a notable whip," she told him. "It was always a part of your reputation."

"One day soon," he said, "when we are in the country, I will spring the horses and risk both our lives as they dash along at a neck-or-nothing pace."

"Oh, *will* you?" she said. "Thank you, Charles. I am not a staid old lady quite yet, you know."

"I have noticed," he said, and he risked horrible scandal by leaning toward her and kissing her briefly on the lips while windows in numerous houses all around them looked accusingly on and his young groom pretended to be looking intently elsewhere.

As the curricle moved off in the direction of Hyde Park, Matilda, in marvelous ladylike fashion, threw back her head and laughed.

Nine

Several times over the following month, Charles sat alone in his library, wishing that he had not suddenly found himself at the center of a whirlpool or a tornado—both seemed appropriate metaphors. For of course the notice of his betrothal appeared in every London paper and perhaps a few provincial ones too. And wherever he went, he faced congratulations or—at his clubs—endless witticisms over which he was forced to laugh. His son and one of his sons-in-law dragged him off to his tailor and his boot maker and his hatmaker and Lord knew where else so that on his wedding day he would be able to astonish the *ton* with new and fashionable everything.

His daughters and every female on earth who had a connection with the Westcott family, no matter how slim, held meeting after meeting to discuss every aspect of the wedding that women invariably found to discuss and wrangle over. Though to be fair, he heard no reports of arguments or raised voices or heated discussions or rivalries between the two families. Early predictions proved quite accurate. The wedding breakfast was to be served at Westcott House, the home of Alexander, Earl of Riverdale, on South Audley Street. Invitations were sent. If any member of the *ton* then staying in or within a twenty-mile radius of London had been omitted, Charles would be enormously surprised. Relatives from farther afield had been summoned, including a few cousins he scarcely knew but whose presence on his wedding day was deemed by his daughters to be essential to his happiness.

Charles would just as happily have done what the Netherbys had once done and sneaked off to marry Matilda in an obscure church somewhere, special license in hand, while their families were in a flurry of plotting and planning for a grand wedding to outdo all others this year. But despite ever-changing misgivings and second and third and sixth thoughts through which Matilda suffered during the course of the month, he understood that a big public wedding was what she really wanted. And what Matilda wanted she would have. She had waited long enough for her wedding—thirty-six years.

What she had feared most was being laughed at. Charles felt no doubt that there were certain elements of society that ridiculed her behind her back. There always were. The world would never be rid of unkind people who compensated for their own insecurities by dragging down other happier, more successful people to their own level through their gossip. They were to be heartily ignored. She was well received wherever she went. Barbara held a soiree in her honor, and Jane had her as a special guest in Wallace's private box at the theater the very evening after the announcement appeared in the papers. The Duke and Duchess of Netherby hosted a betrothal party at their home, and the Marquess and Marchioness of Dorchester organized an afternoon tea. Charles took her driving in the park several times and escorted her to a private concert and a literary evening.

She received well-wishers with quiet dignity wherever she went. No longer was she the fussy spinster forever in her mother's shadow, though perhaps that had something to do with the fact that her mother flatly refused to have her there any longer. And Matilda need not fear for her care, her mother informed Charles when he broached the subject of her coming to live with them after their marriage.

"You need not fear either, Lord Dirkson," she had added. "I am quite capable of looking after myself. And has Matilda not told you? My sister is coming to live with me when I return to the country after the Season is over. She will be bringing her longtime companion with her, an estimable lady who will offer companionship without trying to worry me into my grave."

Charles had understood immediately that life had been about to change very much for the worse for Matilda, who would no doubt have found herself constantly being compared unfavorably with her aunt's ideal companion.

"I really do not know how I would have borne it," Matilda had admitted to him when he mentioned what her mother had told him. "I would have gone mad. Adelaide Boniface is the gloomiest creature of my acquaintance. And she *sniffs*."

"Now I know," he had said, "why you accepted my marriage proposal."

"Oh, absolutely!" she had assured him, and laughed gleefully.

He loved her laughter. He loved her happiness. Oh, she behaved in public with quiet dignity, though even then he was aware of an inner glow in her that warmed him too. In private she smiled a great deal, and the glow was brighter. Her eyes when she looked at him had a sparkle that made them appear to smile even if the rest of her face was in repose.

He felt awed and humbled by her happiness.

And by the fact that he shared it.

He had never given much thought to being happy. It was not a word much in his vocabulary—though he *had* been happy when each of his children was born and whenever he had spent time with them during their growing years. He had been happy when his daughters married and when his grandchildren were born. He had just not used that particular word to describe his feelings. He had not known the conscious exuberance of happiness since Matilda had disappeared from his life when he was still no more than a puppy.

Now he knew himself happy again. Even if he *did* spend great swaths of time shut up in his library during the month before his nuptials wishing he did not have the ghastly ordeal of a grand *ton* wedding to face before he could bear Matilda off home and live out his life with her there. He was even dreaming of happily-ever-after, though fortunately it was contained inside him. Sometimes he could still think and feel like that young puppy he had been. It was downright embarrassing.

He was going to be very glad when the wedding was over.

In the meanwhile, he was equally glad that Matilda, despite all her frequent misgivings, was at last going to have the wedding she ought to have had more than thirty years ago.

CHARLES WAS QUITE RIGHT IN HIS PERCEPTIONS. THERE HAD been no wrangling, no unpleasantness between his daughters on the one hand and the ladies of the Westcott family on the other as they planned the wedding. All of them, once the Westcotts had recovered from the shock they had felt upon learning that Matilda, that most confirmed of spinsters, was going to marry at last, had thrown themselves with enthusiasm into the planning of the wedding of the Season. And if Louise and Mildred, Matilda's younger sisters, still felt wary of the bridegroom's notorious past, they soon set their fears aside in favor of rejoicing that their precious Matilda, that rock of sisterly support upon which they had leaned since they were girls, was to find happiness of her own at last. The bridegroom's daughters were genuinely pleased for their father, having concluded that Lady Matilda Westcott was vastly different from any of the other ladies he had escorted about London since their mother's passing. And vastly preferable too.

There was no wrangling, then. There was, however, an awkward moment. It came when they were making lists of potential guests and everyone was throwing out suggestions, most of which were accepted without question. Viola, Marchioness of Dorchester, had suggested Harry—Major Harry Westcott, her son—who was not far away at Hinsford Manor in Hampshire, and Camille, her elder daughter, who was in Bath with her husband and family. She was interrupted before she could say more.

"I certainly hope Camille and Joel will come," Wren, Countess of Riverdale, said. "But will they, Viola? With all seven children?"

All but one of those children were under ten years of age. Four of them were adopted, three Camille and Joel's own.

"They came to Hinsford a few months ago to see Harry when he came home from war at last," Viola said. "Whether they will now come all the way to London for Matilda's wedding is another matter, of course."

"They must be invited anyway," Elizabeth, Wren's sister-in-law, said. "It will be up to them whether they come or not."

"That sounds sensible," Mildred said.

"And what about Abby?" Jessica asked. "She and Gil must be invited too."

That was when the suggestion of an awkward moment happened. Jessica and Abigail had always been the closest of friends. Jessica had been as hurt as her cousin when Abigail's illegitimacy had been revealed just as she was about to make her come-out into society.

"They have only recently gone home to Gloucestershire," Louise said quickly. "It is too much to expect them to return so soon. I am sure you will write to them with the news, of course, Viola, if you have not already done so."

"But—" Jessica said.

"Who else?" her mother said more loudly than seemed necessary, directing a pointed look her daughter's way.

There was an awkward pause before Mildred rushed in with a new suggestion. "How about—"

But Barbara Dewhurst interrupted her. "No, really," she said. "We are quite well aware of who Gil Bennington is, are we not, Jane? He is married to the former Abigail Westcott, your daughter, ma'am." She nodded in Viola's direction. "And he is our father's natural son."

"There is really no need—" Louise began.

"No, there really is no need to hush up all mention of his existence, ma'am," Jane, Lady Frater, said, interrupting her. "We know of him. Our father has told us. We also know that he will have nothing to do with Papa. That hurts him, though he has not openly admitted it. Our brother, Adrian, however, is determined to meet him sometime. It has been a shock to discover this late in our lives that we have a half brother. But we do feel as curious about him as Adrian does."

"We do," Barbara agreed. "And now there is this extraordinary circumstance of our father being about to marry Abigail Bennington's aunt."

"He has a young daughter," Jane said, sounding almost wistful. "Our niece. I do long to see her."

"Are you suggesting, then," Anna, Duchess of Netherby, asked, "that they be invited to the wedding?"

"Well," Barbara said, frowning, "our father would doubtless be horrified. And it seems almost certain Gil himself would refuse to come. But—"

"Perhaps Abigail will come alone," Wren suggested. "Though it would be a shame."

"*Shall* we invite them?" Anna asked.

"I really do not see why not," Jessica said. "Abby is as much a part of our family as any of us."

"And we *are* inviting Camille," Elizabeth said, "even though it seems equally doubtful that she will come. Perhaps we ought to send an invitation and let Abigail and Gil decide for themselves."

"What do you think?" Viola asked Charles's daughters. "Please be honest. And will you inform your father if we do invite them?"

Barbara smiled. "He has told us," she said, "that we may do anything we wish for this wedding provided we do nothing of which Lady Matilda would disapprove, and provided we do not expect him to have his ears assailed with details."

"Ah," Mildred said, smiling back. "Then we need to consult Matilda, do we? And let *her* decide."

"We know what her answer will be," Elizabeth said.

"Do we?" Mildred asked.

"Of course," Elizabeth said, laughing. "Matilda is a romantic. She always has been. She will certainly want them to be invited to her wedding."

"Oh, I hope so," Jessica said. "I *do* hope they come."

MATILDA HAD ASSERTED HERSELF, SOMETHING SHE HAD RARELY done all her life, at least on her own account. Oh, she had allowed the women of her family and Charles's to organize her wedding according to their wishes, it was true. She had made the decision to have a grand society wedding, despite the fact that privately she changed her mind at least once every waking hour. Having done so, she was content to leave the details to the grand committee—of which she would have been a leading member if it had been anyone else's wedding.

But she had asserted herself in other ways. She had selected an outfit for the occasion, a simple, elegant walking dress of pale blue when her sisters had wanted her to wear a finer, more elaborate gown, one more suited to the occasion. And they had wanted her to choose a more vivid color, since pastel shades were associated with youth and she surely would not wish to be accused of trying to minimize her age.

She was now—on her wedding day—wearing the pale blue walking dress. She was also wearing a straw hat—*not* a bonnet—which was held on her head with pins and was tipped slightly forward over her eyes. It was trimmed with silk cornflowers, which were a slightly darker shade than her dress. Louise had described it as frivolous, and Mildred had suggested that she change the trim to a simple ribbon instead of the flowers. Matilda was wearing it this morning—complete with flowers.

She was also wearing silver gloves and silver slippers and silver earrings, something she rarely wore because after an hour or two she invariably found that the earrings pinching her earlobes caused excruciating pain if she did not pull them off. But that always left the lobes red and painful-looking, often with the imprints of the earrings upon them. This morning she had donned the earrings the last of all her accessories in the hope that she could get through her wedding and maybe even the breakfast afterward without screaming in agony. They were in the form of bells and tinkled slightly when she moved her head. Another frivolity.

And she had asserted herself over Abigail and Gil. *Of course* they must be invited, she had assured the delegation that had come to put the question to her—Viola and Anna and Louise and Mildred. It was very probable, she agreed, that Gil would refuse to come and that Abigail would not come without him. And it was altogether possible that if they *did* come, Charles would be horribly embarrassed and perhaps Adrian and Barbara and Jane too despite what the latter two had said to the contrary. But *of course* they must be invited. Rational adults ought to be allowed to make up their own minds about what they wished to do with their lives. It ought not to be up to their families to try to live their lives for them.

"Matilda," Mildred asked, looking thoughtful, "is that what happened to you? Was it Mama and Papa who tore you away from Viscount Dirkson when the two of you were young?"

"What happened more than thirty years ago no longer matters," Matilda told her firmly. "It is *now* that matters. We are together *now*, Charles and I, and we are to be married, and I want a wedding day that is perfect. Will it be more perfect if Gil and Abigail are the only family members *not* present or if they *are*? It is impossible to know the answer. But the decision ought not to be ours to make. It must be Gil's and Abigail's."

"Not Viscount Dirkson's?" Viola asked.

"He will say no," Matilda told her, "while his heart will yearn to say yes."

"We must do all in our power, then," Anna said, smiling, "to make sure he gets his heart's desire. And you too, Aunt Matilda."

"Well, I *do* want them to come," Matilda admitted, "though I would ask that the invitation not be sent until tomorrow. I ought, I suppose, to call upon Barbara and Jane first."

But those two young ladies, as well as Adrian, who happened to be with his sisters when Matilda called first upon Barbara, were genuinely curious to meet the half brother of whose existence they had not even known until recently.

"And if they come and Papa does not want them here," Adrian said, "I would really be very surprised. I believe he longs to be reconciled."

"But that would not make you unhappy?" Matilda asked.

"No." He frowned in thought for a moment. "Papa said something the day he told me about Gil Bennington. He told me how he had fallen in love with me the moment he saw me after I was born. And I daresay he fell in love in just the same way with my sisters. All my childhood memories confirm me in the belief that he was telling the truth. He spent more time with us than most fathers of my acquaintance spend with their children, and he always gave the impression that he was as happy with our company as we were with his. I do not believe love has limits. Do you, Lady Matilda? I mean, the fact that there was always Gil and that our father obviously cared for him does not mean he cared the less for us. If Gil comes back into Papa's life now, it will not mean that we are diminished. Will it?"

"Not by one iota," Matilda assured him, remembering how, when Anna arrived unexpectedly in their family at the age of twenty-five, it had seemed at first that Humphrey's newly illegitimate offspring—Camille and Harry and Abigail—would be displaced. It had not been so. Just the opposite had happened, in fact. The whole family had bonded more firmly than ever before under the threat of attack. They had routed the threat with love.

Matilda did what never came quite naturally to her. She got to her feet and hugged first Adrian and then his sisters. And because Mr. Dewhurst, Barbara's husband, was also in the room, she hugged him too.

"*Diminished,*" she said. "What a foolish notion. Your family love is about to *expand*, not contract. Your father is about to marry me, is he not?"

At which they all laughed, Matilda included.

And she asserted herself over which man of the family would give her away at her wedding. Thomas, Mildred's husband, had offered. So had Alexander, as head of the family. Harry—Major Harry Westcott, the eldest of her nephews—had written from Hinsford to offer his services. Avery, Duke of Netherby, had informed her one afternoon that she doubtless had dozens of family members fighting duels over the honor of leading her along the nave of St. George's, but if not—or if she did not much fancy any of the contestants—he would be happy to make himself available. Colin, Lord Hodges, Elizabeth's husband, had offered, as had Marcel, Marquess of Dorchester, Viola's husband. Even young Bertrand Lamarr had offered, grinning at her cheekily as he did so.

"After all, Aunt Matilda," he had said, "I believe I started the renewal of your romance when I agreed to escort you to Viscount Dirkson's house when you wished him to attend the custody hearing for Gil's daughter."

And since he had spoken publicly, the whole secret story came out and the family discovered that not long ago Matilda had taken the truly scandalous step of calling upon a gentleman in his own home with no one to chaperon her except a very young man who was not even related to her by blood.

Trust the young to keep a secret!

Matilda made her choice and announced it during the family dinner that preceded the betrothal party Avery and Anna gave for her at Archer House.

"Thank you to all of you," she said, looking at each man in turn—though Harry had not yet come up from the country. "I am touched that each of you is willing to stand in place of my father. However, I am fifty-six years old. The notion that someone—someone male—needs to give me away is a strange one. Give me away from *what*? I have been of age for thirty-five years. Although I have always lived with Mama, I have independent means. I can and will give myself away to the man of my choice. So I shall walk alone along the nave of the church."

"Matilda," her mother said, reproach in her voice. "It just is not *done*."

"It will be done by me," Matilda said. "And that is my final word."

"Oh, bravo, Aunt Matilda," Jessica said.

"Jessica!" her mother said.

"I say," Boris said. "You are a jolly fine fellow, Aunt Matilda."

"A *fellow*, Boris?" Mildred asked. "A *jolly fine* one? Wherever do you get such language?"

But her son merely grinned at her and waggled his eyebrows.

"It cannot be allowed, Matilda," Louise said firmly. "You will be the—"

"I believe," Avery said in his usual languid voice, his jeweled quizzing glass in his hand, though he was not actually looking through it, "there is a little-known statute on the books to the effect that after the age of—ah—fifty-five, a woman must be considered entirely her own person and may do whatever she wishes without running the risk of being exiled for life for doing what no one has done before her."

"Oh, Avery," Estelle said, giggling. "You made that up on the spot."

"Well, of course he did, idiot," said her fond twin.

"Then that settles the matter," Matilda said. "Thank you, Avery. Though I would have done it anyway, you know, even if there had been no such statute."

"Quite so," he said.

And so here she was now, dressed in pale blue and silver, wearing a frivolous hat at a jaunty angle on her head, knowing—though Charles did not—that Gil and Abigail and Katy had arrived late yesterday afternoon at Viola and Marcel's London home, and knowing too that no man awaited her downstairs to offer her a steady male arm to help her totter her way along the nave of St. George's to meet her bridegroom.

Her bridegroom! Her heart leaped within her bosom and performed a couple of headstands and a number of tumble tosses before leaving her simply breathless. Surely he would have changed his mind at the last moment and would not be there awaiting her when she arrived.

What utter nonsense and drivel!

Her bridegroom! Charles. Ah. At last. At long, long last.

And if she stood here, one glove on and one off, still in the hand of her maid, and entertained more of such idiotic thoughts, it was *she* who would not be turning up on time. Not that brides were expected to be on time. But she was not just any bride. She was Matilda Westcott. And Matilda had gone through life being punctual, on the theory that it was bad mannered to be late and waste other people's time when they might be using it to better effect elsewhere.

She was not going to start being late with her own wedding. She was not going to be early either. That would be embarrassing. She would be on time. To the minute.

And it was time to leave.

"Thank you," she said, taking her glove from her maid and pulling it on as she drew a few deep breaths.

Her wedding day!

Perhaps she would perform a few twirls on her way along the nave. Now *that* would make for a memorable wedding.

How dreadfully the mind babbled when one was nervous.

And she was very, very nervous.

Oh, Charles!

She straightened her shoulders, stepped out of her dressing room, and made her way downstairs and outdoors to the awaiting carriage.

Ten

Charles was resigned to his fate as he awaited the arrival of his bride at St. George's. Behind him the pews had filled with family and the very crème de la crème of aristocratic society. At least, he assumed they had filled. He did not turn his head to look. But he could hear the rustling of silks and satins, the muted conversations, the cleared throats.

Given the choice, he would still opt for a quiet wedding. He was also still glad Matilda was to have her grand wedding at last. He sat in the front pew, wondering how her life would have proceeded if her father had not refused his suit quite so adamantly or if she had not refused to discuss the matter with him afterward. Or if he had had the gumption to fight for what he wanted instead of turning peevishly away to nurse his bruised heart by becoming one of England's most notorious rakes and hellions. Would they have married? Would his children be hers too—but different children, of course? But children of her own—and his. Would she have been happy? Would he? Her life would certainly have been different. Would his?

They were pointless thoughts, of course. Ifs were always point-less when applied to the past. If the past had been different, then so would the present be. He would not now be sitting here on full display before the *ton*, awaiting the arrival of his bride. She would not be living through her wedding day now, today.

He was glad it was now. He felt suddenly happy even as a twinge of anxiety nudged at him lest she be going through one of her many doubting moments and would simply not come.

Impossible! Of course she would come.

"Nervous?" Adrian murmured from beside him. His son was his best man.

"Of course," Charles murmured back. "Today is the start of a wholly new life."

But before anxiety could take hold of him, he heard a stirring from the back of the church and guessed that it heralded the arrival of Matilda, who was apparently coming alone. Her mother had ar-rived earlier with Mrs. Monteith, her sister, and Miss Boniface, her paragon of a companion who also, according to Matilda, sniffed. They had come earlier than originally planned in order to take up residence with the dowager countess and console her for the loss of her eldest daughter to marriage.

The clergyman, fully robed, appeared from somewhere and Charles rose with the rest of the congregation and the great pipe organ began to play. Charles turned to look along the nave. And sure enough, she came alone, a straight-backed woman of middle years, proceeding with slow—but not too slow—dignity along the aisle, her eyes fixed forward until they found and held upon him. She was dressed decently, elegantly, almost severely in pale blue—as he might have expected had he given the matter thought—with an absurdly pretty straw hat tipped forward over her forehead and with her silver-gloved hands clasped before her. Her face was pale, her mouth in a prim line until she was a few steps away from him. Then, unseen by all except the closest of the congregation, she smiled at him with all the sunshine of a summer's day behind her eyes.

He saw in that smile the vivid girl she had been. And he saw in the quiet poise of her demeanor the woman she had become.

He saw Matilda. His love. Always and ever his love.

She set her hand in his, giving herself to him because, as she had explained, she did not need any man to do it for her, no matter how closely related to her that man was or how well meaning. She let her fingers curl about his own in a firm grip.

"Here I am," she murmured for his ears only.

"And at last," he said just as quietly, "so am I."

They turned together to face the clergyman.

"Dearly beloved," he began.

And just like that, within a very few minutes, they were married.

Charles was after all glad they had done it this way, with all the pomp of a high church service, with all their family and friends and acquaintances in attendance. He was glad for himself, for he wanted the world to know that he married this woman from choice and from love. He was glad for Matilda, for she glowed from the moment she first smiled at him until the moment when the clergyman pronounced them man and wife. And even then she glowed as he led her to the vestry for the signing of the register. When Alexander, Earl of Riverdale, witnessed her signature and then hugged her, and Adrian witnessed his signature and hugged her too, she glowed at them. She glowed as they left the vestry and proceeded, her arm drawn through Charles's, back along the nave, smiling from one side to the other as they passed the pews. It was impossible to see everyone who was there. But they would do that at the wedding breakfast in a short while.

She smiled still as they passed through the church doors and emerged into sunshine at the top of the long flight of steps down to their awaiting carriage—an open barouche decorated almost beyond recognition with flowers. She smiled at the crowd of onlookers that had gathered down there to applaud and even cheer. And she laughed when she saw her young nephews and his sons-in-law waiting farther down the steps to pelt them with flower petals before they could reach the dubious safety of the open carriage. And then, halfway down, when the petals were already raining about them in a brightly colored shower, she looked back up to where the congregation was beginning to spill outdoors after them and she lost her smile.

"Ah," she said, and Charles had the curious impression that she saw something she had been looking for. He looked backward even as he laughed at another shower of petals that was fluttering from the brim of his hat.

Quite a few people had come outside, his daughters and grandchildren, Matilda's mother and aunt and sisters among them. And one group a little separate from the others, three steps down from the top. A man and a woman, and a child between them, holding a hand of each.

When he thought about it afterward, Charles did not suppose that silence had really descended upon the congregation above, the gathering of the curious below, and the young people on the steps with their handfuls of petals. But it seemed to him at the time that they were suddenly cocooned in silence, Matilda and he, her arm through his, her face turned to look into his—with anxiety?

God. Oh good God.

Neither group moved for what was perhaps a second or two but seemed far longer at the time. Then the woman took a step down, impelling the child and the man to descend too. And Matilda took one step back up, forcing him to do likewise. Who descended or ascended the other steps between them Charles did not afterward know, or who first extended a hand. But suddenly he felt the warm, firm clasp of his son's hand even as he gripped it in return.

His elder son, that was.

Gil.

"Congratulations, sir," he said stiffly.

"You came," Charles said foolishly.

"We came."

And then Matilda was hugging first his son's wife and then his son and was then bending down to smile at the child—Katy—and say something to her. And Abigail was hugging Charles and lifting Katy to say *how do you do* to her grandpapa, and somehow—oh, somehow his son was hugging him too. Briefly, awkwardly, improbably, surely unintentionally, unforgettably.

"Congratulations, sir," he said again.

"You came," Charles said, just to be original.

After every wedding Charles had ever attended, the bride and groom left the church and ran the gamut of mischievous relatives who went out ahead of them in order to decorate their carriage with noisy hardware and throw flowers. The carriage was always on its way by the time large numbers of the congregation left the church behind them. All the greetings and congratulations, all the hugs and kisses, and slapping of backs, and laughter, came later as the guests arrived at the venue for the wedding breakfast.

This wedding was the exception to that tradition. It was too late to escape. Within moments they were surrounded by wedding guests. Matilda was being hugged and kissed and wept over by her mother and her sisters and sister-in-law and cousins and nieces and aunt. She had children about her—most of them, he believed, the offspring of her niece Camille from Bath—all trying to tell her things in piping yells while brushing at the flower petals with which she was strewn. His own daughters and grandchildren were soon gathered about her too. She was bright eyed and rosy cheeked and laughing and lovely. Her brother-in-law and nephews and cousins meanwhile were pumping him by the hand and slapping him on the back, as were his sons-in-law, having abandoned their petal throwing for the moment—or perhaps they had no more to throw. Adrian and Charles's daughters and grandchildren were hugging him. Other people were calling greetings.

Matilda, some little distance away from Charles, turned to find him and smiled at him in a way that would put sunshine to shame.

She was, he realized, elbowing her way closer to him until she could take his hand in hers, utterly happy.

As was he.

"We had better leave while we still may," he said, laughing.

"Oh, must we?" But she slid her arm through his and allowed him to lead her down through the path that opened for them and hand her into the barouche.

"I have just one wish remaining," she said as he sat beside her and took her hand in his, lacing their fingers. "I hope the young people tied a whole arsenal of pots and pans and old boots beneath the carriage. I want to make an unholy din on the way to Westcott House. I have always envied—"

But what or whom she had always envied was drowned out as the coachman gave the horses the signal to start and the barouche rocked into motion. So was Charles's laughter. And so were the church bells pealing out the good news of a new marriage.

Matilda's one remaining wish had come true.

She turned her face toward him, and he saw that she was laughing—until the laughter faded and her eyes became luminous beneath the brim of her hat.

Matilda.

What part had she played in bringing his elder son to him today of all days? What part had his younger son and his daughters played in it? Surely they had been consulted. What on earth had persuaded Gil to come for the wedding of the father he had not wanted to know? What did it mean exactly that he had come? Would he also come to the wedding breakfast?

It was impossible to ask any of these questions. The noise coming from beneath the carriage was deafening.

And the answers would wait.

He smiled at his bride, and her eyes filled with tears even as she smiled back at him.

"I love you," he said, and her eyes lowered to read his lips.

"I love you," her lips said in return.

And he dipped his head and kissed her. Propriety be damned. If he must suffer this din, which proclaimed to the world that a newly wedded couple was on its way through the streets of London, then at least he was going to let the world know that he was happy about it.

He lifted his head and grinned at her. Her eyes brimmed with tears and laughter.

He kissed her again. Or she kissed him.

They kissed each other.

READ ON FOR AN EXCERPT FROM THE
FIRST NOVEL IN THE WESTCOTT SERIES,

Someone to Love

AVAILABLE NOW FROM JOVE

Despite the fact that the late Earl of Riverdale had died without having made a will, Josiah Brumford, his solicitor, had found enough business to discuss with his son and successor to be granted a face-to-face meeting at Westcott House, the earl's London residence on South Audley Street. Having arrived promptly and bowed his way through effusive and obsequious greetings, Brumford proceeded to find a great deal of nothing in particular to impart at tedious length and with pompous verbosity.

Which would have been all very well, Avery Archer, Duke of Netherby, thought a trifle peevishly as he stood before the library window and took snuff in an effort to ward off the urge to yawn, if he had not been compelled to be here too to endure the tedium. If Harry had only been a year older—he had turned twenty just before his father's death—then Avery need not be here at all and Brumford could prose on forever and a day as far as he was concerned. By some bizarre and thoroughly irritating twist of fate, however, His Grace had found himself joint guardian of the new earl with the countess, the boy's mother.

It was all remarkably ridiculous in light of Avery's notoriety for indolence and the studied avoidance of anything that might be dubbed work or the performance of duty. He had a secretary and numerous other servants to deal with all the tedious business of life for him. And there was also the fact that he was a mere eleven years older than his ward. When one heard the word *guardian,* one conjured a mental image of a gravely dignified graybeard. However, it seemed he had inherited the guardianship to which his father had apparently agreed—in writing—at some time in the dim distant past when the late Riverdale had mistakenly thought himself to be at death's door. By the time he did die a few weeks ago, the old Duke of Netherby had been sleeping peacefully in his own grave for more than two years and was thus unable to be guardian to anyone. Avery might, he supposed, have repudiated the obligation since he was not the Netherby mentioned in that letter of agreement, which had never been made into a legal document anyway. He had not done so, however. He did not dislike Harry, and really it had seemed like too much bother to take a stand and refuse such a slight and temporary inconvenience.

It felt more than slight at the moment. Had he known Brumford was such a crashing bore, he might have made the effort.

"There really was no need for Father to make a will," Harry was saying in the sort of rallying tone one used when repeating oneself in order to wrap up a lengthy discussion that had been moving in unending circles. "I have no brothers. My father trusted that I would provide handsomely for my mother and sisters according to his known wishes, and of course I will not fail that trust. I will certainly see to it too that most of the servants and retainers on all my properties are kept on and that those who leave my employ for whatever reason—Father's valet, for example—are properly compensated. And you may rest assured that my mother and Netherby will see that I do not stray from these obligations before I arrive at my majority."

He was standing by the fireplace beside his mother's chair, in a relaxed posture, one shoulder propped against the mantel, his arms crossed over his chest, one booted foot on the hearth. He was a tall lad and a bit gangly, though a few more years would take care of that deficiency. He was fair-haired and blue-eyed with a good-humored countenance that very young ladies no doubt found impossibly handsome. He was also almost indecently rich. He was amiable and charming and had been running wild during the past several months, first while his father was too ill to take much notice and again during the couple of weeks since the funeral. He had probably never lacked for friends, but now they abounded and would have filled a sizable city, perhaps even a small county, to overflowing. Though perhaps *friends* was too kind a word to use for most of them. *Sycophants* and *hangers-on* would be better.

Avery had not tried intervening, and he doubted he would. The boy seemed of sound enough character and would doubtless settle to a bland and blameless adulthood if left to his own devices. And if in the meanwhile he sowed a wide swath of wild oats and squandered a small fortune, well, there were probably oats to spare in the world and there would still be a vast fortune remaining for the bland adulthood. It would take just too much effort to intervene, anyway, and the Duke of Netherby rarely made the effort to do what was inessential or what was not conducive to his personal comfort.

"I do not doubt it for a moment, my lord." Brumford bowed from his chair in a manner that suggested he might at last be conceding that everything he had come to say had been said and perhaps it was time to take his leave. "I trust Brumford, Brumford & Sons may continue to represent your interests as we did your dear departed father's and his father's before him. I trust His Grace and Her Ladyship will so advise you."

Avery wondered idly what the other Brumford was like and just how many young Brumfords were included in the "& Sons." The mind boggled.

Harry pushed himself away from the mantel, looking hopeful. "I see no reason why I would not," he said. "But I will not keep you any longer. You are a very busy man, I daresay."

"I will, however, beg for a few minutes more of your time, Mr. Brumford," the countess said unexpectedly. "But it is a matter that does not concern you, Harry. You may go and join your sisters in the drawing room. They will be eager to hear details of this meeting. Perhaps you would be good enough to remain, Avery."

Harry directed a quick grin Avery's way, and His Grace, opening his snuffbox again before changing his mind and snapping it shut, almost wished that he too were being sent off to report to the countess's two daughters. He must be very bored indeed. Lady Camille Westcott, age twenty-two, was the managing sort, a forthright female who did not suffer fools gladly, though she was handsome enough, it was true. Lady Abigail, at eighteen, was a sweet, smiling, pretty young thing who might or might not possess a personality. To do her justice, Avery had not spent enough time in her company to find out. She was his half sister's favorite cousin and dearest friend in the world, however—her words—and he occasionally heard them talking and giggling together behind closed doors that he was very careful never to open.

Harry, all eager to be gone, bowed to his mother, nodded politely to Brumford, came very close to winking at Avery, and made his escape from the library. Lucky devil. Avery strolled closer to the fireplace, where the countess and Brumford were still seated. What the deuce could be important enough that she had voluntarily prolonged this excruciatingly dreary meeting?

"And how may I be of service to you, my lady?" the solicitor asked.

The countess, Avery noticed, was sitting very upright, her spine arched slightly inward. Were ladies taught to sit that way, as though the backs of chairs had been created merely to be decorative? She was, he estimated, about forty years old. She was also quite perfectly beautiful in a mature, dignified sort of way. She surely could not have been happy with Riverdale—who could?—yet to Avery's knowledge she had never indulged herself with lovers. She was tall, shapely, and blond with no sign yet, as far as he could see, of any gray hairs. She was also one of those rare women who looked striking rather than dowdy in deep mourning.

"There is a girl," she said, "or, rather, a woman. In Bath, I believe. My late husband's . . . daughter."

Avery guessed she had been about to say *bastard,* but had changed her mind for the sake of gentility. He raised both his eyebrows and his quizzing glass.

Brumford for once had been silenced.

"She was at an orphanage there," the countess continued. "I do not know where she is now. She is hardly still there, since she must be in her middle twenties. But Riverdale supported her from a very young age and continued to do so until his death. We never discussed the matter. It is altogether probable he did not know I was aware of her existence. I do not know any details, nor have I ever wanted to. I still do not. I assume it was not through you that the support payments were made?"

Brumford's already florid complexion took on a distinctly purplish hue. "It was not, my lady," he assured her. "But might I suggest that since this . . . person is now an adult, you—"

"No," she said, cutting him off. "I am not in need of any suggestion. I have no wish whatsoever to know anything about this woman, even her name. I certainly have no wish for my son to know of her. However, it seems only just that if she has been supported all her life by her . . . father, she be informed of his death if that has not already happened, and be compensated with a final settlement. A handsome one, Mr. Brumford. It would need to be made perfectly clear to her at the same time that there is to be no more—ever, under any circumstances. May I leave the matter in your hands?"

"My lady." Brumford seemed almost to be squirming in his chair. He licked his lips and darted a glance at Avery, of whom—if His Grace was reading him correctly—he stood in considerable awe.

Avery raised his glass all the way to his eye. "Well?" he said. "*May* her ladyship leave the matter in your hands, Brumford? Are you or the other Brumford or one of the sons willing and able to hunt down the bastard daughter, name unknown, of the late earl in order to make her the happiest of orphans by settling a modest fortune upon her?"

"Your Grace." Brumford's chest puffed out. "My lady. It will be a difficult task, but not an insurmountable one, especially for the skilled investigators whose services we engage in the interests of our most valued clients. If the . . . person indeed grew up in Bath, we will identify her. If she is still there, we will find her. If she is no longer there—"

"I believe," Avery said, sounding pained, "her ladyship and I get your meaning. You will report to me when the woman has been found. Is that agreeable to you, Aunt?"

The Countess of Riverdale was not, strictly speaking, his aunt. His stepmother, the duchess, was the late Earl of Riverdale's sister, and thus the countess and all the others were his honorary relatives.

"That will be satisfactory," she said. "Thank you, Avery. When you report to His Grace that you have found her, Mr. Brumford, he will discuss with you what sum is to be settled upon her and what legal papers she will need to sign to confirm that she is no longer a dependent of my late husband's estate."

"That will be all," Avery said as the solicitor drew breath to deliver himself of some doubtless unnecessary and unwanted monologue. "The butler will see you out."

He took snuff and made a mental note that the blend needed to be one half-note less floral in order to be perfect.

"That was remarkably generous of you," he said when he was alone with the countess.

"Not really, Avery," she said, getting to her feet. "I am being generous, if you will, with Harry's money. But he will neither know of the matter nor miss the sum. And taking action now will ensure that he never discovers the existence of his father's by-blow. It will ensure that Camille and Abigail not discover it either. I care not the snap of my fingers for the woman in Bath. I *do* care for my children. Will you stay for luncheon?"

"I will not impose upon you," he said with a sigh. "I have . . . things to attend to. I am quite sure I must have. Everyone has things to do, or so everyone is in the habit of claiming."

The corners of her mouth lifted slightly. "I really do not blame you, Avery, for being eager to escape," she said. "The man is a mighty bore, is he not? But his request for this meeting saved me from summoning him and you on this other matter. You are released. You may run off and busy yourself with . . . things."

He possessed himself of her hand—white, long fingered, perfectly manicured—and bowed gracefully over it as he raised it to his lips.

"You may safely leave the matter in my hands," he said—or in the hands of his secretary, anyway.

"Thank you," she said. "But you will inform me when it is accomplished?"

"I will," he promised before sauntering from the room and taking his hat and cane from the butler's hands.

The revelation that the countess had a conscience had surprised him. How many ladies in similar circumstances would voluntarily seek out their husbands' bastards in order to shower riches upon them, even if they did convince themselves that they did so in the interests of their own, very legitimate children?

ANNA SNOW HAD BEEN BROUGHT TO THE ORPHANAGE IN BATH when she was not quite four years old. She had no real memory of her life before that beyond a few brief and disjointed flashes—of someone always coughing, for example, or of a lych-gate that was dark and a bit frightening inside whenever she was called upon to pass through it alone, and of kneeling on a window ledge and looking down upon a graveyard, and of crying inconsolably inside a carriage while someone with a gruff, impatient voice told her to hush and behave like a big girl.

She had been at the orphanage ever since, though she was now twenty-five. Most of the other children—there were usually about forty of them—left when they were fourteen or fifteen, after suitable employment had been found for them. But Anna had lingered on, first to help out as housemother to a dormitory of girls and a sort of secretary to Miss Ford, the matron, and then as the schoolteacher when Miss Rutledge, the teacher who had taught her, married a clergyman, and moved away to Devonshire. She was even paid a modest salary. However, the expenses of her continued stay at the orphanage, now in a small room of her own, were still provided for by the unknown benefactor who had paid them from the start. She had been told that they would continue to be paid as long as she remained.

Anna considered herself fortunate. She had grown up in an orphanage, it was true, with not even a full identity to call her own, since she did not know who her parents were, but in the main it was not a charity institution. Almost all her fellow orphans were supported through their growing years by someone—usually anonymous, though some knew who they were and why they were there. Usually it was because their parents had died and there was no other family member able or willing to take them in. Anna did not dwell upon the loneliness of not knowing her own story. Her material needs were taken care of. Miss Ford and her staff were generally kind. Most of the children were easy enough to get along with, and those who were not could be avoided. A few were close friends, or had been during her growing years. If there had been a lack of love in her life, or of that type of love one associated with a family, then she did not particularly miss it, having never consciously known it.

Or so she always told herself.

She was content with her life and was only occasionally restless with the feeling that surely there ought to be more, that perhaps she should be making a greater effort to *live* her life. She had been offered marriage by three different men—the keeper of the shop where she went occasionally, when she could afford it, to buy a book; one of the governors of the orphanage, whose wife had recently died and left him with four young children; and Joel Cunningham, her lifelong best friend. She had rejected all three offers for varying reasons and wondered sometimes if it had been foolish to do so, as there were not likely to be many more offers, if any. The prospect of a continuing life of spinsterhood sometimes seemed dreary.

Joel was with her when the letter arrived.

She was tidying the schoolroom after dismissing the children for the day. The monitors for the week—John Davies and Ellen Payne—had collected the slates and chalk and the counting frames. But while John had stacked the slates neatly on the cupboard shelf allotted for them and put all the chalk away in the tin and replaced the lid, Ellen had shoved the counting frames haphazardly on top of paintbrushes and palettes on the bottom shelf instead of arranging them in their appointed place side by side on the shelf above so as not to bend the rods or damage the beads. The reason she had put them in the wrong place was obvious. The second shelf was occupied by the water pots used to swill paint brushes and an untidy heap of paint-stained cleaning rags.

"Joel," Anna said, a note of long-suffering in her voice, "could you at least try to get your pupils to put things away where they belong after an art class? And to clean the water pots first? Look! One of them even still has water in it. Very *dirty* water."

Joel was sitting on the corner of the battered teacher's desk, one booted foot braced on the floor, the other swinging free. His arms were crossed over his chest. He grinned at her.

"But the whole point of being an artist," he said, "is to be a free spirit, to cast aside restricting rules and draw inspiration from the universe. My job is to teach my pupils to be true artists."

She straightened up from the cupboard and directed a speaking glance his way. "What utter rot and nonsense," she said.

He laughed outright. "Anna, Anna," he said. "Here, let me take that pot from you before you burst with indignation or spill it down your dress. It looks like Cyrus North's. There is always more paint in his water jar than on the paper at the end of a lesson. His paintings are extraordinarily pale, as though he were trying to reproduce a heavy fog. Does he know the multiplication tables?"

"He does," she said, depositing the offending jar on the desk and then wrinkling her nose as she arranged the still-damp rags on one side of the bottom shelf, from which she had already removed the counting frames. "He recites them louder than anyone else and can even apply them. He has almost mastered long division too."

"Then he can be a clerk in a countinghouse or perhaps a wealthy banker when he grows up," he said. "He will not need the soul of an artist. He probably does not possess one anyway. There—his future has been settled. I enjoyed your stories today."

"You were listening," she said in a mildly accusatory tone. "You were supposed to be concentrating upon teaching your art lesson."

"Your pupils," he said, "are going to realize when they grow up that they have been horribly tricked. They will have all these marvelous stories rolling around in their heads, only to discover that they are not fiction after all but that driest of all realities—*history*. And geography. And even arithmetic. You get your characters, both human and animal, into the most alarming predicaments from which you can extricate them only with a manipulation of numbers and the help of your pupils. They do not even realize they are learning. You are a sly, devious creature, Anna."

"Have you noticed," she asked, straightening the counting frames to her liking before closing the cupboard doors and turning toward him, "that at church when the clergyman is giving his sermon everyone's eyes glaze over and many people even nod off to sleep? But if he suddenly decides to illustrate a point with a little story, everyone perks up and listens. We were made to tell and listen to stories, Joel. It is how knowledge was passed from person to person and generation to generation before there was the written word, and even afterward, when most people had no access to manuscripts or books and could not read them even if they did. Why do we now feel that storytelling should be confined to fiction and fantasy? Can we enjoy only what has no basis in fact?"

He smiled fondly at her as she stood looking at him, her hands clasped at her waist. "One of my many secret dreams is to be a writer," he said. "Have I ever told you that? To write truth dressed up in fiction. It is said one ought to write about what one knows. I could invent endless stories about what I know."

Secret dreams! It was a familiar, evocative phrase. They had often played the game as they grew up—*What is your most secret dream?* Usually it was that their parents would suddenly appear to claim them and whisk them off to the happily-ever-after of a family life. Often when they were very young they would add that they would then discover themselves to be a prince or princess and their home a castle.

"Stories about growing up as an orphan in an orphanage?" Anna said, smiling back at him. "About not knowing who you are? About dreaming of your missing heritage? Of your unknown parents? Of what might have been? And of what still might be if only . . . ? Well, if only."

He shifted his position slightly and moved the paint jar so that he would not accidentally tip it.

"Yes, about all that," he said. "But it would not be all wistful sadness. For though we do not know who we were born as or who our parents or their families were or are, and though we do not know exactly why we were placed here and never afterward claimed, we do know that we *are*. I am not my parents or my lost heritage. I am myself. I am an artist who ekes out a reasonably decent living painting portraits and volunteers his time and expertise as a teacher at the orphanage where he grew up. I am a hundred or a thousand other things too, either despite my background or because of it. I want to write stories about it all, Anna, about characters finding themselves without the hindrance of family lineage and expectations. Without the hindrance of . . . love."

Anna gazed at him in silence for a few moments, the soreness of what felt very like tears in her throat. Joel was a solidly built man, somewhat above average in height, with dark hair cut short— because he did not want to fulfill the stereotypical image of the flamboyant artist with flowing locks, he always explained whenever he had it cut—and a round, pleasant face with a slightly cleft chin, sensitive mouth when it was relaxed, and dark eyes that could blaze with intensity and darken even further when he felt passionately about something. He was good-looking and good-natured and talented and intelligent and extremely dear to her, and because she had known him most of her life, she knew about his woundedness, though any casual acquaintance would not have suspected it.

It was a woundedness shared in one way or another by all orphans.

"There are institutions far worse than this one, Joel," Anna said, "and probably not many that are better. We have not grown up without love. Most of us love one another. I love you."

His grin was back. "Yet on a certain memorable occasion you refused to marry me," he said. "You broke my heart."

She clucked her tongue. "You were not really serious," she said. "And even if you were, you know we do not love each other *that* way. We grew up together as friends, almost as brother and sister."

He smiled ruefully at her. "Do you never dream of leaving here, Anna?"

"Yes and no," she said. "Yes, I dream of going out there into the world to find out what lies beyond these walls and the confines of Bath. And no, I do not want to leave what is familiar to me, the only home I have known since infancy and the only family I can remember. I feel safe here and needed, even loved. Besides, my . . . benefactor agreed to continue supporting me only as long as I remain here. I—Well, I suppose I am a coward, paralyzed by the terror of destitution and the unknown. It is as though, having been abandoned, I really cannot bear the thought of now abandoning the one thing that has been left me, this orphanage and the people who live here."

Joel got to his feet and strolled over to the other side of the room, where the easels were still set up so that today's paintings could dry properly. He touched a few at the edges to see if it was safe to remove them.

"We are both cowards, then," he said. "I did leave, but not entirely. I still have one foot in the door. And the other has not moved far away, has it? I am still in Bath. Do you suppose we are afraid to move away lest our parents come for us and not know where to find us?" He looked up and laughed. "Tell me it is not that, Anna, please. I am *twenty-seven* years old."

Anna felt rather as if he had punched her in the stomach. The old secret dream never quite died. But the most haunting question was never really *who* had brought them here and left them, but *why*.

"I believe most people live their lives within a radius of a few miles of their childhood homes," she said. "Not many people go adventuring. And even those who do have to take themselves with them. That must turn out to be a bit of a disappointment."

Joel laughed again.

"I am useful here," Anna continued, "and I am happy here. You are useful—and successful. It is becoming quite fashionable when in Bath to have your portrait painted by Joel Cunningham. And wealthy people are always coming to Bath to take the waters."

His head was tipped slightly to one side as he regarded her. But before he could say anything more, the classroom door was flung open without the courtesy of a knock to admit Bertha Reed, a thin, flaxen-haired fourteen-year-old who acted as Miss Ford's helper now that she was old enough. She was bursting with excitement and waving a folded paper in one raised hand.

"There is a letter for you, Miss Snow," she half shrieked. "It was delivered by special messenger from London and Miss Ford would have brought it herself but Tommy is bleeding all over her sitting room and no one can find Nurse Jones. Maddie punched him in the nose."

"It is high time someone did," Joel said, strolling closer to Anna. "I suppose he was pulling one of her braids again."

Anna scarcely heard. A letter? From London? By special messenger? For *her*?

"Whoever can it be from, Miss Snow?" Bertha screeched, apparently not particularly concerned about Tommy and his bleeding nose. "Who do you know in London? No, don't tell me—that ought to have been *whom*. *Whom* do you know in London? I wonder what they are writing about. And it came by *special messenger*, all that way. It must have cost a *fortune*. Oh, do open it."

Her blatant inquisitiveness might have seemed impertinent, but really, it was so rare for any of them to receive a letter that word always spread very quickly and everyone wanted to know all about it. Occasionally someone who had left both the orphanage and Bath to work elsewhere would write, and the recipient would almost invariably share the contents with everyone else. Such missives were kept as prized possessions and read over and over until they were virtually threadbare.

Anna did not recognize the handwriting, which was both bold and precise. It was a masculine hand, she felt sure. The paper felt thick and expensive. It did not look like a personal letter.

"Oliver is in London," Bertha said wistfully. "But I don't suppose it can be from him, can it? His writing does not look anything like that, and why would he write to you anyway? The four times he has written since he left here, it was to me. And he is not going to send any letter by special messenger, is he?"

Oliver Jamieson had been apprenticed to a boot maker in London two years ago at the age of fourteen and had promised to send for Bertha and marry her as soon as he got on his feet. Twice each year since then he had faithfully written a five- or six-line letter in large, careful handwriting. Bertha had shared his sparse news on each occasion and wept over the letters until it was a wonder they were still legible. There were three years left in his apprenticeship before he could hope to be on his feet and able to support a wife. They were both very young, but the separation did seem cruel. Anna always found herself hoping that Oliver would remain faithful to his childhood sweetheart.

"Are you going to turn it over and over in your hands and hope it will divulge its secrets without your having to break the seal?" Joel asked.

Stupidly, Anna's hands were trembling. "Perhaps there is some mistake," she said. "Perhaps it is not for me."

He came up behind her and looked over her shoulder. "Miss Anna Snow," he said. "It certainly sounds like you. I do not know any other Anna Snows. Do you, Bertha?"

"I do not, Mr. Cunningham," she said after pausing to think. "But whatever can it be about?"

Anna slid her thumb beneath the seal and broke it. And yes, indeed, the letter was written on a thick, costly vellum. It was not a long letter. It was from Somebody Brumford—she could not read the first name, though it began with a *J*. He was a solicitor. She read through the letter once, swallowed, and then read it again more slowly.

"The day after tomorrow," she murmured.

"In a private chaise," Joel added. He had been reading over her shoulder.

"*What* is the day after tomorrow?" Bertha demanded, her voice an agony of suspense. "*What* chaise?"

Anna looked at her blankly. "I am being summoned to London to discuss my future," she said. There was a faint buzzing in her ears.

"Oh! By who?" Bertha asked, her eyes as wide as saucers. "By *whom*, I mean."

"Mr. J. Brumford, a solicitor," Anna said.

"Josiah, I think that says," Joel said. "Josiah Brumford. He is sending a private chaise to fetch you, and you are to pack a bag for at least a few days."

"To *London*?" Bertha's voice was breathless with awe.

"Whatever am I to do?" Anna's mind seemed to have stopped working. Or, rather, it *was* working, but it was whirring out of control, like the innards of a broken clock.

"What you are to do, Anna," Joel said, pushing a chair up behind her knees and setting his hands on her shoulders to press her gently down onto it, "is pack a bag for a few days and then go to London to discuss your future."

"But what future?" she asked.

"That is what is to be discussed," he pointed out.

The buzzing in her ears grew louder.

READ ON FOR AN EXCERPT FROM THE
SECOND NOVEL IN THE WESTCOTT SERIES,

Someone to Hold

AVAILABLE NOW FROM JOVE

A fter several months of hiding away, wallowing in misery and denial, anger and shame, and any other negative emotion anyone cared to name, Camille Westcott finally took charge of her life on a sunny, blustery morning in July. At the grand age of twenty-two. She had not needed to take charge before the great catastrophe a few months before because she had been a lady—*Lady* Camille Westcott to be exact, eldest child of the Earl and Countess of Riverdale—and ladies did not have or need control over their own lives. Other people had that instead: parents, maids, nurses, governesses, chaperons, husbands, society at large—especially society at large with its myriad rules and expectations, most of them unwritten but none the less real on that account.

But she needed to assert herself now. She was no longer a lady. She was now simply *Miss* Westcott, and she was not even sure about the name. Was a bastard entitled to her father's name? Life yawned ahead of her as a frightening unknown. She had no idea what to expect of it. There were no more rules, no more expectations. There was no more society, no more place of belonging. If she did not take charge and *do* something, who would?

It was a rhetorical question, of course. She had not asked it aloud in anyone's hearing, but no one would have had a satisfactory answer to give her even if she had. So she was doing something about it herself. It was either that or cower in a dark corner somewhere for the rest of her natural days. She was no longer a lady, but she was, by God, a person. She was alive—she was breathing. She was *someone*.

Camille and Abigail, her younger sister, lived with their maternal grandmother in one of the imposing houses in the prestigious Royal Crescent in Bath. It stood atop a hill above the city, splendidly visible from miles around with its great sweeping inward curve of massive Georgian houses all joined into one, open parkland sloping downward before it. But the view worked both ways. From any front-facing window the inhabitants of the Crescent could gaze downward over the city and across the river to the buildings beyond and on out to the countryside and hills in the distance. It was surely one of the loveliest views in all England, and Camille had delighted in it as a child whenever her mother had brought her with her brother and sister on extended visits to their grandparents. It had lost much of its appeal, however, now that she was forced to live here in what felt very like exile and disgrace, though neither she nor Abigail had done anything to deserve either fate.

She waited on that sunny morning until her grandmother and sister had gone out, as they often did, to the Pump Room down near Bath Abbey to join the promenade of the fashionable world. Not that the fashionable world was as impressive as it had once been in Bath's heyday. A large number of the inhabitants now were seniors, who liked the quiet gentility of life here in stately surroundings.

Even the visitors tended to be older people who came to take the waters and imagine, rightly or wrongly, that their health was the better for imposing such a foul-tasting ordeal upon themselves. Some even submerged themselves to the neck in it, though that was now considered a little extreme and old-fashioned.

Abigail liked going to the Pump Room, for at the age of eighteen she craved outings and company, and apparently her exquisite, youthful beauty was much admired, though she did not receive many invitations to private parties or even to more public entertainments. She was not, after all, quite respectable despite the fact that Grandmama was eminently so. Camille had always steadfastly refused to accompany them anywhere they might meet other people in a social setting. On the rare occasions when she did step out, usually with Abby, she did so with stealth, a veil draped over the brim of her bonnet and pulled down over her face, for more than anything else she feared being recognized.

Not today, however. And, she vowed to herself, never again. She was done with the old life, and if anyone recognized her and chose to give her the cut direct, then she would give it right back. It was time for a new life and new acquaintances. And if there were a few bumps to traverse in moving from one world to the other, well, then she would deal with them.

After Grandmama and Abby had left, she dressed in one of the more severe and conservative of her walking dresses, and donned a bonnet to match. She put on comfortable shoes, since the sort of dainty slippers she had always worn in the days when she traveled everywhere by carriage were useless now except to wear indoors. Finally taking up her gloves and reticule, she stepped out onto the cobbled street without waiting for a servant to open and hold the door for her and look askance at her lone state, perhaps even try to stop her or send a footman trailing after her. She stood outside for a few moments, assailed by a sudden terror bordering upon panic and wondering if perhaps after all she should scurry back inside to hide in darkness and safety. In her whole life she had rarely stepped beyond the confines of house or walled park unaccompanied by a family member or a servant, often both. But those days were over, even though Grandmama would doubtless argue the point. Camille squared her shoulders, lifted her chin, and strode off downhill in the general direction of Bath Abbey.

Her actual destination, however, was a house on Northumberland Place, near the Guildhall and the market and the Pulteney Bridge, which spanned the river Avon with grandiose elegance. It was a building indistinguishable from many of the other Georgian edifices with which the city abounded, solid yet pleasing to the eye and three stories high, not counting the basement and the attic, except that this one was actually three houses that had been made into one in order to accommodate an institution.

An orphanage, to be precise.

It was where Anna Snow, more recently Lady Anastasia Westcott, now the Duchess of Netherby, had spent her childhood. It was where she had taught for several years after she grew up. It was from there that she had been summoned to London by a solicitor's letter. And it was in London that their paths and their histories had converged, Camille's and Anastasia's, the one to be elevated to heights beyond her wildest imaginings, the other to be plunged to depths lower than her worst nightmares.

Anastasia, also a daughter of the Earl of Riverdale, had been consigned to the orphanage—by him—at a very young age on the death of her mother. She had grown up there, supported financially but quite ignorant of who she was. She had not even known her real name. She had been Anna Snow, Snow being her mother's maiden name—though she had not realized that either. Camille, on the other hand, born three years after Anastasia, had been brought up to a life of privilege and wealth and entitlement with Harry and Abigail, her younger siblings. None of them had known of Anastasia's existence. Well, Mama had, but she had always assumed that the child Papa secretly supported at an orphanage in Bath was the love child of a mistress. It was only after his death several months ago that the truth came out.

And what a catastrophic truth it was!

Alice Snow, Anastasia's mother, had been Papa's legitimate wife. They had married secretly in Bath, though she had left him a year or so later when her health failed and she returned to her parents' home near Bristol, taking their child with her. She had died sometime later of consumption, but not until four months after Papa married Mama in a bigamous marriage that had no legality. And because the marriage was null and void, all issue of that marriage was illegitimate. Harry had lost the title he had so recently inherited; Mama had lost all social status and had reverted to her maiden name—she now called herself Miss Kingsley and lived with her clergyman brother, Uncle Michael, at a country vicarage in Dorsetshire. Camille and Abigail were no longer *Lady* Camille and *Lady* Abigail. Everything that had been theirs had been stripped away. Cousin Alexander Westcott—he was actually a second cousin—had inherited the title and entailed property despite the fact that he had genuinely not wanted either, and Anastasia had inherited everything else. That *everything else* was the vast fortune Papa had amassed after his bigamous marriage to Mama. It also included Hinsford Manor, the country home in Hampshire where they had always lived when they were not in London, and Westcott House, their London residence.

Camille, Harry, Abigail, and their mother had been left with nothing.

As a final crushing blow, Camille had lost her fiancé. Viscount Uxbury had called upon her the very day they heard the news. But instead of offering the expected sympathy and support, and instead of sweeping her off to the altar, a special license waving from one hand, he had suggested that she send a notice to the papers announcing the ending of their betrothal so that she would not have to suffer the added shame of being cast off. Yes, a crushing blow indeed, though Camille never spoke of it. Just when it had seemed there could not possibly be any lower to sink or greater pain to be borne, there could be and there was, but the pain at least was something she could keep to herself.

So here she and Abigail were, living in Bath of all places on the charity of their grandmother, while Mama languished in Dorsetshire and Harry was in Portugal or Spain as a junior officer with the 95th Foot Regiment, also known as the Rifles, fighting the forces of Napoleon Bonaparte. He could not have afforded the commission on his own, of course. Avery, Duke of Netherby, their stepcousin and Harry's guardian, had purchased it for him. Harry, to his credit, had refused to allow Avery to set him up in a more prestigious, and far more costly, cavalry regiment and had made it clear that he would not allow Avery to purchase any promotions for him either.

By what sort of irony had she ended up in the very place where Anastasia had grown up, Camille wondered, not for the first time, as she descended the hill. The orphanage had acted like a magnet ever since she came here, drawing her much against her will. She had walked past it a couple of times with Abigail and had finally— over Abby's protests—gone inside to introduce herself to the matron, Miss Ford, who had given her a tour of the institution while

Abby remained outside without a chaperon. It had been both an ordeal and a relief, actually seeing the place, walking the floors Anastasia must have walked a thousand times and more. It was not the sort of horror of an institution one sometimes heard about. The building was spacious and clean. The adults who ran it looked well-groomed and cheerful. The children she saw were decently clad and nicely behaved and appeared to be well-fed. The majority of them, Miss Ford had explained, were adequately, even generously, supported by a parent or family member even though most of those adults chose to remain anonymous. The others were supported by local benefactors.

One of those benefactors, Camille had been amazed to learn, though not of any specific child, was her own grandmother. For some reason of her own, she had recently called there and agreed to equip the schoolroom with a large bookcase and books to fill it. Why she had felt the need to do so, Camille did not know, any more than she understood her own compulsion to see the building and actually step inside it. Grandmama could surely feel no more kindly disposed toward Anastasia than she, Camille, did. Less so, in fact. Anastasia was at least Camille's half sister, perish the thought, but she was nothing to Grandmama apart from being the visible evidence of a marriage that had deprived her own daughter of the very identity that had apparently been hers for longer than twenty years. Goodness, Mama had been Viola Westcott, Countess of Riverdale, for all those years, though in fact the only one of those names to which she had had any legal claim was Viola.

Today Camille was going back to the orphanage alone. Anna Snow had been replaced by another teacher, but Miss Ford had mentioned in passing during that earlier visit that Miss Nunce might not remain there long. Camille had hinted with an impulsiveness that had both puzzled and alarmed her that she might be interested in filling the post herself, should the teacher resign. Perhaps Miss Ford had forgotten or had not taken her seriously. Or perhaps she had judged Camille unsuited to the position. However it was, she had not informed Camille when Miss Nunce did indeed leave. It was quite by chance that Grandmama had seen the notice for a new teacher in yesterday's paper and had read it aloud to her granddaughters.

What on earth, Camille asked herself as she neared the bottom of the hill and turned in the direction of Northumberland Place, did she know about teaching? Specifically, what did she know about teaching a supposedly large group of children of all ages and abilities and both genders? She frowned, and a young couple approaching her along the pavement stepped smartly out of her way as though a fearful presence were bearing down upon them. Camille did not even notice.

Why on earth was she going to beg to be allowed to teach orphans in the very place where Anastasia had grown up and taught? She still disliked, resented, and—yes—even hated the former Anna Snow. It did not matter that she knew she was being unfair—after all, it was not Anastasia's fault that Papa had behaved so despicably, and she had suffered the consequences for twenty-five years before discovering the truth about herself. It did not matter either that Anastasia had attempted to embrace her newly discovered siblings as family and had offered more than once to share everything she had inherited with them and to allow her two half sisters to continue to live with their mama at Hinsford Manor, which now belonged to her. In fact, her generosity merely made it harder to like her. How dared she offer them a portion of what had always been theirs by right, as though she were doing them a great and gracious favor? Which in a sense she was.

It was a purely irrational hostility, of course, but raw emotions were not often reasonable. And Camille's emotions were still as raw as open wounds that had not even begun to heal.

So why exactly was she coming here? She stood on the pavement outside the main doors of the orphanage for a couple of minutes, debating the question just as though she had not already done so all yesterday and through a night of fitful sleep and long wakeful periods. Was it just because she felt the need to *do* something with her life? But were there not other, more suitable things she could do instead? And if she must teach, were there not more respectable positions to which she might aspire? There were genteel girls' schools in Bath, and there were always people in search of well-bred governesses for their daughters. But her need to come here today had nothing really to do with any desire to teach, did it? It was . . . Well, what was it?

The need to step into Anna Snow's shoes to discover what they felt like? What an absolutely ghastly thought. But if she stood out here any longer, she would lose her courage and find herself trudging back uphill, lost and defeated and abject and every other horrid thing she could think of. Besides, standing here was decidedly uncomfortable. Though it was July and the sun was shining, it was still only morning and she was in the shade of the building. The street was acting as a type of funnel too for a brisk wind.

She stepped forward, lifted the heavy knocker away from the door, hesitated for only a moment, then let it fall. Perhaps she would be denied employment. What a huge relief that would be.

JOEL CUNNINGHAM WAS FEELING ON TOP OF THE WORLD WHEN he got out of bed that morning. July sunshine poured into his rooms as soon as he pulled back the curtains from every window to let it in, filling them with light and warmth. But it was not just the perfect summer day that had lifted his mood. This morning he was taking the time to appreciate his home. His *rooms*—plural.

He had worked hard in the twelve years since he left the orphanage at the age of fifteen and taken up residence in one small room on the top floor of a house on Grove Street just west of the river Avon. He had taken employment at a butcher's shop while also attending art school. The anonymous benefactor who had paid his way at the orphanage throughout his childhood had paid the school fees too and covered the cost of basic school supplies, though for everything else he had been on his own. He had persevered at both school and employment while working on his painting whenever he could.

Often after paying his rent he had had to make the choice between eating and buying extra supplies, and eating had not always won. But those days were behind him. He had been sitting outside the Pump Room in the abbey yard one afternoon a few years ago, sketching a vagabond perched alone on a nearby bench and sharing a crust of bread with the pigeons. Sketching people he saw about him on the streets was something Joel loved doing, and something for which one of his art teachers had told him he had a genuine talent. He had been unaware of a gentleman sitting down next to him until the man spoke. The result of the ensuing conversation had been a commission to paint a portrait of the man's wife. Joel had been terrified of failing, but he had been pleased with the way the painting turned out. He had made no attempt to make the lady appear younger or lovelier than she was, but both husband and wife had seemed genuinely delighted with what they called the realism of the portrait. They had shown it to some friends and recommended him to others.

The result had been more such commissions and then still more, until he was often fairly swamped by demands for his services and wished there were more hours in the day. He had been able to leave his employment two years ago and raise his fees. Recently he had raised them again, but no one yet had complained that he was over-charging. It had been time to begin looking for a studio in which to work. But last month the family that occupied the rest of the top floor of the house in which he had his room had given notice, and Joel had asked the landlord if he could rent the whole floor, which came fully furnished. He would have the luxury of a sizable studio in which to work as well as a living room, a bedchamber, a kitchen that doubled as a dining room, and a washroom. It seemed to him a true palace.

The family having moved out the morning before, last night he had celebrated his change in fortune by inviting five friends, all male, to come and share the meat pies he had bought from the butcher's shop, a cake from the bakery next to it, and a few bottles of wine. It had been a merry housewarming.

"You will be giving up the orphanage, I suppose," Marvin Silver, the bank clerk who lived on the middle floor, had said after toasting Joel's continued success.

"Teaching there, do you mean?" Joel had asked.

"You do not get paid, do you?" Marvin had said. "And it sounds as though you need all your time to keep up with what you *are* being paid for—quite handsomely, I have heard."

Joel volunteered his time two afternoons a week at the orphan-age school, teaching art to those who wanted to do a little more than was being offered in the art classes provided by the regular teacher. Actually, *teach* was somewhat of a misnomer for what he did with those children. He thought of his role to be more in the nature of inspiring them to discover and express their individual artistic vision and talent. He used to look forward to those afternoons. They had not been so enjoyable lately, however, though that had nothing to do with the children or with his increasingly busy life beyond the orphanage walls.

"I'll always find the time to go there," he had assured Marvin, and one of the other fellows had slapped him with hearty good cheer on the back.

"And what of Mrs. Tull?" he had asked him, waggling his eyebrows. "Are you thinking of moving her in here to cook and clean for you among other things, Joel? As Mrs. Cunningham, perhaps? You can probably afford a wife."

Edwina Tull was a pretty and amiable widow, about eight years Joel's senior. She appeared to have been left well-off by her late husband, though in the three years Joel had known her he had come to suspect that she entertained other male friends apart from him and that she accepted gifts—monetary gifts—from them as she did from him. The fact that he was very possibly not her only male friend did not particularly bother him. Indeed, he was quite happy that there was never any suggestion of a commitment between them. She was respectable and affectionate and discreet, and she provided him with regular female companionship and lively conversation as well as good sex. He was satisfied with that. His heart, unfortunately, had long ago been given elsewhere, and he had not got it back yet even though the object of his devotion had recently married someone else.

"I am quite happy to enjoy my expanded living quarters alone for a while yet," he had said. "Besides, I believe Mrs. Tull is quite happy with her independence."

His friends had finished off the food and wine and stayed until after midnight. It had felt very good indeed to be able to entertain in his own rooms and actually have enough chairs for them all to sit on.

Now he strolled about his living and working quarters in the morning sunshine and reveled anew in the realization that all this space was his. He had come a long way in twelve years. He stood before the easel in the studio and gazed at the portrait he had been able to leave propped on it. Apart from a few small finishing touches, it was ready to be delivered. He was particularly pleased with it because it had given him problems. Mrs. Dance was a faded lady who had probably never been pretty. She was bland and amiable, and at the beginning he had asked himself how the devil he was going to paint her in such a way that both she and her husband would be satisfied. He had wrestled with the question for several weeks while he sketched her and talked with her and discovered that her amiability was warm and genuine and had been hard-won—she had lost three of her seven children in infancy and another just before he finished school. Once Joel had erased the judgmental word *bland* as a descriptor, he came to see her as a genuinely lovely person and had had great pleasure painting her portrait. He hoped he had captured what he saw as the essence of her well enough that others would see it too.

But though his fingers itched to pick up his brush to make those finishing touches, he had to resist. He had made arrangements with Miss Ford to go to the orphanage school early today, since he had an appointment with another client this afternoon, which he had been unable to shift to a different time. But even the thought of going to school early could not dampen his mood, for he would have the schoolroom to himself and his small group today and, if he was fortunate, for the rest of the summer.

While Miss Nunce had taught at the orphanage school, Joel and his group had had to squeeze into a strictly calculated third of the schoolroom—she had actually measured it with a long tape borrowed from Roger, the porter, and marked it out with chalk. They had crowded in with their easels and all the other necessary paraphernalia of an art class while she conducted her lessons in the other two-thirds. Her reasoning had been that he had one-third of the total number of schoolchildren while she had two-thirds. The art equipment did not factor into her view. But last week, Miss Nunce had resigned in high dudgeon before she could be forcibly ejected.

Joel had not been there at the time, but he did not mourn her departure. It had not been beyond the woman to intrude upon his third of the room, stepping carefully over the chalk line so as not to smudge it, to give her verdict on the paintings in progress, and invariably it was a derogatory judgment. She was an opinionated, joyless woman who clearly despised all children, and orphans in particular. She appeared to have seen it as her personal mission to prepare them to be humble and servile and to know their place—that place being the bottom rung of the social ladder, or perhaps somewhat below the bottom rung. Sometimes he had thought she resented even having to teach them to read, write, and figure. She had done her utmost to quell dreams and aspirations and talent and imagination, all of which in her view were inappropriate to their parentless condition.

She had walked out after Mary Perkins went running to find Miss Ford to tell her that Miss Nunce was beating Jimmy Dale. When Miss Ford had arrived on the scene, Jimmy was standing in the corner, his back to the room, squirming from the pain of a sore bottom. Miss Nunce, it seemed, had discovered him reading one of the new books—unfortunately for him, one of the larger, heavier volumes—and actually chuckling over something within its pages.

She had taken it from him, instructed him to stand and bend over his desk, and walloped him a dozen times with it before sending him to the corner to contemplate his sins. She had still been holding the book aloft and haranguing the class on the evils of the trivial use of one's time and of empty-minded levity when Miss Ford appeared. Seeing her, Miss Nunce had turned her triumphant glare upon the matron.

"And *this*," she had pronounced, "is what comes of allowing *books* in the schoolroom."

The books, together with a large bookcase to display them, had been donated a short while ago by a Mrs. Kingsley, a wealthy and prominent citizen of Bath. Miss Nunce had been quite vocal in her opposition at the time. Books, she had warned, would merely give the orphans ideas.

Miss Ford had crossed the room to Jimmy, turned him by the shoulders, and asked him why he had been reading in class. He had explained that his arithmetic exercise was finished and he had not wanted to sit idle. Sure enough, all his sums were completed and all were correct. She had sent him back to his seat after first removing her shawl and folding it several times into a square for him to sit on. She had asked the day's monitors to take charge of the room and invited Miss Nunce to step outside, much to the disappointment of the children. Joel would have been disappointed too if he had been there. But then, the incident would not have happened if he had been there. No child at the orphanage was ever struck. It was one of Miss Ford's immutable rules.

Less than fifteen minutes later—the children and some of the staff in other parts of the building had heard the teacher's raised voice alternating with silences that probably indicated Miss Ford was speaking—Miss Nunce had stridden from the building with

Roger a few steps behind her to lock the door, lest she change her mind.

Joel had rejoiced, not just because he had found it difficult to work with her, but because he cared for the children—all of them. He had been greatly relieved too, because Miss Nunce had succeeded Anna Snow, who had left a few months ago, and who had been everything she was not. Anna had brought sunshine to the schoolroom.

It was Anna whom he loved, though he tried doggedly to use the past tense whenever he considered his feelings for her. She was a married lady now. She was the Duchess of Netherby.

Read on for an excerpt from the
third novel in the Westcott series,

Someone to Wed

Available now from Jove

T he Earl of Riverdale," the butler announced after opening wide the double doors of the drawing room as though to admit a regiment and then standing to one side so that the gentleman named could stride past him.

The announcement was not strictly necessary. Wren had heard the arrival of his vehicle, and guessed it was a curricle rather than a traveling carriage, although she had not got to her feet to look. And he was almost exactly on time. She liked that. The two gentlemen who had come before him had been late, one by all of half an hour. Those two had been sent on their way as soon as was decently possible, though not only because of their tardiness. Mr. Sweeney, who had come a week ago, had bad teeth and a way of stretching his mouth to expose them at disconcertingly frequent intervals even when he was not actually smiling. Mr. Richman, who had come four days ago, had had no discernible personality, a fact that had been quite as disconcerting as Mr. Sweeney's teeth. Now here came the third.

He strode forward a few paces before coming to an abrupt halt as the butler closed the doors behind him. He looked about the room with apparent surprise at the discovery that it was occupied only by two women, one of whom—Maude, Wren's maid—was seated off in a corner, her head bent over some needlework, in the role of chaperon. His eyes came to rest upon Wren and he bowed.

"Miss Heyden?" It was a question.

Her first reaction after her initial approval of his punctuality was acute dismay. One glance told her he was not at all what she wanted.

He was tall; well formed; immaculately, elegantly tailored; dark haired; and impossibly handsome. And young—in his late twenties or early thirties, at a guess. If she were to dream up the perfect hero for the perfect romantic fairy tale, she could not do better than the very real man standing halfway across the room, waiting for her to confirm that she was indeed the lady who had invited him to take tea at Withington House.

But this was no fairy tale, and the sheer perfection of him alarmed her and caused her to lean back farther in her chair and deeper into the shade provided by the curtains drawn across the window on her side of the fireplace. She had not wanted a handsome man or even a particularly young man. She had hoped for someone older, more ordinary, perhaps balding or acquiring a bit of a paunch, pleasant-looking but basically . . . well, ordinary. With decent teeth and at least *something* of a personality. But she could hardly deny her identity and dismiss him without further ado.

"Yes," she said. "How do you do, Lord Riverdale? Do have a seat." She gestured to the chair across the hearth from her own. She knew something of social manners and ought, of course, to have risen to greet him, but she had good reason to keep to the shadows, at least for now.

He eyed the chair as he approached it and sat with obvious reluctance. "I do beg your pardon," he said. "I appear to be early. Punctuality is one of my besetting sins, I am afraid. I always make the mistake of assuming that when I am invited somewhere for half past two, I am expected to arrive at half past two. I hope some of your other guests will be here soon, including a few ladies."

She was further alarmed when he smiled. If it was possible to look more handsome than handsome, he was looking it. He had perfect teeth, and his eyes crinkled attractively at the corners when he smiled. And his eyes were very blue. Oh, this was wretched. Who was number four on her list?

"Punctuality is a virtue as far as I am concerned, Lord Riverdale," she said. "I am a businesswoman, as perhaps you are aware. To run a successful business, one must respect other people's time as well as one's own. You are on time. You see?" She swept one hand toward the clock ticking on the mantel. "It is twenty-five minutes to three. And I am not expecting any other guests."

His smile disappeared and he glanced at Maude before looking back at Wren. "I see," he said. "Perhaps you had not realized, Miss Heyden, that neither my mother nor my sister came into the country with me. Or perhaps you did not realize I have no wife to accompany me. I beg your pardon. I have no wish to cause you any embarrassment or to compromise you in any way." His hands closed about the arms of his chair in a signal that he was about to rise.

"But my invitation was addressed to you alone," she said. "I am no young girl to need to be hedged about with relatives to protect her from the dangerous company of single gentlemen. And I do have Maude for propriety's sake. We are neighbors of sorts, Lord Riverdale, though more than eight miles separate Withington House from Brambledean Court and I am not always here and you are not always there. Nevertheless, now that I am owner of Withington and have completed my year of mourning for my aunt and uncle, I have taken it upon myself to become acquainted with some of my neighbors. I entertained Mr. Sweeney here last week and Mr. Richman a few days after. Do you know them?"

He was frowning, and he had not removed his hands from the arms of his chair. He still looked uncomfortable and ready to spring to his feet at the earliest excuse. "I have an acquaintance with both gentlemen," he said, "though I cannot claim to *know* either one. I have been in possession of my title and property for only a year and have not spent much time here yet."

"Then I am fortunate you are here now," she said as the drawing room doors opened and the tea tray was carried in and set before her. She moved to the edge of her chair, turning without conscious intent slightly to her left as she did so, and poured the tea. Maude came silently across the room to hand the earl his cup and saucer and then to offer the plate of cakes.

"I did not know Mr. and Mrs. Heyden, your aunt and uncle," he said, nodding his thanks to Maude. "I am sorry for your loss. I understand they died within a very short while of each other."

"Yes," she said. "My aunt died a few days after taking to her bed with a severe headache, and my uncle died less than a week later. His health had been failing for some time, and I believe he simply gave up the struggle after she had gone. He doted upon her." And Aunt Megan upon him despite the thirty-year gap in their ages and the hurried nature of their marriage almost twenty years ago.

"I am sorry," he said again. "They raised you?"

"Yes," she said. "They could not have done better by me if they had been my parents. Your predecessor did not live at Brambledean, I understand, or visit often. I speak of the late Earl of Riverdale, not his unfortunate son. Do you intend to take up permanent residence there?"

The unfortunate son, Wren had learned, had succeeded to the title until it was discovered that his father had contracted a secret marriage as a very young man and that the secret wife had still been alive when he married the mother of his three children. Those children, already adult, had suddenly found themselves to be illegitimate, and the new earl had lost the title to the man now seated on the other side of the hearth. The late earl's first marriage had produced one legitimate child, a daughter, who had grown up at an orphanage in Bath, knowing nothing of her identity. All this and more Wren had learned before adding the earl to her list. The story had been sensational news last year and had kept the gossip mills grinding for weeks. The details had not been difficult to unearth when there were servants and tradespeople only too eager to share what came their way.

One never knew quite where truth ended and exaggeration or misunderstanding or speculation or downright falsehood began, of course, but Wren did know a surprising amount about her neighbors, considering the fact that she had absolutely no social dealings with them. She knew, for example, that both Mr. Sweeney and Mr. Richman were respectable but impoverished gentlemen. And she knew that Brambledean had been almost totally neglected by the late earl, who had left it to be mismanaged almost to the point of total ruin by a lazy steward who graced the taproom of his local inn more often than his office. By now the house and estate needed the infusion of a vast sum of money.

Wren had heard that the new earl was a conscientious gentleman of comfortable means, but that he was not nearly wealthy enough to cope with the severity of the disaster he had inherited so unexpectedly. The late earl had not been a poor man. Far from it, in fact. But his fortune had gone to his legitimate daughter. She might have saved the day by marrying the new earl and so reuniting the entailed property with the fortune, but she had married the Duke of Netherby instead. Wren could well understand why the many-faceted story had so dominated conversation both above- and below-stairs last year.

"I do intend to live at Brambledean," the Earl of Riverdale said. He was frowning into his cup. "I have another home in Kent, of which I am dearly fond, but I am needed here, and an absentee landlord is rarely a good landlord. The people dependent upon me here deserve better."

He looked every bit as handsome when he was frowning as he did when he smiled. Wren hesitated. It was not too late to send him on his way, as she had done with his two predecessors. She had given a plausible reason for inviting him and had plied him with tea and cakes. He would doubtless go away thinking her eccentric. He would probably disapprove of her inviting him alone when she was a single lady with only the flimsy chaperonage of a maid. But he would shrug off the encounter soon enough and forget about her. And she did not really care what he might think or say about her anyway.

But now she remembered that number four on her list, a man in his late fifties, had always professed himself to be a confirmed bach-elor, and number five was reputed to complain almost constantly of ailments both real and imagined. She had added them only because the list had looked pathetically short with just three names.

"I understand, Lord Riverdale," she said, "that you are not a wealthy man." Now perhaps it was too late—or very nearly so. If she sent him away now, he would think her vulgar as well as eccentric and careless of her reputation.

He took his time about setting his cup and saucer down on the table beside him before turning his eyes upon her. Only the slight flaring of his nostrils warned her that she had angered him. "Do you indeed?" he said, a distinct note of hauteur in his voice. "I thank you for the tea, Miss Heyden. I will take no more of your time." He stood up.

"I could offer a solution," she said, and now it was very definitely too late to retreat. "To your relatively impoverished state, that is. You need money to undo the neglect of years at Brambledean and to fulfill your duty to the people dependent upon you there. It might take you years, perhaps even the rest of your life, if you do it only through careful management. It is unfortunately necessary to put a great deal of money into a business before one can get money out of it. Perhaps you are considering taking out a loan or a mortgage if the property is not already mortgaged. Or perhaps you intend to marry a rich wife."

He stood very straight and tall, and his jaw had set into a hard line. His nostrils were still flared. He looked magnificent and even slightly menacing, and for a moment Wren regretted the words she had already spoken. But it was impossible to unsay them.

"I beg to inform you, Miss Heyden," he said curtly, "that I find your curiosity offensive. Good day to you."

"You are perhaps aware," she said, "that my uncle was enormously rich, much of his wealth deriving from the glassworks he owned in Staffordshire. He left everything to me, my aunt having predeceased him. He taught me a great deal about the business, which I helped him run during his last years and now run myself. The business has lost none of its momentum in the last year, and is, indeed, gradually expanding. And there are properties and investments even apart from that. I am a very wealthy woman, Lord

Riverdale. But my life lacks something, just as yours lacks ready money. I am twenty-nine years old, very nearly thirty, and I would like . . . someone to wed. In my own person I am not marriageable, but I do have money. And you do not."

She paused to see if he had something to say, but he looked as though he were rooted to the spot, his eyes fixed upon her, his jaw like granite. She was suddenly very glad Maude was in the room, though her presence was also embarrassing. Maude did not approve of any of this and did not scruple to say so when they were alone.

"Perhaps we could combine forces and each acquire what we want," Wren said.

"You are offering me . . . *marriage?*" he asked.

Had she not made herself clear? "Yes," she said. He continued to stare at her, and she became uncomfortably aware of the ticking of the clock.

"Miss Heyden," he said at last, "I have not even seen your face."

ALEXANDER WESTCOTT, EARL OF RIVERDALE, FELT RATHER AS though he had wandered into one of those bizarre dreams that did not seem to arise from anything he had ever experienced in the waking world. He had come in answer to an invitation from a distant neighbor. He had accepted many such invitations since coming into Wiltshire to the home and estate he really would very much rather not have inherited. It was incumbent upon him to meet and establish friendly relationships with the people among whom he intended to live.

No one he had asked knew anything much about Miss Heyden beyond the fact that she was the niece of a Mr. and Mrs. Heyden, who had died within days of each other a year or so ago and left

her Withington House. They had attended some of the social func-
tions close to Brambledean, his butler seemed to recall, though not
many, probably because of the distance. He had heard no mention
of their niece's ever being with them, though. William Bufford,
Alexander's steward, had not been able to add anything. He
had held the position for only four months, since the former steward had been let go with a generous bonus he had in no way earned.
Mr. Heyden had been a very elderly gentleman, according to the
butler. Alexander had assumed, then, that the niece was probably
in late middle age and was making an effort to establish herself in
the home that was now hers by inviting neighbors from near and
far to tea.

He had certainly not expected to be the lone guest of a lady who
was almost surely younger than he had estimated. He was not quite
sure how much younger. She had not risen to greet him but had
remained seated in a chair that had been pushed farther to the side
of the hearth than the one across from it and farther into the shade
provided by a heavily curtained window. The rest of the room was
bright with sunlight, making the contrast more noticeable and making the lady less visible. She sat gracefully in her chair and appeared
youthfully slim. Her hands were slender, long fingered, well manicured, and young. Her voice, soft and low pitched, was not that of a
girl, but neither was it that of an older woman. His guess was confirmed when she told him she was almost thirty—his own age.

She was wearing a gray dress, perhaps as half mourning. It was
stylish and becoming enough. And over her head and face she wore
a black veil. He could see her hair and her face through it, but neither with any clarity. It was impossible to know what color her hair
was and equally impossible to see her features. She had eaten nothing with her tea, and when she drank, she had held the veil outward

with one hand gracefully bent at the wrist and moved her cup beneath it.

To say that he had been uncomfortable since entering the room would be hugely to understate the case. And more and more as the minutes passed he had been wishing he had simply turned around and left as soon as he had understood the situation. It might have appeared ill-mannered, but good God, his being here alone with her—he hardly counted the presence of the maid—was downright improper.

But now, in addition to feeling uncomfortable, he was outraged. She had spoken openly about the desperate condition of Brambledean and his impoverished state. Not that he was personally impoverished. He had spent five years after his father's death working hard to bring Riddings Park in Kent back to prosperity, and he had succeeded. He had been settling into the comfortable life of a moderately prosperous gentleman when the catastrophe of last year had happened and he had found himself with his unwelcome title and the even more unwelcome encumbrance of an entailed estate that was on the brink of ruin. His moderate fortune had suddenly seemed more like a pittance.

But how dared she—a stranger—make open reference to it? The vulgarity of it had paralyzed his brain for a few moments. She had provided a solution, however, and his head was only just catching up to it. She was wealthy and wanted a husband. He was not wealthy and needed a rich wife. She had suggested that they supply each other's needs and marry. But—

Miss Heyden, I have not even seen your face.

It was bizarre. It was very definitely the stuff of that sort of dream from which one awoke wondering where the devil it had come from. Some other words of hers suddenly echoed in his mind.

In my own person I am not marriageable. What in thunder had she meant?

"No," she said, breaking the silence, "you have not, have you?" She turned her head to the left to look at her maid. "Maude, will you open the curtains, please?" The maid did so and Miss Heyden was suddenly bathed in light. Her dress looked more silver than gray. Her veil looked darker in contrast. She raised her hands. "I suppose you must see what you would be getting with my money, Lord Riverdale."

Was she being deliberately offensive? Or were her words and her slightly mocking manner actually a defense, her way of hiding discomfort? She *ought* to be uncomfortable. She raised her veil and threw it back over her head to land on the seat of the chair behind her. For a few moments her face remained half turned to the left.

Her hair was a rich chestnut brown, thick and lustrous, smooth at the front and sides, gathered into a cluster of curls high on the back of her head. Her neck was long and graceful. In profile her face was exquisitely beautiful—wide browed with long eyelashes that matched her hair, a straight nose, finely sculpted cheek, soft lips, firmly chiseled jaw, pale, smooth skin. And then she turned full face toward him and raised her eyelids. Her eyes were hazel, though that was a detail he did not notice until later. What he did notice was that the left side of her face, from forehead to jaw, was purple.

He inhaled slowly and mastered his first impulse to frown, even to recoil or actually take a step back. She was looking very directly into his face. There was no distortion of features, only the purple marks, some clustered and darker in shade, some fainter and more isolated. She looked rather as though someone had splashed purple paint down one side of her and she had not yet had a chance to wash it off.

"Burns?" he asked, though he did not think so. There would have been other damage.

"A birthmark," she said.

He had seen birthmarks, but nothing to match this. What would otherwise have been a remarkably beautiful face was severely, cruelly marred. He wondered if she always wore the veil in public. *In my own person I am not marriageable.*

"But I am wealthy," she said.

And he knew that it was indeed self-defense, that look of disdain, that boast of wealth, that challenge of the raised chin and very direct gaze. He knew that the coldness of her manner was the thinnest of veneers. *I am twenty-nine years old, very nearly thirty, and I would like someone to wed.* And because she was wealthy after the death of her uncle, she could afford to purchase what she wanted. It seemed startlingly distasteful, but was his own decision to go to London this year as soon as the Season began in earnest after Easter to seek a wealthy bride any the less so?

He suddenly remembered something she had said earlier. "Did you also make this offer to Mr. Sweeney and Mr. Richman?" he asked her. Ironic name, that—*Richman.* His question was ill-mannered, but there was nothing normal about this situation. "Did they refuse?"

"I did not," she told him, "and so they did not. Although neither was here for longer than half an hour, I knew long before that time expired that neither would suit me. I may wish to wed, Lord Riverdale, but I am not desperate enough to do so at all costs."

"You have judged, then, that I *will* suit you, that I am worth the cost?" he asked, raising his eyebrows and clasping his hands behind his back. He was still standing and looking down at her. If she found that fact intimidating, she was not showing it. He would suit her because of his title, would he? Then why had he been third on her list?

"It is impossible to know after just half an hour," she said, "but I believe so. I believe you are a gentleman, Lord Riverdale."

And the other two were not? "What exactly does that mean?" he asked. Good God, was he willing to stand here discussing the matter with her?

"I believe it means you would treat me with respect," she said.

He looked down at her disfigured face and frowned. "And that is all you ask of a marriage?" he asked. "Respect?"

"It is a large something," she said.

Was it? Was it enough? It was something he would surely be asking himself a number of times in the coming months. It was actually a good answer. "And would you treat me with respect if I married you for your money?" he asked.

"Yes," she said after pausing to think about it. "For I do not believe you would squander that money on your own pleasures."

"And upon what information do you base that judgment?" he asked her. "By your own admission you have a half hour's acquaintance with me."

"But I do know," she said, "that you have your own well-managed estate in Kent and could choose to live there in comfort for the rest of your life and forget about Brambledean Court. It is what your predecessor chose to do despite the fact that he was a very wealthy man. His wealth went to his daughter instead of to you, however. All you inherited was the title and the entailed property. Yet you have come here and employed a competent steward and clearly intend to take on the Herculean task of restoring the property and the farms and bettering the lives of the numerous people who rely upon you for their livelihood. Those are not the actions of a man who would use a fortune for riotous living."

She had more than a half hour's acquaintance with him, then. She had the advantage of him. They looked speculatively at each other.

"The question is," she said when he did not respond to her words, "could you live with *this*, Lord Riverdale?" She indicated the left side of her face with one graceful movement of her hand.

He gave the question serious consideration. The birthmark seriously disfigured her. More important, though, it must have had some serious impact upon the formation of her character if it had been there all her life. He had already seen her defensive, slightly mocking manner, her surface coldness, her isolation, the veil. The blemish on her face might be the least of the damage done to her. Her face might be easy enough to live with. It would be cruel to think otherwise. But how easy to live with would *she* be?

And was he giving serious consideration to her offer? But he must think seriously about some such marriage. And soon. The longer he lived at Brambledean, the more he saw the effects of poverty upon those whose well-being depended upon him.

"Do you wish to give me a definite no, Lord Riverdale?" Miss Heyden asked. "Or a possible maybe? Or a definite maybe, perhaps? Or even a yes?"

But he had not answered her original question. "We all have to learn to live behind the face and within the body we have been given," he said. "None of us deserves to be shunned—or adulated— upon looks alone."

"Are you adulated?" she asked with a slight mocking smile.

He hesitated. "I am occasionally told that I am the proverbial tall, dark, handsome man of fairy tales," he said. "It can be a burden."

"Strange," she said, still half smiling.

"Miss Heyden," he said, "I cannot possibly give you any answer now. You planned this long before I came. You have had time to think and consider, even to do some research. You have a clear advantage over me."

"A possibly possible maybe?" she said, and he was arrested for the moment by the thought that perhaps she had a sense of humor. "Will you come back, Lord Riverdale?"

"Not alone," he said firmly.

"I do not entertain," she told him.

"I understand that this has not been an entertainment," he said, "despite the invitation and the tea and cakes. It has been a job interview."

"Yes." She did not argue the point.

"I shall arrange something at Brambledean," he said. "A tea, perhaps, or a dinner, or a soiree—*something*—and I shall invite you with several other neighbors."

"I do not mingle with society or even with neighbors," she told him.

He frowned again. "As Countess of Riverdale, you would have no choice," he told her.

"Oh," she said, "I believe I would."

"No."

"You would be a tyrant?" she asked.

"I would certainly not allow my wife to make a hermit of herself," he said, "merely because of some purple marks on her face."

"You would not *allow*?" she said faintly. "Perhaps I need to think more carefully about whether you will suit me."

"Yes," he said, "perhaps you do. It is the best I can offer, Miss Heyden. I shall send an invitation within the next week or so. If you have the courage to come, perhaps we can discover whether your suggestion is something we wish to pursue more seriously. If you do not, then we both have an answer."

"If I have the courage," she said softly.

"Yes," he said. "I beg to take my leave with thanks for the tea. I shall see myself out."

He bowed and strode across the room. She neither got to her feet nor said anything. A few moments later he shut the drawing room doors behind him, blew out his breath from puffed cheeks, and descended the stairs. He informed the butler that he would fetch his own curricle and horses from the stables.

READ ON FOR AN EXCERPT FROM THE
FOURTH NOVEL IN THE WESTCOTT SERIES,

Someone to Care

AVAILABLE NOW FROM JOVE

Marcel Lamarr, Marquess of Dorchester, was not at all pleased when his carriage turned abruptly into the yard of an undistinguished country inn on the edge of an undistinguished country village and rocked to a halt. He made his displeasure felt, not in words, but rather in a cold, steady gaze, his quizzing glass raised almost but not quite to his eye, when his coachman opened the door and peered apologetically within.

"One of the leaders has a shoe coming loose, my lord," he explained.

"You did not check when we stopped for a change of horses an hour ago that all was in order?" his lordship asked. But he did not wait for an answer. "How long?"

His coachman glanced dubiously at the inn and the stables off to one side, from which no groom or hostler had yet emerged eagerly rushing to their aid. "Not long, my lord," he assured his employer.

"A firm and precise answer," his lordship said curtly, lowering his glass. "Shall we say one hour? And not a moment longer? We will step inside while we wait, André, and sample the quality of the ale served here." His tone suggested that he was not expecting to be impressed.

"A glass or two will not come amiss," his brother, André, replied cheerfully. "It has been a dashed long time since breakfast. I never understand why you always have to make such an early start and then remain obstinately inside the carriage when the horses are being changed."

The quality of the ale was indeed not impressive, but the quantity could not be argued with. It was served in large tankards, which foamed over to leave wet rings on the table. Quantity was perhaps the inn's claim to fame. The landlord, unbidden, brought them fresh meat pasties, which filled the two plates and even hung over the edges. They had been cooked by his own good wife, he informed them, bowing and beaming as he did so, though his lordship gave him no encouragement beyond a cool, indifferent nod. The good woman apparently made the best meat pasties, and, indeed, the best pies of any and all descriptions, for twenty miles around, probably more, though the proud husband did not want to give the appearance of being boastful in the singing of his woman's praises. Their lordships must judge for themselves, though he had no doubt they would agree with him and perhaps even suggest that they were the finest in all England—possibly even in Wales and Scotland and Ireland too. He would not be at all surprised. Had their lordships ever traveled to those remote regions? He had heard—

They were rescued from having to listen to whatever it was he had heard, however, when the outer door beyond the taproom opened and a trio of people, followed almost immediately by a steady stream of others, turned into the room. They were presumably villagers, all clad in their Sunday best, though it was not Sunday, all cheerful and noisy in their greetings to the landlord and one another. All were as dry as the desert and as empty as a beggar's bowl in a famine—according to the loudest of them—and in need of sustenance in the form of ale and pasties, it being not far off noon and the day's festivities not due to begin for another hour or so yet. They fully expected to be stuffed for the rest of the day once the festivities *did* begin, of course, but in the meanwhile . . .

But someone at that point—with a chorus of hasty agreement from everyone else—remembered to assure the host that nothing would or could compare with his wife's cooking. That was why they were here.

Each of the new arrivals became quickly aware that there were two strangers in their midst. A few averted their eyes in some confusion and scurried off to sit at tables as far removed from the strangers as the size of the room allowed. Others, somewhat bolder, nodded respectfully as they took their seats. One brave soul spoke up with the hope that their worships had come to enjoy the entertainments their humble village was to have on offer for the rest of the day. The room grew hushed as all attention was turned upon their worships in anticipation of a reply.

The Marquess of Dorchester, who neither knew the name of the village nor cared, looked about the dark, shabby taproom with disfavor and ignored everyone. It was possible he had not even heard the question or noticed the hush. His brother, more gregarious by nature, and more ready to be delighted by any novelty that presented itself, nodded amiably to the gathering in general and asked the inevitable question.

"And what entertainments would those be?" he asked.

It was all the encouragement those gathered there needed. They were about to celebrate the end of the harvest with contests in everything under the sun—singing, fiddle playing, dancing, arm wrestling, archery, wood sawing, to name a few. There were to be races for the children and pony rides and contests in needlework and cooking for the women. And displays of garden produce, of course, and prizes for the best. There was going to be something for everyone. And all sorts of booths with everything one could wish for upon which to spend one's money. Most of the garden produce and the women's items were to be sold or auctioned after the judging. There was to be a grand feast in the church hall in the late afternoon before general dancing in the evening. All the proceeds from the day were to go into the fund for the church roof.

The church roof apparently leaked like a sieve whenever there was a good rain, and only five or six of the pews were safe to sit upon. They got mighty crowded on a wet day.

"Not that some of our younger folk complain too loud about the crowding," someone offered.

"Some of them pray all week for rain on Sunday," someone else added.

André Lamarr joined in the general guffaw that succeeded these witticisms. "Perhaps we will stay an hour or two to watch some of the contests," he said. "Log sawing, did you say? And arm wrestling? I might even try a bout myself."

All eyes turned upon his companion, who had neither spoken nor shown any spark of interest in all the supposedly irresistible delights the day held in store.

They offered a marked contrast to the beholder, these two brothers. There was a gap of almost thirteen years in their ages, but it was not just a contrast in years. Marcel Lamarr, Marquess of Dorchester, was tall, well formed, impeccably elegant, and austerely handsome. His dark hair was silvering at the temples. His face was narrow, with high cheekbones and a somewhat hawkish nose and thin lips. His eyes were dark and hooded. He looked upon the world with cynical disdain, and the world looked back upon him—when it dared look at all—with something bordering upon fear. He had a reputation as a hard man, one who did not suffer fools gladly or at all. He also had a reputation for hard living and deep gambling among other vices. He was reputed to have left behind a string of brokenhearted mistresses and courtesans and hopeful widows during the course of his almost forty years. As for unmarried ladies and their ambitious mamas and hopeful papas, they had long ago given up hope of netting him. One quelling glance from those dark eyes of his could freeze even the most determined among them in their tracks. They consoled themselves by fanning the flames of the rumor that he lacked either a heart or a conscience, and he did nothing to disabuse them of such a notion.

André Lamarr, by contrast, was a personable young man, shorter, slightly broader, fairer of hair and complexion, and altogether more open and congenial of countenance than his brother. He liked people, and people generally liked him. He was always ready to be amused, and he was not always discriminating about where that amusement came from. At present he was charmed by these cheerful country folk and the simple pleasures they anticipated with such open delight. He would be perfectly happy to delay their journey by an hour or three—they had started out damnably early, after all. He glanced inquiringly at his brother and drew breath to speak. He was forestalled.

"No," his lordship said softly.

The attention of the masses had already been taken by a couple of new arrivals, who were greeted with a hearty exchange of pleasantries and comments upon the kindness the weather was showing them and a few lame flights of wit, which drew disproportionate shouts of merry laughter. Marcel could not imagine anything more shudderingly tedious than an afternoon spent at the insipid entertainment of a country fair, admiring large cabbages and crocheted doilies and watching troops of heavy-footed dancers prancing about the village green.

"Dash it all, Marc," André said, his eyebrows knitting into a frown. "I thought you were none too eager to get home."

"Nor am I," Marcel assured him. "Redcliffe Court is too full of persons for whom I feel very little fondness."

"With the exception of Bertrand and Estelle, I would hope," André said, his frown deepening.

"With the exception of the twins," Marcel conceded with a slight shrug as the innkeeper arrived to refill their glasses. Once more they brimmed over with foam, which swamped the table around them. The man did not pause to wipe the table.

The twins. Those two were going to have to be dealt with when he arrived home. They were soon to turn eighteen. In the natural course of events Estelle would be making her come-out during the London Season next year and would be married to someone eligible within a year or so after that, while Bertrand would go up to Oxford, idle away three or four years there, absorbing as little knowledge as possible, and then take up a career as a fashionable young man about town. *In the natural course of events . . .* There was, in fact, nothing natural about his children. They were both almost morbidly serious minded, perhaps even pious, perish the thought. Sometimes it was hard to believe he could have begotten them. But then he had not had a great deal to do with their upbringing, and doubtless that was where the problem lay.

"I am going to have to exert myself with them," he added.

"They are not likely to give you any trouble," André assured him. "They are a credit to Jane and Charles."

Marcel did not reply. For *that* was precisely the trouble. Jane Morrow was his late wife's elder sister—straitlaced and humorless and managing in her ways. Adeline, who had been a careless, fun-loving girl, had detested her. He still thought of his late wife as a girl, for she had died at the age of twenty when the twins were barely a year old. Jane and her husband had stepped dutifully into the breach to take care of the children while Marcel fled as though the hounds of hell were at his heels and as though he could outpace his grief and guilt and responsibilities. Actually, he had more or less succeeded with that last. His children had grown up with their aunt and uncle and older cousins, albeit at his home. He had seen them twice a year since their mother's death, almost always for fairly short spans of time. That home had borne too many bad memories. One memory, actually, but that one was very bad indeed. Fortunately, that home in Sussex had been abandoned and leased out after he inherited the title. They all now lived at Redcliffe Court in Northamptonshire.

"Which I am not," André continued with a rueful grin after taking a long pull at his glass and wiping froth off his upper lip with the back of his hand. "Not that anyone would expect me to be a credit to Jane and Charles, it is true. But I am not much of a credit to you either, am I, Marc?"

Marcel did not reply. It would not have been easy to do even if he had wanted to. The noise in the taproom was deafening. Everyone was trying to speak over one another, and it seemed that every second utterance was hilarious enough to be deserving of a prolonged burst of merriment. It was time to be on their way. Surely his coachman had had sufficient time to secure one loose shoe on one leg of one horse. He had probably done it in five minutes and was enjoying a tankard of ale of his own.

Beyond the open door of the taproom, Marcel could see that someone else had arrived. A woman. A lady, in fact. Undoubtedly a lady, though surprisingly she seemed to be alone. She was standing at the desk out in the hallway, looking down at the register the innkeeper was turning in her direction. She was well formed and elegant, though not young, at a guess. His eyes rested upon her with indifference until she half turned her head as though something at the main doors had taken her attention and he saw her face in profile. Beautiful. Though definitely not young. And . . . familiar? He looked more intently, but she had turned back to the desk to write in the register before stooping to pick up a bag and turning in the direction of the staircase. She was soon lost to view.

"Not that you are much of a credit to yourself sometimes," André said, apparently oblivious to Marcel's inattention to their conversation.

Marcel fixed his brother with a cool gaze. "I would remind you that my affairs are none of your concern," he said.

His brother added to the general din by throwing back his head and laughing. "An apt choice of words, Marc," he said.

"But still not your concern," Marcel told him.

"Oh, it may yet be," André said, "if a certain husband and his brothers and brothers-in-law and other assorted relatives and neighbors should happen to be in pursuit and burst in upon us."

They were coming from Somerset, where they had spent a few weeks at a house party hosted by a mutual acquaintance. Marcel had alleviated his boredom by flirting with a neighbor of his host who was a frequent visitor to the house, though he had stopped well short of any sexual intimacy with her. He had kissed the back of her hand once in full view of at least twenty other guests, and once when they were alone on the terrace beyond the drawing room. He had a reputation for ruthless and heartless womanizing, but he did make a point of not encouraging married ladies, and she was married. Someone, however—he suspected it was the lady herself—had told some highly embellished tale to the husband, and that worthy had chosen to take umbrage. All his male relatives to the third and fourth generations, not to mention his neighbors and several local dignitaries, had taken collective umbrage too, and soon it had been rumored that half the county was out for the blood of the lecherous Marquess of Dorchester. A challenge to a duel was not out of the question, ridiculous as it had seemed. Indeed, André and three of the other male house guests had offered their services as his second.

Marcel had written to Redcliffe Court to give notice of his intention to return home within the week and had left the house party before all the foolishness could descend into downright farce. He had no desire whatsoever either to kill a hotheaded farmer who neglected his wife or to allow himself to be killed. And he did not care the snap of two fingers if his departure was interpreted as cowardice.

He had been planning to go home anyway, even though home was full of people who had never been invited to take up residence there—or perhaps because of that fact. He had inherited the title from his uncle less than two years ago, and with it Redcliffe Court. He had inherited its residents too—the marchioness, his widowed aunt, and her daughter, and the daughter's husband with their youngest daughter. The three elder ones had already married and—mercifully—flown the nest with their husbands. Since he had little interest in making his home at Redcliffe, Marcel had not deemed it important to suggest that they remove to the dower house, which had been built at some time in the past for just this sort of situation. Now Jane and Charles Morrow were there too with their son and daughter, both of whom were adults but neither of whom had shown any sign of launching out into a life independent of their parents. The twins were at Redcliffe too, of course, since it was now rightfully their home.

One big, happy family.

"What *is* my concern," Marcel said into a slight lull in the noise level after the landlord had distributed steaming pasties from a giant platter and everyone had tucked in, "is your debts, André."

"Yes, I thought we would get to those," his brother said with a resigned sigh. "I would have had them paid off long before now if I had not had a run of bad luck at the tables just before we left for the country. I will come about, though, never fear. I always do. You know that. *You* always come about. If my creditors have the sheer impudence to come after you again, just ignore 'em. I always do."

"I have heard that debtors' prison is not the most comfortable of residences," Marcel said.

"Oh, I say, Marc. That was uncalled-for." His brother sounded both shocked and indignant. "You surely do not expect me to appear in company dressed in rags and wearing scuffed boots, do you? I would be a reproach to you if I patronized an inferior tailor or boot maker. Or, worse, none at all. I really cannot be faulted on *those* bills. As for the gaming, what is a fellow supposed to do for amusement? Read improving books at his fireside each night? Besides, it is a family failing, you must confess. Annemarie is forever living beyond her means and then dropping a whole quarter's allowance at the tables."

"Our sister," Marcel said, "has been the concern of William Cornish for the past eight or nine years." Though that did not stop her from begging the occasional loan when she had been more than usually extravagant or unlucky and quailed at the prospect of confessing all to her sober-minded husband. "He knew what he was getting into when he married her."

"She tells me he never scolds and never threatens her with debtors' prison," André said. "Extend me a loan, if you will be so good, Marc. Just enough to cover the gaming debts and perhaps a bit extra to get the more pressing of my creditors off my back, damn their eyes. I will pay back every penny. With interest," he added magnanimously.

The lady had reappeared. The door from the taproom into the dining room was also open, and Marcel could see her seating herself at a table in there, the room's sole occupant as far as he could see. She was facing him, though there was the width of two rooms and many persons between them. And by God, he really did know her. The marble goddess whom he had once upon a time tried his damnedest to turn to flesh and blood—with no success whatsoever. Well, almost none. She had been married at the time, of course, but he had tried flirting with her nevertheless. He was an accomplished flirt and rarely failed when he set his mind to a conquest. He had begun to think that she might be interested, but then she had told him to go away. Just that, in those exact words.

Go away, Mr. Lamarr, she had said.

And he had gone, his pride badly bruised. For a while he had feared that his heart had been too, but he had been mistaken. His heart had already been stone-cold dead.

Now, all these years later, she had fallen a long way from the pedestal of pride from which she had ruled her world then. And she was no longer young. But she was still beautiful, by God. The Countess of Riverdale. No, not that. She was no longer the countess, or even the dowager countess. He did not know what she called herself now. Mrs. Westcott? She was not that either. Mrs. Somebody

Else? He could take a look at the inn register, he supposed. If he was sufficiently interested, that was.

"You do not believe me," André said, sounding aggrieved. "I know I did not repay you the last time. Or the time before, if I am going to be perfectly honest, though I would not have lost such a vast sum at the races if the horse I bet on had not run lame out of the starting gate. He was as sure a thing as there ever was, Marc. You would have bet a bundle on him yourself if you had been there. It was just dashed rotten luck. But *this* time I will definitely repay you. I have a tip on a sure thing coming up next month. A *real* sure thing this time," he added when he saw his brother's skeptically raised eyebrow. "You ought to take a look at the horse yourself."

Hers was the face of someone who had suffered, Marcel thought, and was strangely more beautiful as a result. Not that he was interested in suffering women. Or women who must be close to forty or even past it, for all he knew. She was taking a look around, first at the presumably empty dining room and then through the door at the noisy crowd gathered in the taproom. Her eyes alit upon him for a moment, passed onward, and then returned. She looked directly at him for a second, perhaps two, and then turned sharply away as the innkeeper appeared at her elbow with the coffeepot.

She had both seen him and recognized him. If he was not mistaken—he did not raise his quizzing glass to observe more closely—there was a flush of color in her cheeks.

"I hate it," André said, "when you give me the silent treatment, Marc. It is dashed unfair, you know. You of all people."

"Me of all people?" Marcel turned his attention to his brother, who squirmed under his gaze.

"Well, you are not exactly a saint, are you?" he said. "Never have been. Throughout my boyhood I listened to tales of your extravagance and womanizing and reckless exploits. You were my idol, Marc. I did not expect that you would stand in judgment when I do only what you have always done."

André was twenty-seven, their sister two years older. They all had the same mother, but there had been an eleven-year span during which no live child had been born to her. And then, when she had given up hope of adding to her family, along had come first Annemarie and then André.

"Someone was careless in allowing such unsavory gossip to reach the ears of children," Marcel said. "And to make it sound like something that ought to be emulated."

"Not so young either," André said. "We used to listen at doors. Don't all children? Annemarie adored you too. She still does. I have no idea why she married Cornish. Every time he moves he is obscured by a cloud of dust."

"Dear me," Marcel said. "Not literally, I hope."

"Oh, I say," André said, suddenly distracted. "There is Miss Kingsley. I wonder what she is doing here."

Marcel followed the line of his gaze—toward the dining room. Kingsley. *Miss* Kingsley. She had never been married, except bigamously for twenty years or so to the Earl of Riverdale. He wondered if she had known. Probably not. Undoubtedly not, in fact. Her son had inherited his father's title and property after the latter's death and then been disinherited in spectacular fashion when his illegitimacy was exposed. Her daughters had been disinherited too and cast out of society like lepers. Had not one of them been betrothed and dropped like a hot potato?

Across the two rooms, he saw her look up and directly at him this time before looking away, though not hurriedly.

She was aware of him, then. Not just as someone she had

recognized. She was *aware* of him. He was almost certain of it, just as he had been all those years ago, though her final words to him had seemed to belie that impression. *Go away, Mr. Lamarr.*

"Well," André said cheerfully, picking up his tankard and draining its contents, "you can come and visit me in debtors' prison, Marc. Bring some clean linen when you come, will you? And take the soiled away with you to be laundered and deloused. But as for today, are we going to stay for a while and watch some of the contests? We are in no big hurry, after all, are we?"

"Your debts will be paid," Marcel said. "All of them. As you know very well, André." He did not add that the debt to him would also be forgiven. That went without saying, but his brother must be left with some pride.

"I am much obliged to you," André said. "I will pay you back within the month, Marc. Depend upon it. At least you are unlikely ever to have a similar problem with Bertrand. Or Estelle."

Quite right. Perhaps it was illogical to half wish that he would.

"But then," André added with a laugh, "they would not have been brought up to idolize you or emulate you, would they? If there is one person more dusty than William Cornish, it is Jane Morrow. And Charles. A well-matched couple, those two. *Are* we staying?"

Marcel did not answer immediately. He was looking at the former Countess of Riverdale, whom he could not quite think of as Miss Kingsley. She was eating, though he did not think that was one of the landlady's famous but somewhat overhearty meat pasties on her plate. And she was glancing up to look straight at him again, a sandwich suspended a short distance from her mouth. She half frowned, and he cocked one eyebrow before she looked away once more.

"I am staying," he said on a sudden impulse. "You are not, however. You may take the carriage."

"Eh?" André said inelegantly.

"I am staying," Marcel repeated. "You are not."

She was not wearing her bonnet and there was no other outdoor garment in sight. He could not see her bag beside her. She had signed the register—he had seen her do it—surely proof that she was staying, though why on earth she had chosen this particular inn in this particular village he could not imagine. Carriage trouble? Nor could he imagine why she was alone. Surely she had not fallen on such hard times that she could not afford servants. It was hardly likely she had come for the express purpose of participating in the harvest celebrations. He might soon be kicking himself from here to eternity, though, if she was *not* staying. Or if she repeated her famous reproof and sent him away.

But since when had he lacked confidence in himself, especially when it came to women? Not since Lady Riverdale herself, surely, and that must be fifteen years or more ago.

"Miss Kingsley," André said suddenly and with a clicking of his fingers and great indignation. He looked from his brother to her and back again. "Marc! Surely you are not . . ."

Marcel turned a cold gaze upon his brother, eyebrows raised, and the sentence was not completed. "You may take the carriage," he said again. "Indeed, you *will* take it. When you reach Redcliffe Court, you will inform Jane and Charles and anyone else who may be interested that I will arrive when I arrive."

"What sort of message is that?" André asked. "Charles will turn purple in the face and Jane's lips will disappear, and one of them is sure to say it is just like you. And Bertrand and Estelle will be disappointed."

Marcel doubted it. Did he wish André were right? For a moment he hesitated, but only for a moment. He had done nothing to earn their disappointment, and it was a bit late now to think of yearning for it.

"You hate this sort of country entertainment," André said. "Really, this is too bad of you, Marc. I am the one who suggested staying awhile. And I left that house party before I intended to in order to give you my company just when I was making some progress with the redhead."

"Did I ask for your company?" Marcel asked, his quizzing glass in his hand.

"Oh, I say. Next time I will know better," his brother told him. "I might as well go on my way, then. I always know when arguing with you is useless, Marc, which is most of the time. Or all the time. I hope she intends to be back on the road within the half hour. I hope she will have nothing to do with you. I hope she spits in your eye."

"Do you?" Marcel asked softly.

"Marc," his brother said. "She is *old*."

Marcel raised his eyebrows. "But so am I, brother," he said. "Forty on my next birthday, which is lamentably close. Positively decrepit."

"It is different for a man," his brother said, "and you very well know it. Good Lord, Marc."

He left a few minutes later, striding off without a backward glance and with only a cursory wave of the hand for the villager who asked redundantly if he was leaving. Marcel did not accompany him out to the innyard. He heard his carriage leave five minutes or so after that. He was stranded here, then. That was more than a bit foolish of him. The crowd was eyeing him uncertainly and then began to disperse, the platter of meat pasties having been reduced to a few crumbs and the festivities beyond the inn doors apparently being imminent. The former countess was drinking her coffee. Soon there were a mere half dozen villagers left in the taproom, and none of them occupied the tables between him and her. He gazed steadily at her, and she looked back once over the rim of her cup and held his gaze for a few moments.

Marcel got to his feet, strolled out into the hallway, turned the register to observe that yes, she had indeed signed it for a one-night stay as Miss Kingsley, and then strolled to the outside door to glance out. He crossed to the dining room and entered it by the hallway door. She looked up as he closed the door behind him and then set her cup down carefully in its saucer, her eyes on what she was doing. Her hair, swept back and upward into an elegant chignon, was still the color of honey. Unless his advanced age had dimmed his excellent eyesight, there was not a single strand of gray there yet. Or any lines on her face or sagging of chin. Or of bosom.

"You told me to go away," he said. "But that was fifteen years or so ago. Was there a time limit?"

There was nothing like a family Christmas to make a person feel warm about the heart—oh, and a little wistful too. And perhaps just a bit melancholy.

Brambledean Court in Wiltshire was the scene of just such a gathering for the first time in many years. All the Westcotts were gathered there, from Eugenia, the seventy-one-year-old Dowager Countess of Riverdale, on down to her newest great-grandson, Jacob Cunningham, the three-month-old child of the former Camille Westcott and her husband, Joel. They had all been invited by Alexander Westcott, the present Earl of Riverdale and head of the family, and Wren, his wife of six months.

The house had been unlived in for more than twenty years before Alexander inherited the title, and had been shabby even back then. By the time he arrived it had grown shabbier, and the park surrounding it had acquired a sad air of general neglect. It had been a formidable challenge for Alexander, who took his responsibilities seriously but did not have the fortune with which to carry them out.

That problem had been solved with his marriage, since Wren was vastly wealthy. The fortune she had brought to their union enabled them to repair the damage of years and restore the house and park on the one hand and the farms on the other to their former prosperity and glory. But Rome was not built in a day, as the dowager countess was not hesitant to remark after her arrival. There was still a great deal to be done. A very great deal. But at least the house now had a lived-in air.

There were a few other guests besides the Westcotts and their spouses and children. There were Mrs. Kingsley from Bath and her son and daughter-in-law, the Reverend Michael and Mary Kingsley from Dorsetshire. They were the mother, brother, and sister-in-law of Viola, a former Countess of Riverdale, whose marriage of upward of twenty years to the late earl had been exposed spectacularly after his death as bigamous. There had been many complications surrounding that whole ugly episode. But all had ended happily for Viola. For on this very day, Christmas Eve, she had married Marcel Lamarr, Marquess of Dorchester, in the village church. The newlyweds were at the house now, as well as Dorchester's eighteen-year-old twin son and daughter.

And Colin Handrich, Baron Hodges, Wren's brother, was here too. For the first time in his twenty-six years he was experiencing a real family Christmas, and after some feeling of awkwardness yesterday despite a warm welcome from everyone, he was now enjoying it greatly.

The house was abuzz with activity. There had been the wedding this morning—a totally unexpected event, it must be added. The marquess had burst in upon them without any prior warning last evening, armed with a special license and an urgent proposal of marriage for Viola a mere couple of months after he had broken off their engagement in spectacularly scandalous fashion during their betrothal party at his own home. But that was another story, and Colin had not been there to experience it firsthand. The wedding had been followed by a wedding breakfast hastily and impressively thrown together by Riverdale's already overworked staff under Wren's supervision.

This afternoon had been one of laughter-filled attempts to add to yesterday's decorations. Fragrant pine boughs and holly and ivy and mistletoe, not to mention ribbons and bells and bows and all the other paraphernalia associated with the season, were everywhere, it seemed—in the drawing room, on the stairs, in the hall, in the dining room. A kissing bough, fashioned under the guidance of Lady Matilda Westcott, unmarried eldest daughter of the dowager countess, hung in the place of honor from the center of the drawing room ceiling and had been causing laughter and whistles and blushes ever since yesterday as it was put to use. There had been the Yule log to haul in today and position in the large hearth in the great hall, ready to be lit in the evening.

And all the while as they moved about and climbed and perched, pinned and balanced, pricked fingers and kissed and blushed, tantalizing smells had been wafting up from the kitchens below of Christmas puddings and gingerbread and mince pies and the Christmas ham, among other mouthwatering delights.

And there had been the snow as a constant wonder and distraction, drawing them to every available window far more often than was necessary to assure themselves that it had not stopped falling and was not melting as fast as it came down. It had been threatening for days and had finally begun during the wedding this morning. It had continued in earnest all day since then, until by now it must be knee-deep.

Snow, especially such copious amounts of it, was a rarity in England, especially for Christmas. They did not stop telling one another so all afternoon.

And now, this evening, the village carolers had waded up the driveway to sing for them. The Yule log had been lit and the family had gathered and the carolers had come against all expectation, exclaiming and stamping boots and shaking mufflers and slapping mittens and rubbing at red noses to make them redder—and then quieting down and growing self-conscious as they looked around at the family and friends gathered in the great hall to listen to them.

They sang for half an hour, and their audience listened and occasionally joined in. The dowager countess and Mrs. Kingsley were seated in ornately carved and padded wooden chairs close to the great fireplace to benefit from the logs that flamed and crackled around the Yule log in the hearth. It gave more the effect of cheerfulness than actual warmth to the rest of the hall, but everyone else was happy to stand until the carolers came to the end of their repertoire and everyone applauded. Alexander gave a short speech wishing everyone a happy and healthy New Year. Then they all moved about, mingling and chatting and laughing merrily as glasses of wassail and trays of warm mince pies were brought up from belowstairs and offered first to the carolers and then to the house guests.

After a while Colin found himself standing in the midst of it all, alone for the moment, consciously enjoying the warm, festive atmosphere of the scene around him. From what he could observe, there was not one discordant note among the happy crowd—if one ignored the impatience with which the dowager was batting away the heavy shawl Lady Matilda was attempting to wrap about her shoulders.

This was what family should be like.

This was what Christmas should always be like.

It was an ideal of perfection, of course, and ideals were not often attained and were not sustainable for long when they were. Life could never be unalloyed happiness, even for a family that was close, such as this one. But there were moments when it was, and this was surely one of them. It deserved to be recognized and enjoyed and savored.

And envied.

He smiled at the three young ladies across the hall who had their heads together, chattering and laughing and stealing glances his way. It was not altogether surprising. He was not unduly conceited, but he *was* a young, single gentleman in possession of a title and fortune. Single gentlemen above the age of twenty were in short supply here at Brambledean. Indeed, he was the only one, with the exception of Captain Harry Westcott, Viola's son, who had arrived back from the wars in the Peninsula two days ago—also unexpectedly—on recruitment business for his regiment. Unfortunately for the three ladies, however, the captain was the brother of one of them and the first cousin of another. Only Lady Estelle Lamarr, the Marquess of Dorchester's daughter, was unrelated to him by blood, though she had become his stepsister this morning.

When they saw Colin smile, they all ducked their heads, while above the general hubbub he could hear one of them giggling. But why would he not look and be pleased with what he saw—and flattered by their attention? They were all remarkably pretty in different ways, younger than he and unattached, as far as he knew. They were all eligible, even Abigail Westcott, Viola and the late Earl of Riverdale's daughter, whose birth had been declared illegitimate almost three years ago after the disastrous revelation concerning her father's bigamy. Colin did not care a fig for that supposed stain upon her name. Lady Jessica Archer was half sister of the Duke of Netherby and daughter of the former duke and his second wife, one of the Westcott sisters.

It had not been easy during the six months since Wren had married Alexander to sort out the complex relationships within this family, but Colin believed he had finally mastered them, even the step and half connections.

He was about to stroll across the hall to ask the three young ladies how they had enjoyed the caroling when his sister appeared at his side and handed him a glass of wassail.

"You are going to have to stay here tonight after all, thanks to the snow, Colin," she said, sounding smug.

"But you already have a houseful, Roe," he protested, though in truth he knew it would be impossible to go home tonight and even more impossible to return tomorrow. Home was Withington House, nine miles away, where he had been living since the summer. It belonged to Wren, but he had gladly moved in there when she had offered it, rather than stay in London, where he had lived throughout the year for the past five years.

"*Roe*," she said softly and fondly. She had been christened Rowena as a baby. *Roe* had been Colin's childhood name for her, and he still called her that when in conversation with her, even though her name had been legally changed to Wren. "One more guest will cause no upheaval, and it will make us all a lot happier. Me in particular. Was not the carol singing wonderful?"

"Wonderful," he agreed, though the singers had been more hearty than musical.

"And the wedding this morning was perfect," she said with a happy sigh. "And the wedding breakfast after it. And the snow and putting up more decorations and . . . oh, and *everything*. Have you ever lived through a happier day?"

He pretended to think about it, his eyes raised to the high ceiling of the great hall, his forefinger tapping his chin. He raised the finger. "Yes, I have, actually," he said. "The day Alexander came to call at my rooms in London and I discovered that you were still alive, and I went with him to meet you for the first time in almost twenty years."

"Ah. Yes." She beamed at him, her eyes luminous with memory. "Oh yes, indeed, Colin, you are right. When I looked at you, and you spoke my name, and I realized you were that little mop-haired boy I remembered . . . It was indeed an unforgettable day."

He had been told when he was six years old that ten-year-old Rowena had died shortly after their aunt took her away from Roxingley, supposedly to consult a physician about the great strawberry birthmark that swelled over one side of her face, disfiguring her quite horribly. In reality there had been no physician and no death. Aunt Megan had taken Rowena from a home in which she had been isolated and frequently locked in her room so that no one would have to look at her. Aunt Megan had married Reginald Heyden, a wealthy gentleman of her acquaintance, soon after, and the two of them had adopted Rowena Handrich, changed her name to Wren Heyden, and raised her as their own. Colin, meanwhile, had grieved deeply for his beloved sister and playmate. He had discovered the truth only this year, when Alexander had sought him out soon after marrying her.

Wren was lovely despite the purple marks down the left side of her face where the strawberry swelling had been when she was a child. And she was looking more beautiful than ever these days. Alexander had lost no time in getting her with child.

"Was Christmas a happy time for you when you were a boy, Colin?" Her face turned a little wistful as she gazed into his.

He had grown up as part of a family—there were his mother and father, an elder brother, and three older sisters. Roxingley Park was a grand property where there had always been an abundance of the good things in life. The material things, that was. His father had been a wealthy man, just as Colin was now. Christmases had come and gone, even after the supposed death of Rowena, the youngest of his sisters, and the real death of his brother Justin nine years later. But he did not remember them as warm family occasions. Not like this one. Not even close.

"I am sorry," she said. "You are looking suddenly melancholy. Aunt Megan and Uncle Reggie always made Christmas very special for me and for each other. Not like this, of course. There were just the three of us. But very lovely nevertheless and abounding with love. Life will get better for you, Colin. I promise. And you will be staying tonight. You will be here all day tomorrow and probably all of Boxing Day too. *Definitely*, in fact, for we will press ahead with the plans for our Boxing Day evening party even if some of our invited guests find it impossible to get here. This is going to be the best Christmas ever. I have decided, and I will not take no for an answer. It already is the best, in fact, though I do wish Aunt Megan and Uncle Reggie were still alive to be a part of it. You would have loved them, and they would have loved you."

He opened his mouth to reply, but Alexander had caught her eye from his position behind the refreshments and she excused herself to weave her way back toward him in order to distribute more of the wassail to the carolers before they left.

Colin looked about the hall again, still feeling warm and happy—and a bit melancholy at having been reminded of the brokenness that was and always had been his own family. And perhaps too at the admission that, though he was now Baron Hodges himself and therefore head of his family, and though he was twenty-six years old and no longer had the excuse of being a mere boy, he had done nothing to draw its remaining members together—his mother and his three sisters and their spouses and children. He had not been to Roxingley since he was eighteen, when he had gone for his father's funeral. He had done nothing to perpetuate his line, to create his own family, something more like this one. The Westcotts had suffered troubles enough in the last few years and no doubt before that too. Life was like that. But their troubles had seemed to strengthen rather than loosen the bonds that held them.

Not so with the Handrich family.

Could it be done? Was it possible? Was he ready at least to try? To do something positive with his life instead of just drifting from day to day and more or less hiding from the magnitude of what doing something would entail? His eyes alit again upon the group across the hall. The young ladies had been joined by the three schoolboy sons of Lord and Lady Molenor. Winifred Cunningham, Abigail's young niece, was with them too, as were a couple of the younger carolers. They were all merrily chatting and laughing and behaving as though this Christmas Eve was the very happiest of days—as indeed it was.

Colin felt suddenly as though he were a hundred years older than the oldest of them.

"A penny for them," a voice said from close by, and he turned toward the speaker.

Ah. Lady Overfield.

Just the sight of her lifted his mood and brought a smile to his face. He liked and admired her more than any other woman of his acquaintance, perhaps more than any other person of either gender. For him she lived on a sort of pedestal, above the level of other mortals. He might have been quite in love with her if she had been of an age with him or younger. Though even then it would have seemed somehow disrespectful. She was his ideal of womanhood.

She was Alexander's elder sister, Wren's sister-in-law, and beautiful through and through. He was well aware that other people might not agree. She was fair-haired and trim of figure and had a face that was amiable more than it was obviously lovely. But his life experiences had taught him to look deeper than surface appearances to discover beauty or its lack. Lady Overfield was perhaps the most beautiful woman he had ever met. There was something about her manner that exuded a seemingly unshakable tranquility combined with a twinkling eye. But she did not hoard it. Rather, she turned it outward to touch other people. She did not draw attention to herself but bestowed it upon others. She was everyone's best friend in the family, the one with whom all felt appreciated and comfortable, the one who would always listen and never judge. She had been Wren's first friend ever—Wren had been close to thirty at the time—and had remained steadfast. Colin would have loved her for that alone.

He had liked her since his rediscovery of his sister, but he had felt particularly warm toward her since yesterday. He had felt a bit awkward being among the members of a close family, though everyone had made him welcome. Lady Overfield had singled him out, though, for special attention. She had talked with him all evening from her perch on the window seat in the room where they were all gathered, drawing him out on topics he would not normally have raised with a woman, talking just enough herself to make it a conversation. He had soon relaxed. He had also felt honored, for to her he must appear little more than a gauche boy. He guessed she must be somewhere in her mid-thirties to his twenty-six. He did not know how long she had been a widow, but she must have been quite young when she lost her husband, poor lady. She had no children. She lived with Mrs. Westcott, her mother, at Alexander's former home in Kent.

She had asked him a question.

"I was trying to decide," he said, nodding in the direction of the group of young people, "which of the three ladies I should marry."

She looked startled for a moment and then laughed with him as she glanced across the room.

"Oh, indeed?" she said. "But have you not heard, Lord Hodges, that when one gazes across a crowded room at the one and only person destined to be the love of one's life, one feels no doubt whatsoever? If you look and see *three* possible candidates for the position, then it is highly probable that none of them is the right choice."

"Alas," he said. "Are you quite sure?"

"Well, not *quite*," she admitted. "They are all remarkably pretty, are they not? I must applaud your taste. I have observed too that they are not indifferent to your charms. They have been stealing glances at you and exchanging nudges and giggles since yesterday—at least Abby and Jessica have. Estelle came only today after the wedding, but she seems equally struck by you. But Lord Hodges, *are* you in search of a wife?"

"No," he said after a slight hesitation. "Not really. I am not, but I am beginning to feel that perhaps I ought to be. Sometime. Maybe soon. Maybe not for a few years yet. And how is that for a firm, decisive answer?"

"Admirable," she said, and laughed again. "I expect the young female world and that of its mamas will go into raptures when you do begin the search in earnest. You must know that you are one of

England's most eligible bachelors and not at all hard on the eyes either. Wren is over the moon with delight that you will be staying here tonight, by the way. She was disappointed last evening when you insisted upon returning home."

"I believe the snow is still coming down out there, Lady Overfield," he said. "If I tried to get home, there might be nothing more than my eyebrows showing above the snow when someone came in search of me. It would appear that I am stuck here for at least a couple of days."

"Better here than there even if you could get safely home," she said. "You would be stuck there and all alone for Christmas. The very thought makes me want to weep. But will you call me Elizabeth? Or even Lizzie? My brother is, after all, married to your sister, which fact makes us virtually brother and sister, does it not? May I call you Colin?"

"Please do, Elizabeth," he said, feeling a bit awkward at saying her name. It seemed an imposition. But she had requested it, a particular mark of acceptance. What a very happy Christmas this was turning out to be—and it was not even Christmas Day yet. How could he even consider feeling melancholy?

"You ought to be very thankful for the snow," she said. "Now you will not have to waste part of the morning in travel. Christmas morning is always one of my favorites of the year, if not my *very* favorite. Is it not a rare treat indeed to have a white Christmas? And has that been remarked upon a time or two already today? But I cannot remember the last time it happened. And it is not even a light dusting to tease the hopes of children everywhere, but a massive fall. I would wager upon the sudden appearance of an army of snowmen and perhaps snowladies tomorrow, as well as a heavenly host of snow angels. And snowball fights and sleigh rides—there is an ancient sleigh in the carriage house, apparently. And sledding down the hill. There are sleds too, which really ought to be in a museum somewhere, according to Alex, but which will doubtless work just as well as new ones would. There is even a hill, though not a very mountainous one, alas. It will do, however. You will not be sorry you stayed."

"Perhaps," he said, "I will choose to spend a more traditional Christmas in a comfortable chair by the fire, eating rich foods and imbibing spiced wine and napping."

She looked at him, startled again. "Oh, you could not possibly be so poor-spirited," she said, noticing the twinkle in his eye. "You would be the laughingstock. A pariah. Expelled from Brambledean in deep disgrace, never to be admitted within its portals again even if you *are* Wren's brother."

"Does that also mean none of your young cousins would be willing to marry me?" he asked.

"It absolutely means just that," she assured him. "Even I would not."

"Ah," he said, slapping a hand to the left side of his chest. "My heart would be broken."

"I would have no pity on you," she said, "even if you came to me with the pieces in your hand."

"Cruel." He sighed. "Then I had better be prepared to go out tomorrow and make a few snow angels and hurl a few snowballs, preferably at you. I warn you, though, that I was the star bowler on my cricket team at school."

"What modesty," she said. "Not to mention gallantry. But I see that two of the footmen are lighting the carolers' lanterns. They are about to leave. Shall we go and see them on their way?"

She took the arm he offered and they joined the throng about the great doors. The noise level escalated as everyone thanked the carolers again and the carolers thanked everyone in return and everyone wished one another a happy Christmas.

He *was* happy, Colin decided. He was a part of all this. He was an accepted member of the Westcott family, even if merely an extended member. Lady Overfield—Elizabeth—had remarked that they were virtually brother and sister. She had joked and laughed with him. Her hand was still tucked through his arm. There was surely no greater happiness.

There were a snowball fight and sledding to look forward to tomorrow.

And gifts to exchange.

And goose and stuffing and Christmas pudding.

Yes, it felt very good to belong.

To a family that was not really his own.

Read on for an excerpt from the
sixth novel in the Westcott series,

Someone to Honor

Available now

H ome at last!

Well, back in England, at least. Twenty months had passed since his last brief, disastrous stay here, after the Battle of Waterloo, in 1815. Now he was back.

But as Lieutenant Colonel Gilbert Bennington, Gil to his friends and acquaintances, disembarked from the packet in Dover after making the night crossing from Calais, he felt only weariness, irritation, and a heavy foreboding that coming home was not going to bring happily-ever-after with it.

He grimaced at the sight of an elegant traveling carriage, ducal crests emblazoned upon its doors, standing on the dock, for it was obviously awaiting him. Or, more specifically, Avery Archer, Duke of Netherby, one of his three traveling companions. Gil would have far preferred to hire a chaise for the journey ahead, but he might have guessed that nothing but opulent splendor would do for His Grace on his own native soil. And it had to be admitted, grudgingly, that this conveyance would be far better than a hired chaise for one of their other companions, Harry. Harry was looking gray with exhaustion.

Gil had not intended to have three companions for the journey. He had recently spent a year on the island of St. Helena as part of the garrison that guarded Napoleon Bonaparte during his second exile. When he had returned, on a ship bound for France rather than England for the simple reason that it was the first outward-bound vessel after his term of duty was over, he had gone to Paris. There he had discovered, quite by chance, that his old friend and comrade Major Harry Westcott, who he thought had died at Waterloo, was convalescing at a facility for military officers. Gil had last seen him after the battle, when his injuries had seemed mortal. But against all odds Harry had survived—barely. And after more than a year and a half he was itching to go home, though his physicians advised strongly against the strenuous journey. He was still not fully recovered.

Gil had offered to escort him, and Harry had jumped at the opportunity. He had invited Gil to stay with him for a while once they were back home, and Gil had accepted. He wanted to be in England. He *needed* to be there. But he was reluctant to go all the way to his own home. There were things that must be done first.

But then, at the last possible moment, two of Harry's kinsmen had arrived in Paris with the purpose of conveying him home themselves. And although Harry himself was a mere illegitimate member of his family, his kinsmen were powerful men. Aristocrats. They were Avery Archer, who had once been Harry's guardian—before the illegitimacy was discovered—and was now his brother-in-law; and Alexander Westcott, Earl of Riverdale, head of the family and holder of the title that had once been Harry's—also before the discovery of the illegitimacy.

It was a bit of a complicated family, Gil understood. Harry had never spoken much about it.

They had traveled together, the four of them, though Gil had tried to bow out. He did *not* feel comfortable in aristocratic company. Despite his senior military rank, he was in reality a nobody from nowhere and as illegitimate as Harry. A gutter rat, if one chose to call a spade a spade. But Harry had begged him not to change his mind, so Gil had come. His friend would need him after his relatives had conveyed him home and returned to their own families.

"Ah," the Duke of Netherby said now, looking at his carriage through the quizzing glass he raised to his eye. "A sight for sore eyes. How much did you wager, Harry, that my carriage would not be here?"

"Absolutely nothing, if you will recall," Harry said. "It would be more than the life of your coachman is worth, or his livelihood anyway, to be late."

"Quite so," His Grace said with a sigh. "Let us go find a nearby inn and enjoy a good English breakfast. I daresay there will be a meaty bone somewhere on the premises too."

The meaty bone would be for Gil's dog, a great lump of a canine of indeterminate breed that had followed him from Waterloo to England to St. Helena, to France, and now back to England. She stood panting at Gil's side, happy, he believed, to have her paws on firm soil again. Within moments she was inside the Duke of Netherby's carriage with the rest of them, draped over Gil's feet like a large sheepskin rug and half over Riverdale's boots too.

The carriage transported them the short distance to what Gil did not doubt was the best inn in Dover, where three of them ate a hearty breakfast and Harry nibbled without enthusiasm upon a piece of toast. His Grace then called for pen, ink, and paper and wrote a brief note to inform his duchess of their safe return to England and of the change in their planned destination. His relatives had intended to take Harry to London, where other relatives awaited him, including his mother, the Marchioness of Dorchester, and one of his sisters. But Harry had insisted upon going to Hinsford Manor in Hampshire, where he had grown up. He wanted the quiet of the countryside, he had explained to Gil. More to the point, he wanted to avoid being fussed over, and fussed over he would be if he went to London.

Having arranged for the note to be sent, His Grace joined the other three in his carriage and it proceeded northward without further delay. It was certainly a comfortable carriage, Gil conceded. It also attracted the gawking attention of everyone it passed.

Harry, on the seat opposite, next to Riverdale, was even paler than usual, if that was possible, and thin almost to the point of emaciation. His good looks and ever-cheerful, energetic charm had deserted him. He was twenty-six years old, eight years younger than Gil. Apparently for the six months following Waterloo the army physicians had been in daily expectation of his dying. He had been taken to Paris after the first month—why not back to England none of the military authorities seemed to know. Even after the six months he was being assailed by one infection and fever after another, only to have to face a painful, life-threatening surgery five months ago to remove an embedded bullet, which his surgeons judged had shifted closer to his heart. Having it removed would very possibly kill him, they had warned. Not doing so certainly would. He had survived the excruciatingly painful ordeal, but the renewed infections and fevers had almost killed him anyway.

Gil hoped the ordeal of their trip would not accomplish what all the fevers and infections had been unable to do. He hoped Harry would survive the journey, which Gil had encouraged and arranged.

"You must be happy to be back in England, Harry," Riverdale said. "Though it is unfortunate you are being treated to a typical English welcome." He gestured toward the window. Heavy clouds hung low over a landscape that was being buffeted by a west wind and assaulted by a slanting rain.

"It is indeed a good feeling," Harry said, gazing out upon the scene. "But I have been thinking and wondering. I suppose it is altogether possible I will be descended upon not just by rain in the next week or so. Do you think there is any chance the family will come visiting since I am not going to London to visit them?"

"I would certainly not wager against it," Alexander said. "They have all been eagerly awaiting your arrival in London. I doubt your choosing to go to Hinsford instead will deter them. It is not terribly far from London, after all."

"The devil!" Harry muttered, closing his eyes and setting his head back against the plush cushions.

"I suppose," Riverdale added, "you have chosen to go straight to Hinsford at least partly in order to avoid the commotion awaiting you in town."

"Yes, at least partly," Harry admitted—and then laughed unexpectedly without opening his eyes. "I ought to have known better. And if I *had* known better, I would have felt obliged to warn you, Gil. There is possibly no other family on earth that rallies around its members as the Westcotts do—and that includes those who are married to Archers and Cunninghams and Handriches and Lamarrs and . . . Did I miss anyone? Once a Westcott, always a Westcott, it seems. Even if one is a bastard."

"You know that is a word we never use within the family, Harry," Riverdale said. "Think of your sisters when you use it, if you please, even if not of yourself."

Gil, without showing any outer sign, was wishing like hell that Harry *had* thought to warn him that his fond family was likely to descend upon him en masse even though Hinsford was some distance from London. Most of them would be gathered in London now for the spring session of parliament and the social whirl of the Season. He might have guessed, of course, when these two men turned up unexpectedly in Paris as emissaries of the family. But it had not occurred to him even then that the rest of them would actually journey into the country to see Harry when he arrived home.

After all, no family had ever rallied around him, either on his mother's side—they had turned her out, never to relent, after she conceived him—or on his father's. The most his father had ever done for him was purchase his ensign's commission in a foot regiment after word had reached him of the death of Gil's mother. Gil had been at that time a sergeant with a British regiment in India. Later he had purchased a lieutenancy for his son too, but Gil had written to him on that occasion, and not to thank him—why should he thank a father who had ignored his very existence for more than twenty years, only to swoop down seemingly from nowhere with a gift his son had neither wanted nor asked for? Gil had written to inform the man that he need supply no further patronage and that it would be refused if it was offered. By that time Gil had been wishing heartily that he were still a sergeant. He had been happier with his own kind.

He and Harry had fought together in the Peninsula and at Toulouse and Waterloo. They had been friends from the start, perhaps because they had one thing in common apart from their regiment and military experiences: They were both bastards—yes, it was always as well to call a spade a spade—in a gentlemen's army. In the officer ranks of the army, that was. Hard work and prowess, talent and dedication to one's men and mission, counted for far less in the officers' tents and messes than did birth and fortune. Oh, Gil and Harry had never been ostracized outright, it was true, but they had always been made in subtle and sometimes not-so-subtle ways to feel that they were outsiders. That they did not quite belong. That they were a bit of an embarrassment. Occasionally more than a bit.

He gazed out the window on his side of the carriage at the gloomy countryside, though it was only the heavy clouds and rain that caused the gloom. It was *England*, and he felt a rush of affection for his native land even if there were not very many happy memories associated with it.

He had a home of his own here, Rose Cottage in Gloucestershire, purchased during the Indian years when he had acquired what had seemed to him—it still seemed—a fabulous fortune in prizes. He had invested what remained of it after the purchase, engaging the services of an agent in London he had been persuaded to trust, happily as it had turned out. He could have lived like a gentleman from that moment on if he had chosen to leave the army. He had not done so, however. Nor had he done so anytime since. The army was all he had known since he left home at the age of fourteen in a recruiting sergeant's untender care, and on the whole it had been good to him. The life had suited him.

He *had* gone home after the Battle of Toulouse in 1814, though, taking his pregnant wife with him. He had taken her to Rose Cottage—a great deal larger actually than a cottage despite its name. And all his own. His anchor to this world. The place where he would send down roots. The place where he would raise his family. Home. The dream of happiness had become even more of a reality when Katy was born—Katherine Mary Bennington. Ah, that achingly happy day following hours of pain for Caroline and anxiety for him. That dark-haired baby. That warm little bundle of squawking humanity.

His daughter.

It was a brief interval in his life almost too painful to look back upon. Therefore, he rarely did. But some memories went deeper than conscious thought. They were *there* always, like a leaden weight, or like an open wound that would not quite kill him but would never heal either.

Happily-ever-after had begun to slip away when Caroline, her confinement over, had become more restless than usual and peevish about the inferior size of the house and the dullness of the village on the edge of which it stood, and the insipid nature of their social life there. It had slipped further a little more than three months after Katy's birth when Gil had been recalled to his regiment following Napoleon Bonaparte's escape from his first exile, on the island of Elba, and his return to France to gather another vast army about him.

Caroline had wanted to go too, leaving the baby with her mother. He had refused. Following the drum was no life for a lady, though Caroline had done it for a few months before he married her when her mother brought her to the Peninsula after she had finished her lady's schooling. And a baby needed her mother and a home and her father's financial support and the promise of his return as soon as he was able. A baby actually needed *both* parents, but life could not always be ideal. He had tried to make it as secure and comfortable as was possible under the circumstances.

By the time he had hurried home after Waterloo, alarmed by

increasingly mutinous letters from his unhappy wife, she was gone. So was their daughter. And her nurse. But no one—not their servants, not any of their neighbors—knew just where they had gone or when they were likely to return. He had not seen either one of them since, though he did know that Katy was in Essex, living with her grandparents, General Sir Edward and Lady Pascoe, to whom, unbeknown to him, she had been taken before Waterloo, soon after his own departure for Belgium. Lady Pascoe had refused to let him see her, however, when he had gone to her home, frantic for news. Caroline, he had discovered later, had gone off to a house party at the invitation of old friends and from there to another party and another. Gil could neither pursue his quest to retrieve his daughter nor go in search of his errant wife before he was abruptly and unexpectedly posted to St. Helena. Doubtless thanks to General Pascoe.

Katy was still with her grandparents. Caroline was dead. Word of her demise had reached him on St. Helena.

Now, more than a year later, the situation had become more fraught. General Pascoe was back at home, and he and his wife were determined to keep custody of Katy. They had acquired a lawyer who intended to see that the whole matter be wrapped up right and tight—and legally—in their favor. They had two angry, threatening letters he had written from St. Helena to use against him in addition to Lady Pascoe's account of the frantic, demanding visits he had made to the general's home and the lies Caroline had told when she took their daughter to her mother. He would be made to appear to be a violent, uncontrolled man and an unfit father.

Gil's first instinct upon leaving St. Helena had been to return as soon as he could to England, where he would rage at his in-laws until they relinquished his daughter into his care and he could take her back home where she belonged. A cooler wisdom had prevailed, however, and he had hired a lawyer of his own, a man recommended by his agent as the best of his kind in London. And Grimes—of the law firm Grimes, Hanson, and Digby—had insisted in the lawyerly letter he had written his client after the contract was signed that Lieutenant Colonel Bennington leave the matter of the custody of his daughter entirely in his hands and do absolutely nothing himself.

Doing nothing was the hardest thing Gil had ever had to do in his life. For a lawyer, even this one—*the best of his kind in London*—might not be enough. The general had considerable power and influence. So did Lady Pascoe. She was the sister of a baron who held a prominent position in the government. Both had been vehemently opposed to their daughter's marrying the bastard son of a blacksmith's daughter, even if he *was* an officer of high rank. They would undoubtedly have withheld their consent had Caroline not already been increasing. That fact had drawn their tight-lipped consent, but it had done nothing to endear him to them. It was also a fact that had deeply shamed him. After becoming a commissioned officer, he had tried hard to behave like a gentleman even if he could never be one.

Gil's offer to accompany Harry home and his agreement to remain with him for a while had been made at least partly for selfish reasons, then. It would take him back to England, not far distant from London, where he would be able to consult his agent more easily and the lawyer who did not really want to be consulted or pressed. Being back in England would give him a sense of purpose, of not simply doing nothing. But the offer had also been made out of genuine friendship and concern, for his friend could not travel alone or *be* alone despite what he might think. Yet he would not go to London, where his mother was living during the spring months.

The arrival of Netherby and Riverdale in Paris had seemed like a relatively minor annoyance at the time. Both had treated Gil with quiet respect, but he had assumed that they would return to their families and parliamentary duties in London as soon as they possibly could after conveying Harry home. Now it appeared he had assumed wrongly. It seemed very likely indeed that the whole of the Westcott family would descend upon Hinsford within days of their arrival and stay for who knew how long. How many of them were there, for God's sake?

It was a daunting prospect and one that might well force him into a change of plans. Indeed, he would surely have changed them at Dover if this conversation had been held over breakfast. But now he was stuck, at least temporarily. He did not have a carriage of his own or even a horse with which to leave Hinsford.

"He is asleep," the Earl of Riverdale said from the seat opposite, his voice little more than a murmur. "He is far weaker than I expected him to be after almost two years."

"He will recover," Netherby said, equally quietly. "If he has been too stubborn to die thus far, he is not going to do it now."

"What is your opinion, Lieutenant Colonel?" Riverdale asked.

"It is my belief," Gil said, gazing at his friend, whose chin had sunk to his chest, "that if Bonaparte were to escape again today and gather another army to lead against the allies, Major Harry Westcott would be volunteering to lead the first charge."

"Not you?" the Duke of Netherby asked. "It has been whispered, Bennington, that you once led a forlorn hope and were promoted from captain to major as a result."

Gil frowned. He never felt comfortable discussing his war exploits. There were thousands of men, many of them dead, just as brave as he. "I had men at my back who would not have allowed me to retreat even if I had wished to do so," he said. "It was not the accomplishment of a single individual, but one of a large group. Most military actions are that way even if only one man is singled out afterward for commendations and honors. Harry was one of the best. If there was ever danger for his men to face, he was there to lead them into it. He looks weak now, but he has a ferocious spirit. It may be lying dormant, but it is not dead, I assure you. He will recover fully."

"Or die in the attempt," the duke said.

Gil looked across into his eyes, keen beneath the sleepy lids, and was surprised by the flash of humor from a man who was an apparently bored aristocrat from his blond, expertly styled hair to his fashionable and immaculately tailored clothes, from his well-manicured, beringed hands to the tips of his supple, highly polished boots. A bit of a dangerous man too, Gil suspected.